MW00984398

Angela,

Never give up on the
dreams that God has
put on your heart!

♡ Erin Elise Kiv

BASED ON A TRUE STORY

One Transforming
LOVE

Erin Elise Kiu

AVIVA
PUBLISHING
New York

Published by:
Aviva Publishing
Lake Placid, NY
(518) 523-1320
www.AvivaPubs.com

Address all inquiries to:
Erin Elise Kiu
erinelisekiu@funandholy.com
www.funandholy.com

This book is a work of fiction. Unless otherwise noted, all people, places, and events are fictional or used fictitiously. Any resemblance to real people is purely coincidental.

Unless otherwise indicated, all Scripture quotations are taken from the Holy Bible, New Living Translation, copyright © 1996, 2004, 2015 by Tyndale House Foundation. Used by permission of Tyndale House Publishers, Inc., Carol Stream, Illinois 60188. All rights reserved.

Hardcover ISBN: 978-1-63618-100-4
eBook ISBN: 978-1-63618-105-9
Library of Congress Control Number: 2021908241

Editor: Tyler Tichelaar, Superior Book Productions
Cover Design and Interior Layout: Fusion Creative Works
Author Photograph: Brooke Preece

This book is dedicated to those who prayed for me to experience the transforming love of Jesus Christ, and to those who showed me grace along the way.

To my mom, thank you for never giving up praying for me to know Jesus.

To my sister in Christ, Nina, thank you for being the invitation back to church and to Jesus I so desperately needed.

To my husband, Jeff, thank you for always believing in me and the dreams God has put on my heart to write.

And lastly, to the One who transformed my life, thank you Jesus for the love and grace you showed me when I needed it most.

Based on a True Story

"And they have defeated him by the blood of the Lamb and by their testimony...."

— Revelation 12:11

Chapter 1

⚓

Aubrey tried to focus on reading her book, but she couldn't help wondering if that good-looking guy walking on the boardwalk was him. Her table at the coffee shop gave her a front row view of everyone who passed along the Pacific Beach boardwalk.

His biceps and chest seemed like they wanted to pop out of his shirt, but he wasn't overly buff like the other gym-obsessed guys on the boardwalk. Guys out here in San Diego really were more fit than guys back in the Midwest—another sign that moving across the country to San Diego had been the right move.

What if he was her Bumble date? They could go on so many cute first dates here in San Diego. They could walk along the beach at sunset, go bike riding along the boardwalk, hike Torrey Pines, or even take a surf lesson together.

Aubrey took a sip of her latte. *Stop being ridiculous. Stop planning the entire first month of dates before you even meet this guy. He may not even have a real job like half the other guys on Bumble.*

Aubrey opened up the app and checked his profile for the tenth time that day. Twenty-nine, originally from Ohio, works in finance, loves hiking, biking, boxing, and running along the beach with his Golden Retriever. She would see if he really did work in finance. And if that really was his dog in his profile pictures. They had so much in common already, but she didn't want to get her hopes up again.

Aubrey had done the whole app dating thing in Chicago for years, but she had never had much luck. While she had heard stories of friends of friends meeting on Tinder and falling in love, and some even getting married, her experience with app dating only left her feeling more single and hopeless.

Romantic and old-fashioned at heart, Aubrey refused to get on the dating apps at first, hoping to meet the one organically in person. But after years of trying to meet a decent guy in Chicago, she had given up. Guys at bars only wanted to hook up—none of them wanted a serious relationship. Every somewhat decent-looking guy at the public accounting firm where she worked was already taken or too young. And cute guys never sat next to her on flights for work like they did in the movies.

As her other friends started to go on dates with guys they met online, she finally gave in and created a dating profile on Bumble. But hours spent swiping left and right and coming up with creative, fun ways to start the conversation only led to frustration and rejection.

What was the point of matching with someone if the guy didn't engage in conversation? What was the point of chatting with someone in the app if he didn't have the balls to ask for her number or ask her out on an actual date? How come all her other friends went on all of these dates? Guys had way too many options in the app dating world. Why would they want to go out with her when they had their pick of hundreds of other girls who were prettier and skinnier?

Aubrey had managed to go on a few first dates from the app, but they didn't end in the romantic fairy tale she wanted. One guy tried to Netflix and chill her on the first date; he didn't understand what was so wrong about suggesting they watch a movie at his house their first time hanging out together.

Another guy was extremely good-looking, had a successful job working for a private equity firm, and seemed promising at first. He took Aubrey to one of the hottest restaurants on the river in Chicago and everything went well with the exception of him talking too much about himself. Aubrey figured he must have been nervous, and she was about to agree to a second date until her friend realized he was actually a coworker's boyfriend.

Interested in a relationship? Clearly not. More like, already in a relationship but dealing with insecurities from the past and unable to commit to one woman.

"Don't give up," Aubrey's friend Brittany from Chicago had encouraged her after Aubrey was about to delete the app altogether. "You're moving to a new city where you don't know anyone, and it will be a completely different scene in San Diego. Keep an open mind and see what happens. Even if the date doesn't work out, you never know who could be a new friend."

The whirl of the espresso machine brought Aubrey back to reality. She had already agreed to meet this guy for a date, and there was no turning back now. Maybe things would be different in the dating scene in San Diego.

As Aubrey scrolled through her own dating profile, she already felt more confident about her appearance after spending hours running on the beach and hiking along the coast. She didn't feel fat, but she wanted to tone the natural thick legs and butt God had given her. She was learning to embrace her curvy figure and natural brown hair instead of comparing herself to the skinny blondes she saw everywhere on the beach. She knew she was a catch, and if the guy didn't see that, then he wasn't the one.

"Hi. Excuse me, is this you?" A guy approached her table, holding his phone out to Aubrey.

She looked down and saw her dating profile on his phone. Crap! Had he seen her looking at her own profile just now?

"Yes! Hi! I'm Aubrey. Nice to meet you." She stood up and gave him an awkward side hug.

"I'm Jordan. Nice to meet you. I'm going to grab a coffee. Do you need a refill?"

Aubrey glanced at her cup. She had already had two cups of coffee today, but she wanted to have something to hold onto.

"Yes, thanks. I'll take a nonfat latte."

She checked him out as he ordered their drinks at the counter. He was tall and athletic like every guy on the boardwalk. Dressed casually in a pair of cargo shorts and a tank top, Jordan looked more like a grown-up frat boy than a twenty-nine-year-old guy who worked in finance.

"So," he said, setting their drinks down on the table before taking a seat, "you mentioned in the app that you just moved to San Diego. First of all, congrats! You officially live in the best place on Earth. How are you settling in so far?"

Jordan's dimples appeared as he smiled over his iced coffee. Aubrey couldn't believe she was on a date already after moving to San Diego only two weeks ago. And not just any date, but a date by the beach overlooking the Pacific Ocean.

"It all feels like a dream come true," Aubrey replied. "I wake up, walk out to the beach, and think, 'Wow, this is my life now. Why did I live in the freezing Midwest for so long?'" They laughed as they stared out toward the beach.

Toddlers were playing along the shore, covered in sand and squealing when the waves caught up to them. A group of guys were diving in the sand, playing Spikeball. Surfers were staring at the horizon, waiting to catch the perfect wave.

"I know, right? I keep telling my parents back in Ohio that they need to move out here. It's a completely different lifestyle, and I can't imagine what it would be like to grow up here, going out to the beach or hiking whenever we wanted."

"Exactly! It's a completely different lifestyle. I keep thinking the same thing. I grew up in Michigan, and we didn't have all these options of things to do outside."

"I totally could tell you're a Midwest girl. A sweet Midwest girl on the beach in sunny San Diego? My favorite."

They both laughed. This was going better than she had hoped.

"So, what made you move to this paradise anyway?" Jordan stirred a sugar into his iced coffee.

Ah, the ultimate question. How should she answer? So many thoughts went through Aubrey's head, but she went with the standard response she had been reciting for the past week.

"I was ready for a change. I lived in Chicago for about four years, and it was a great city, but I wanted to be somewhere more outdoorsy and active. I visited Southern California on a work trip and fell in love with the beach and ocean life. I was eating an acai bowl in Laguna Beach and stumbled across a surfing competition on the beach. It was that moment that I knew I needed to move here."

Those dimples again.

"Laguna Beach! One of my favorite beaches in SoCal. That's awesome you got to visit here for work; you must have a pretty cool job. What do you do again, accounting consulting?"

Aubrey hesitated. Whenever she explained what she did for work, she would see people's eyes glaze over in boredom. Accounting wasn't sexy, no matter how hard she tried to hype it up. But she did get to travel a lot, and everyone loved talking about travel.

"Yeah, I do accounting consulting for Assets & Beyond Consulting. I help companies figure out how to do their accounting for complex transactions, like when they buy or sell a company, and I help them figure out how certain line items should be recorded, like how they should recognize revenue."

Was she rambling about accounting already? Was it too much?

Jordan nodded. "Like accounting or transaction services? A few of my close friends from college work for the big public accounting firms, and I do finance for a large company, so I know what you're talking about. Don't worry—we speak the same business language."

He winked as he sipped his coffee.

Looks like he really did work in finance. And thank God he didn't think she was a nerd for working in accounting.

"So, do you like it?" Jordan asked.

Aubrey shook her head. "I'm not going to lie; I don't really like accounting. Even my boss knows it's not my passion."

"Well, who really does feel passionate about accounting or finance? But it must be a good gig if you get to travel and live by the beach in San Diego."

Aubrey smiled as she raised her latte in the air. "Exactly. Cheers to the beach life."

"I just met you, so I know you love the beach life, but how could you leave all the amazing bars and restaurants in Chicago? My buddies still live there, and I wish San Diego had a nightlife scene like that."

"That's actually another reason I wanted to leave. Chicago does have so many great bars and restaurants, but I wanted to do something more than just working and drinking a lot. It seems like that's what everyone does in Chicago."

Jordan laughed. "Yeah, work hard, play hard; there's nothing wrong with that."

Maybe Jordan was the grown-up frat boy he looked like on the outside. While he did look like a lot of the other guys Aubrey was used to meeting at the bars in Chicago, she didn't want to judge him too soon for being a party boy.

"So," Aubrey asked, "you obviously work hard in finance, but how do you spend your time on the weekends? What does your typical weekend look like?"

"My typical weekend—let's see." He tapped his chin as he stared at the ocean.

"Well, starting on Friday night, I usually hit up a happy hour somewhere downtown either in Gaslamp or Little Italy. Depending on how long the work week was, I may call it an early night or may head to a club if I'm feeling it. On Saturday, depending on how hungover I am from the night before, I may get in a run along the marina or a hike up Cowles Mountain. Or I may head straight to the beach with my buddies for some sun and day drinking.

"We then will eventually make it back downtown, ending the night in Gaslamp, maybe getting a table and a few bottles if the night calls for it. Then on Sundays, I chill, eat lots of wings, and enjoy a few beers while watching football."

Definitely a party boy and not what Aubrey was looking for. Jordan was like the guys she wanted to forget about in Chicago. Guys who only wanted to drink and party on the weekends. She had wasted too many weekends drunk and hungover, and she wasn't about to waste any more that way in beautiful San Diego. It was a fresh start. A new beginning.

Aubrey breathed a sigh of relief; she was glad she hadn't told him the real reason she had moved. He wouldn't understand. He was just like the rest of them.

"What about you?" he asked. "How would you spend your ideal weekend in San Diego?"

Should she carry on and continue to make small talk? At least he asked good questions. Aubrey didn't even want to be friends with him at this point. She knew she needed to meet people who cared about other things besides working and drinking on the weekends. She knew life had to be more than that. She was determined to figure out what she was really meant to do with her life in San Diego. And she was done doing what everyone else did around her just to make friends.

"You seem like a great guy," she said, "but I'm sorry; this isn't going to work out."

Jordan choked on his drink.

"What? We just met like ten minutes ago. What happened?"

There was no turning back now.

"To be honest, I moved here to get away from the party scene. I drank so much in Chicago, and I'm over that scene. Don't you ever wonder if life should be more than just working and drinking a lot?"

Jordan shook his head. "No, I don't wonder that at all. You live in San Diego; what more could you want than a good job and enjoying it on the weekends? It's the best scenario—you can hit up the beach bars and then have fun downtown all in the same day. What more do you need?"

Aubrey needed more. She didn't need any more party boys in her life, but she didn't know what she did need. Now that she lived in San Diego, she could fill her time with hiking, beach walks, and sunsets until she figured out what she was supposed to do with her life. But would that be enough?

"I'm sorry; I have to go. I wish you the best. Enjoy the rest of your Saturday." Aubrey quickly gathered her purse as she stood up to leave.

"No worries; your loss. I'll go join my buddies down the street at the beach bar for some real fun."

Aubrey waved and smiled as she walked away. She didn't need to explain herself. She wasn't going to let this date get to her. San Diego had to have some people who cared about other things besides drinking. It was only the beginning.

Chapter 2

⚓

Aubrey finished her morning walk and sat down on the cliff over-looking the beach. The sun was already warm on her face as the beach started to fill up with surfers and families ready to spend the day at the beach.

Her phone buzzed with a text from her mom.

Have you found a new church yet? Praying and thinking of you. P.S. – the kids miss you like crazy. Kyle keeps asking when you'll come home next.

Aubrey smiled. Even though she was used to living away from her parents and her brother and his family, she felt more homesick living so far away in San Diego. Her nephew Kyle was already seven and her niece Kate was about to turn four. Tyler, her brother, had tried to guilt trip her into staying in the Midwest, telling her she would miss seeing the kids grow up, but she knew she needed to give San Diego a shot. A part of her did feel guilty for not being there to watch her niece and nephew grow up, but she had no desire to move back to Michigan right now.

Her dad had also tried to make her feel guilty for moving across the country. All her life, he had wanted Aubrey to live closer to home. He had finally agreed it was a good idea for her to go away for college to Michigan State University and then to start her career in Chicago, but he hadn't understood her desire to move all the way across the country to California.

"It's too expensive," he had said. "They have too many fires. You'll get sick of the beach there. You'll be homesick too far away from all your friends and family. Why leave a good thing in Chicago to start somewhere new? You'll never meet someone if you're always traveling and moving around."

At least Aubrey's mom had always been supportive of her moving. She knew Aubrey had needed a change from Chicago, and she had always supported her in pursuing her dreams, no matter how crazy they sounded, like moving across the country. In the end, Aubrey was grateful her family all loved each other and she had promised them she would visit them more often with all her free miles she earned from her work travels.

Aubrey texted back.

> I miss you guys too. Tell the kids I can't wait to see them for Christmas. Thanks for the reminder about church. I still need to see what's out here.

Growing up, she had always gone with her family to a Catholic church, but only because her mom expected it of her. Church had been so boring and she never understood what they were saying. As Aubrey got older, during high school and college, she only went to church with her family on holidays. None of her friends or sorority sisters ever went to church or talked about God, so she didn't either. Church hadn't been a part of her life until a few years ago.

One of Aubrey's closest friends, Tina, had started going to a church in Chicago called Soul City Church, and she always made a point of inviting Aubrey. Tina always talked about how great the pastors were and how many new friends she was meeting, but Aubrey didn't want to go.

Tina insisted this church was different—the pastors were actually funny—but Aubrey still didn't want to go. She didn't want to sacrifice waking up early on a Sunday morning, and she was usually too hungover from the night before to get out of bed before noon.

But as the months went on, she had noticed something different about Tina. Tina had stopped drinking and going out with them as much, and she had even stopped going on a lot of dates and hooking up with random guys they would meet at the bars.

At first, the situation had annoyed Aubrey. She had felt like she was losing a friend, but Tina seemed genuinely happier without all those things. She was so excited for church every weekend, and she even came up with dances for the kids' church that she volunteered in.

Tina's new boyfriend, Bryan, even started going to church with her. They seemed so happy together, and he didn't seem to care about missing out on the bar scene. They started to talk more about how God had a plan for their lives and how it was like they had this whole new life with God. They told Aubrey that God had a plan for her life, too, and that he was there any time she was ready.

Aubrey admired how passionate Tina was about the church. She hadn't felt that passionate about anything in a long time. Last year, while Aubrey was still living in Chicago, she had begun to wonder, *What am I doing with my life? I'm already twenty-seven. What is my purpose? Am I supposed to stay in a job I don't really like for the money?*

Aubrey had a great job in public accounting, a handful of close friends, and she could travel anywhere she wanted with the points from her work trips, but she couldn't shake the feeling that something was missing. She felt like she should be happier and grateful for her life, but no matter how much she excelled at work, drank on the weekends, or traveled, nothing seemed able to fill the void she felt. She felt like she was chasing something, but she didn't know what. While she wanted to date someone, she knew having a boyfriend wouldn't replace that void.

Tina and Bryan eventually got married and moved back to Michigan. One night, not long after, something in Aubrey snapped. After a night out of drinking way too many shots and not meeting a single decent guy at the bar, she came home in tears and fell on her knees in her apartment.

God, I know you're there. Is this the plan you have for my life? If this is the plan you have, then why am I still single, God? Why is it so hard to meet a guy who actually wants to date me instead of someone who just wants to hook up?

What's the point of spending hours on these dating apps if nobody wants to go on a real date with me? Why are all these guys so awful? What's wrong with me, God?

And what is my purpose here? Am I supposed to work in accounting forever, feeling unfulfilled and bored? What is the point of working hard if I don't even enjoy it? What am I supposed to do with my life, God?

Aubrey had never cried out to God like that before. She had never prayed out loud, but it felt like something had shifted as she poured her heart out to God. She knew there had to be more to life, and God knew the answer. If God really did create everything on the Earth, including her, then he would reveal her purpose.

If Tina could be this happy from going to church, then Aubrey thought maybe she could too. If Tina and Bryan had gotten out of the bar scene and gotten married, then maybe she could too. God was clearly showing her that she was not about to meet Mr. Right in a bar, twerking on the dance floor. She would much rather meet her husband in a church than in some bar where all the guys walked around trying to get laid.

Aubrey had nothing to lose trying to figure it out by going to church, so she started going to Tina's old church on her own. At first, she felt weird since the church wasn't Catholic, but then she realized she enjoyed it way more than the traditional Catholic Mass she had attended growing up. Her mom had even started going to a non-denominational church once her old pastor had moved to a new church, so she knew her mom would support her decision to explore other churches. Aubrey had been surprised that her mom started going to a non-denominational church after so many years going to a Catholic church, but their neighbor down the street had invited her, and her mom seemed to be enjoying the style and community of her new church more than the traditional Catholic Mass.

At the church in Chicago, Aubrey was surrounded by people her age in jeans and leggings who would smile at her and welcome her to church. She loved the casual, positive vibes the church had. It was so different from the bars she had spent so much time in. People at church seemed genuinely happy and friendly, even without all the alcohol.

Some guys were even cute. Maybe she would even meet her future husband at church, like how her parents had met.

People would raise their hands and sing out loud during worship. A band, complete with a drum set, a few guitarists, and a few singers, would play music on a stage. Aubrey had never heard music played like that in church before. Even though she liked the music, she felt awkward during worship. Why were all these people raising their hands in the air? Why were some dancing? They looked ridiculous.

She didn't dare raise her hands or sing out loud. She had never sung out loud in church. Some people would even cry during worship. It all seemed a bit much, but Aubrey couldn't ignore the peace she felt as she closed her eyes and listened to the music.

The pastors were actually funny, and they spoke in plain English. They would still read and quote scriptures from the Bible like they did in a Catholic church, but she could actually understand what they were talking about now. They always talked about having a transforming relationship with Jesus. That their hope and mission as a church was to lead people to Jesus.

Aubrey knew the story of Jesus, how he was born in a manger and died on a cross. She didn't understand some stuff they talked about like the Holy Spirit or a transformation with God, but she did learn that she needed to start trusting God with the plans he had for her. She believed God had a plan and purpose for her life, and she needed to start spending time with him to figure it out.

Every time Aubrey went to the church, she felt like she was one step closer to figuring out what she was supposed to do with her life. She even stopped going out as much on Saturday nights so she could wake up fresh for church without feeling hungover. Even though none of her friends wanted to go with her, Aubrey didn't care what they thought. It was time to start doing what she wanted to do, even if it meant doing it alone.

Now in San Diego, Aubrey knew she needed to keep going to church. She wanted to figure out the plans God had for her, and church would be a perfect way to meet new people in her new city.

Maybe at her new church, God would show her what her true calling was and who her husband would be.

Aubrey checked the time on her phone. Her friend Morgan, who used to live in San Diego, was visiting in town for work. They had made plans to do a beach workout class and then meet up with some of Morgan's friends after for brunch. Aubrey had a few minutes before she had to meet Morgan at the beach, so she decided to look up churches near her apartment.

Aubrey googled "churches in San Diego," and her phone displayed several churches nearby, but she didn't know what denomination to look for. She dialed Tina on her phone, hoping she would know what to look for.

"Hey, girl! I'm church-shopping in San Diego; what should I look for in a church? I want to find somewhere similar to Soul City in Chicago."

"Ah, church-shopping—so exciting! I'll be praying that God brings you to the right church. I'm so happy you are looking for a new church there."

"I'm so excited to meet some new people and see what God has for me here," Aubrey replied. "I need to meet people who care about other things besides getting drunk on the weekends."

"Absolutely," Tina said. "You're on the right track. Well, most churches have their values or beliefs on their website. You should look for a church similar to Soul City that talks about God, Jesus, and the Holy Spirit. It may be helpful to look for non-denominational churches. Some churches don't talk about the Holy Spirit, but it's important to find a church that preaches from the whole Bible, including the New Testament, that talks about the Holy Spirit."

"Holy Spirit is good. Got it."

Aubrey didn't know which part of the Bible Tina was talking about, but she trusted Tina knew what she should be looking for in a church. She didn't want to end up at another boring church like she had attended growing up.

"You should also be able to see the different types of small groups or ministries the church has. See if the church has anything specifically for young adults or young professionals so you can meet other people our age."

"Yes, young professionals are just what I'm looking for! Especially hot, single, young professional men."

Tina laughed. "Amen! May there be an abundance of hot, professional men at your new church in Jesus' name!"

After Aubrey said goodbye to Tina, she typed "non-denominational churches for young professionals" into Google.

The Freedom Church and Awaken Church San Diego had the most reviews on Google and Yelp. Both churches had a mix of reviews. Some people raved about how God had changed their lives and how the church community was so welcoming. Several reviews mentioned the variety of ministries and small groups both churches had for young adults and families. Other reviews mentioned the churches only wanted people's money and that the pastors were never available.

Aubrey decided to check out Freedom Church the following Sunday since it was closest to the ocean. *God only knows what he has in store for me there.*

Chapter 3

⚓

Aubrey hummed as she walked along the oceanfront path to the park for the workout class. She had already been on a date, made plans with Morgan and her friends, and was going to check out a new church on Sunday. Not bad for her second weekend in her new city.

The park was full of at least a hundred fit people who wanted to breathe in the ocean air and work up a sweat that morning. Most of the men and women had their shirts off, rocking six-pack abs and the latest sports bras from Lululemon. A handful of dogs lingered by their owners' mats, while a few dogs made their way between workout mats, meeting new friends.

Aubrey spotted Morgan stretching on her mat.

"You're finally here! I can't believe it!" Morgan exclaimed.

Aubrey gave her a big hug and then rolled out her workout mat next to Morgan's.

"Oh my gosh," Aubrey said. "I can't believe I actually live in San Diego! And we get to do workouts overlooking the ocean! It feels like a dream." Aubrey spread her arms out, taking in the blue ocean in front of her.

"I'm so excited for you to meet my friends from work," Morgan replied. "We're meeting everyone for brunch at La Playa; they have a rooftop overlooking the ocean. My new crush, Troy, is supposed to be there. We made out a few weeks ago at a happy hour, and he's so hot. We've been texting a little bit, but he hasn't asked me out, so I'm sure tonight will be the night when he really makes a move. I haven't had sex in two months!"

"That sounds great! I can't wait to meet everyone. Do you think Troy will ask you out on a real date?"

Aubrey was excited for Morgan, but she wondered how long they would keep putting up with guys who only wanted to hook up with them. Dating had to be more than settling for hookups that didn't go anywhere. They weren't in their early twenties anymore.

Morgan laughed. "A date would be awesome, but I'm not going to hold my breath. He's like really good-looking and I would totally bang him."

A tanned, buff guy introduced himself as the instructor; then he led everyone in a few warm-up stretches.

Aubrey focused on the ocean in front of her, but she was still thinking about what Morgan had said. She was sick of the hookup culture they lived in. She didn't want to think about all her drunken hookups last year in Chicago and how they had ended. She knew she and her friends were worth more than the guys they ended up with, but somehow, they were all caught in the same hookup cycle.

After the class was over, the two friends freshened up at Aubrey's place before making their way to La Playa for brunch. Aubrey wore her new high-waisted denim shorts, hugging her butt in all the right places, with a casual crop top—the standard beach uniform in Pacific Beach. Ladies sure didn't dress like this in Chicago in November.

The bar was already packed with people dancing and sipping margaritas. Guys were taking shots at the bar while girls dressed in even skimpier shorts and crop tops danced around them.

Aubrey felt like she had stepped into a different world as they made their way up to La Playa's rooftop deck. She was expecting casual mimosas or Bloody Marys at brunch. She wasn't expecting a beach rager on a rooftop in the middle of the day. Aubrey was excited to meet some new people and be on a rooftop by the ocean, but she felt uneasy. This place didn't look like a good scene for brunch.

Morgan handed Aubrey a margarita at the bar and introduced her to a few of her coworkers, who were surrounded by a group of guys who had their tequila shots raised in the air. Aubrey made a mental note not to take any shots or drink too much today. She would have a few drinks meeting some new people, go home, and wake up fresh for church the next day.

"The tall one with the dark curly hair is Troy," Morgan told her. "The guy in the red next to him is the guy Claire has a crush on, so he's off limits. They haven't done anything yet, but she's been crushing on him hard for a few weeks."

Aubrey surveyed the prospects. They seemed attractive, but they looked like every other guy she had met in Chicago—a guy who knew he was good-looking and just wanted to get laid. After their shots, Morgan formally introduced all the guys. None of them were very chatty except for Steve. He was black, tall, and a little stocky. He started talking about his favorite bars in Pacific Beach. He wasn't cute, but he was someone to talk to while Morgan flirted with Troy. Morgan sipped on her margarita while Troy leaned in closer to her by the bar. It looked like Morgan would get what she wanted from Troy by the end of the day.

Steve signaled the bartender for two more margaritas. Aubrey hesitated. She drank the first one fast in an attempt to feel more comfortable around everyone, but she didn't want to turn down a free drink. She would have some water after this one.

"So, can I get your number?" Steve asked, setting the new margarita in her hand. "I would love to hang out sometime and show you around Pacific Beach."

Steve had made an effort to talk to her, but she wasn't interested. He wasn't her type, and he had started to slur his words.

"Um, sure," Aubrey said, not knowing how to say no. She didn't want to make things awkward by turning him down already after he had bought her a drink. Hopefully, he wouldn't even text her after today. Aubrey gave Steve her number and then excused herself to use the restroom. She snaked her way through the crowds of people on the rooftop and made her way downstairs. She couldn't believe there was already a restroom line in the middle of the afternoon.

People knew how to party in Chicago, but this was different. She had never seen day drinking like this. Some of the girls in line were already falling over on each other and spilling their drinks. Everyone looked like they were having fun, but Aubrey couldn't ignore how she felt. She wanted to go home. She didn't want to make small talk with drunk people in hopes of meeting new friends.

At the beginning of the line, Aubrey saw a girl leave a bathroom stall while giving her purse to a friend waiting outside.

"Your turn, have fun!" she winked as she walked out of the restroom without washing her hands.

Was that weed she saw the girl take out of the purse? Some other kind of drug? Who would do drugs in a public restroom in the middle of the day? Aubrey had never gotten into drugs. While she had smoked weed a few times with some of her friends in college, she was glad she was never around friends who did more serious drugs at parties.

Aubrey finally got her turn and quickly headed back upstairs. She felt the buzz kick in from the margaritas and an uneasiness in her stomach after what she had just seen. Seeing Morgan standing by the bar chatting with her coworkers while Troy bought another round of shots, Aubrey approached her.

"Morgan, I think I saw someone doing drugs in the restroom! Who does that?"

Morgan laughed. "Welcome to Pacific Beach! Lots of people do coke here. I haven't done it, but it's all the rage here; lots of people do it in the restrooms at bars."

Claire chimed in. "I see people doing it here all the time. I think Steve and Austin, the guy I like, did it earlier here. I'm not really a fan of drugs, but he's superhot and isn't acting too out of line, so it's not really a big deal."

Steve had done coke in the bathroom? Aubrey made a face as she set her drink down. What was she doing here drinking in the middle of the day with people who were doing drugs and only wanted to get laid? Aubrey looked over at Morgan, who now had her arms around Troy. Claire was talking to her crush, and her other friend was talking to some random guy at the bar, about to take a shot.

Aubrey didn't want to be here anymore. This was exactly the type of scene she had wanted to escape from in Chicago. She didn't want to hang out with people like this. Aubrey wanted to leave without saying goodbye, but she knew she had to say goodbye to Morgan.

"Hey, Morgan," Aubrey said, grabbing her friend's arm to get her attention. "I'm not feeling well. I'm sorry, but I'm going to head home."

"What? No, you have to stay! It's still so early; we have the whole day ahead of us." She smiled suggestively at Troy. She already sounded drunk.

"You won't even miss me; besides, it looks like you're in good hands."

Morgan nodded as she broke into a huge grin. Aubrey fought her way through the crowded bar and made it downstairs to the boardwalk. She was still a little buzzed, but the sound of the waves instantly made her relax.

Tomorrow would be a new day. She would rather explore San Diego alone than meet people in a place like that. When she got home, she ate her favorite Velveeta mac and cheese before falling asleep on her couch.

Chapter 4

⚓

Aubrey spotted the church a few blocks away. She was already running late and felt flustered that she didn't know where to park. Swarms of people were heading inside the church, and several cars were still trying to park.

Why am I so worried? Aubrey thought as she parked her car. She felt more nervous today coming to church than she had meeting all of Morgan's drunk coworkers on the rooftop. Church was supposed to be full of loving people. She didn't need to worry about what other people thought or about fitting in. God was with her, and he wanted her to meet other nice people who could potentially be friends.

Were churches supposed to be this big? Had she picked the right church? She had never been to a church this big. The auditorium looked like it could host Broadway plays. There was even a balcony section.

Aubrey grabbed a program from an usher and sat down. A band was already on the stage playing worship music. It seemed similar to the church back in Chicago with the upbeat Christian music, but more people had their arms raised here. Some ladies were even dancing in the middle of the aisle.

Aubrey stood during worship like everyone else, but she didn't know what to do with her hands. She appreciated that the song lyrics were displayed on a screen, but she still didn't want to sing or raise her hands. She looked at the people worshipping around her. Could she fit in here? Would she meet her new friends here, or even her future husband?

There seemed to be mostly families and couples around her, but the church was so large that there had to be other single people her age as well. After a few more worship songs that seemed never to end, the pastor finally came on stage. Aubrey was glad she had shown up late so she hadn't had to stand there awkwardly for an entire thirty minutes.

Pastor Davis was a former basketball player; he was funny just like the pastors at Soul City in Chicago. He talked about how God had a unique plan to use each one of them for his glory.

"As children of God, you are God's masterpiece. As the Bible talks about in Psalm 139, God had every day of your life written in his book before you were even born. You are wonderfully and re-markably made. You were created by God with unique talents, pas-sions, and gifts to use to fulfill the plans he has for you. When you use those gifts to serve and love others, you are glorifying God and showing him that you are thankful for the gifts he has given you."

Aubrey took notes in her iPhone. She had never thought of her-self as a masterpiece before. She knew she was smart, but she had never thought about the other gifts God had given her.

"Do you realize there is only one of you on this Earth?" Pastor Davis continued. "Your DNA, your fingerprints, your unique makeup—there is only one you, and God needs you to be exactly who he created you to be to fulfill the plans he has for you on this

Earth. God doesn't want you to be like every other person you see on Instagram. He doesn't want you to be doing or copying what your neighbor is doing. He needs you to be you to fulfill the plans he has for you."

Aubrey understood that God had a plan for her, but she didn't know how to figure out what it was. She wanted to figure out God's plan so she could feel fulfilled. She actually wanted to enjoy what she did for a living while feeling like she was making a difference. God had blessed her in college with good grades and had opened up doors for her to do accounting. Even if she was good at her job, wouldn't God want her to enjoy the gifts he had given her? Wouldn't God want her to feel fulfilled using those gifts?

Aubrey was thankful for the career she had, and she knew a lot of people would do anything to have a job like she did. She was thankful God had made her smart enough to handle complicated accounting issues, but she didn't enjoy it. She struggled to understand the importance accounting had in this world. Did God create her to be an accountant so companies could have accurate financial statements? Aubrey cringed. That didn't sound fulfilling at all.

Business had sounded so exciting in college. Earn a degree in accounting, get a good job, and work in the business world. Wear cute pencil skirts and heels, travel the country, and help businesses grow. In reality, Aubrey didn't enjoy the business world as much as she had thought she would. She loved traveling to new places around the country and even the world, but she knew her travel days would come to an end when she was ready to settle down.

Pastor Davis' voice got louder.

"Ephesians talks about how God created you to do the works he knew about long ago. As Christians, we need to live lives worthy of the calling we have received. We cannot neglect the gifts and calling that God has for us. No matter how challenging or how uncomfortable it may feel, we need to respond with obedience to the unique purpose and calling God has for our life. When God called me to be a pastor, do you think I believed him? I thought he was crazy. I thought he had picked the wrong guy. How could someone like me, a former drug addict and frequent customer at strip clubs, become a pastor?"

A drug addict could become a pastor? Aubrey thought.

"For months, I thought God had made a mistake. I didn't feel worthy or qualified enough to be a pastor. But God is so good; he can't wait to reveal the purpose and plans he has for you. If he is calling you to something, he will confirm it again and again. He won't hide it from you when you seek him wholeheartedly. So I prayed, fasted, and prayed some more. And God made it very clear that it was time for me to become a pastor. As a child of God, he has a plan for you, too. A purpose and calling that is bigger than you could ever imagine. And understanding this purpose and calling is one of the things Christians are desperately seeking to find and figure out."

Yes! I am desperate to figure it out. Why is it so hard to figure out what I am supposed to do in this world?

"If you take away anything from today, let it be this," Pastor Davis continued. "Number one, you are unique and created by God to do amazing things for his Kingdom. And two, you don't have to stress about trying to figure out what those amazing things are. When you have a relationship with Jesus Christ and spend time with him regularly, he will reveal the plans he has for you. Jesus already died on the cross for all your mistakes and sins to be forgiven.

He died so you could fulfill these unique, amazing, supernatural plans God has for you.

"If you are still trying to figure out your purpose and calling, you are already found in Jesus. You are a new creation in Jesus Christ, and the old life is buried. You don't have to let your sins and mistakes dictate the future plans God has for you. You can leave those behind, buried in Christ, when you accept Jesus as your Lord and Savior."

Everyone bowed their heads as the pastor prayed. Then he asked if anyone wanted to choose Jesus as their savior. Pastor Davis encouraged them to come down to the front of the church if they wanted to accept Jesus into their life so he could lead them in prayer. A handful of people made their way to the front of the church as everyone clapped and cheered them on.

Aubrey had really enjoyed the sermon, but she didn't understand why people were going up to the front of the church. Couldn't they accept Jesus as their savior and stay in their seats? Why did Pastor Davis make such a big deal about them going down to the front?

Aubrey decided she would prioritize going to church. God had a plan for her in San Diego. He would finally show her what she was supposed to do with her life. God already knew what he created her to do, and it was up to him to reveal it to her as long as she continued seeking him. God had already shown her that drinking was not the plan he had for her. She would pursue things she actually enjoyed doing, and God would reveal the unique plans and calling he had for her.

Aubrey didn't know how she could completely move on from all her poor choices and behavior on all those drunken nights in Chicago, but she was determined not to keep making the same mistakes here. What had happened in Chicago would stay in Chicago. She was ready to move on.

When she got home from church, she texted her mom as she sat on the couch.

> Just got back from church! It was the biggest church I've ever seen. I felt intimidated but I really liked the pastor and the message. I'll be going back. Love and miss you.

Her mom texted back right away.

> So proud of you for checking it out! That's wonderful. What was the message about?

Aubrey replied.

> He talked about how God has a unique plan and purpose for each of our lives. Do you think God created me to do accounting for the rest of my life?

Aubrey was still struggling to understand why God would call her to a job she didn't like. She had already worked at her company for four years but it felt like a lifetime in public accounting years since the turnover was so high.

> I don't know sweetie. But I do know that you are making a difference in your job with the people there. You have such a gift of bringing people together and making them feel welcome. Maybe that's why God has you where you are, for the people, not accounting.

Aubrey sighed as she lay down on the couch. Her mom was right—she did have a gift and passion for people, but that wasn't her job description. Making people feel welcome and planning work happy hours didn't equate to more compensation at year-end. At the end of the day, she was still expected to do accounting and to do it well.

Aubrey closed her eyes and took a few deep breaths. God had a purpose for her and she would figure out what it was. God had brought her out to San Diego, so she could trust God with her future. Yes, God had a plan, and she would continue doing accounting until God told her what she was supposed to do instead.

Chapter 5

⚓

Aubrey made it through the next work week. While she was thankful that she got to work locally from the San Diego office, she still felt like she was wasting her time writing accounting memos and preparing balance sheets.

The next weekend, it was time to explore her new neighborhood. She loved how she could walk to several shops and restaurants right by the beach in Pacific Beach, but she wanted a bike to explore the boardwalk that connected Pacific and Mission Beach.

She bought a bike at the bike shop next door to her apartment building—a mint-colored hybrid—and set off down the boardwalk. Aubrey hadn't ridden a bike since college; she felt like a little kid again, pedaling down the boardwalk next to the ocean.

She sped past the rollercoaster and made her way down to the jetty. Ice cream shops, burger joints, and restaurants with patio dining lined the boardwalk. She couldn't wait to have friends or a boyfriend to go to all these places with.

Soon Aubrey came across a quieter area in Mission Beach with cute cafes and coffee shops. She wasn't in the mood for crowds, so she got an acai bowl from a hole-in-the-wall place. Aubrey locked up her bike and sat on the boardwalk wall eating her bowl. She didn't mind being alone today. She was enjoying the freedom of waking up and exploring wherever she wanted.

As she scanned the people lying out on the beach and the surfers paddling through the waves, she saw something jump quickly out of the water. Was that a shark? Aubrey squinted in the sun, gazing past the surfers and the waves as a dolphin jumped through the waves. A dolphin! In the wild!

She quickly finished the last few bites of the acai bowl and ran to the ocean's edge to get a closer look. Spotting a few more fins, she couldn't believe a pack of dolphins was this close to shore. Aubrey had seen dolphins while snorkeling in Hawaii, but this was different. This was right off the beach in her home. A place where dolphins roamed free. A few surfers sat on their boards only a few feet away from them, so close they could almost touch them.

Aubrey stared at the ocean, waiting for the dolphins to appear again, when she noticed a guy in a red bathing suit laying out his beach towel. He was on the shorter side but still pretty cute. He glanced over at her quickly before walking into the water and diving through the waves. The dolphins jumped right out of the water, but the guy didn't seem to notice.

After a few minutes, the guy made his way back out of the water.

"Did you see the dolphins?" Aubrey asked him. She didn't want him to miss out on the dolphin show right in front of them.

"No, I didn't! Where are they?"

"Right there! You can see a few fins popping out by that surfer!" Aubrey pointed.

"No way! This is my first time seeing dolphins here. How freakin' cool!"

"Mine too!"

They stopped staring at the ocean for a few seconds and turned to each other, both with giddy smiles on their faces.

"I'm Jake. I just moved here from Washington."

"I'm Aubrey. I just moved here from Chicago. Welcome to San Diego!"

Jake had a gorgeous smile. He raised his arms. "We live here now! This is our home!"

It was like seeing the ocean for the first time, seeing a whole new world neither of them thought they would ever be a part of by the beach. They talked nonstop for the next half hour, getting to know each other. Jake lived in Mission Beach, right behind the boardwalk where they were standing. He worked at an online marketing firm and was able to work remotely from San Diego. Ready for a change, he had driven his Jeep all the way down the coast to San Diego.

"So, what are you up to on this gorgeous day?" he asked.

"I've been bike riding, exploring our new home, but I'm about to head home to put my new kitchen table together. I still have to put the legs on the table, so I was planning on heading to the hardware store after my bike ride to get a hexagon wrench."

Jake tilted his head and smiled. "A hexagon wrench? You mean an Allen wrench?"

"Um, sure! Whatever it's called; the hole is a hexagon."

Jake threw his head back and laughed.

Wow, he was pretty cute. He was still shirtless; she couldn't help but check him out. He had nice muscular arms and solid abs with a large tattoo on his upper back and another tattoo that looked like a flame on his shoulder and bicep.

"That's adorable," Jake said. "I know exactly what wrench you are talking about. And you don't have to buy one; I have a few of them laying around my apartment. I moved three weeks ago today and am still building a lot of furniture myself."

Aubrey's eyes lit up. "I moved here exactly three weeks ago too. On November 1."

They stared at each other. Jake started to smile.

"Well, isn't that a coincidence. It's like we were destined to be friends. We should definitely hang out sometime. What's your number?"

Aubrey entered her number in his phone. It was pretty crazy that they had both moved to San Diego on the same day. He seemed fun and they both needed new friends. And he was cute.

"I'm going to get back to building furniture," Jake said, "but you can totally borrow one of my hexagon wrenches. I live behind that building if you want to come grab it."

He pointed to a small apartment building behind the boardwalk. It was a nice gesture, but she hesitated. She had just met him and didn't want to go to his apartment. Jake didn't look like a crazy person, but she knew she needed to be careful all alone here.

"Don't worry—I'm not going to hurt you. Besides, my apartment is a mess with boxes and furniture. I normally wouldn't invite anyone in like this, but I know your apartment must look the same." Jake smiled.

Aubrey followed him up to the boardwalk and to his apartment. She stood in his doorway while he grabbed one of the wrenches. He was telling the truth. Boxes were all over the place; a half-constructed TV stand occupied the middle of the room. He lived in a one-bedroom apartment only a half block from the beach. It had an open kitchen that wasn't very updated, but he must make good money to afford his own place right by the beach.

What were the odds of both of them moving to San Diego on the same day and living only a mile apart on the beach?

"Thanks so much. I'll give it back to you eventually."

Jake smiled. "You can keep it. I have plenty of those laying around. Good luck with the table. I'll see you around the beach by the dolphins."

Aubrey headed back to Mission Beach and grabbed her bike. What a day! She had seen dolphins for the first time and met a cute guy on the beach. It was so refreshing to meet people doing things that she actually enjoyed without having to have a conversation over loud music at a bar. Jake was cute, but she wasn't sure if he was interested in hanging out as more than friends or even at all. She was used to guys asking for her number and then never texting her. But they were both in a new city and needed to make friends. It would be nice to have someone else to hang out with, and they lived so close to each other by the beach.

Aubrey hoped she would hear from him, but she wasn't going to get her hopes up. She realized on her way home that she couldn't even text him if she wanted to. He had saved her number without calling or texting her.

A few hours later, Aubrey was screwing the last leg onto her kitchen table with the hexagon wrench when her phone buzzed with a text from Jake.

How's that table looking?

A huge smile spread across her face. She hadn't expected him to text her right away; it felt flattering that he was thinking of her so soon. She sent him a picture of the table, complete with all four legs screwed on.

Thanks for the hexagon wrench! You're a lifesaver!

Jake sent a picture back of some shelves he had put up with another text.

How about we both call it a day with furniture and celebrate our new city over a few drinks?"

Aubrey's pulse raced. Was he asking her out? He definitely seemed like a great guy, and it would be nice to explore some new bars and restaurants with someone. Aubrey enjoyed doing a lot of things on her own, but eating dinner or going to bars by herself was not one of them. She had originally planned to have a chill night in and was planning on going back to church the next day. But it was only five o'clock. The night was young. Why not explore the town with a new friend? Aubrey replied to Jake's text.

Sure, that would be great!

Jake suggested a rooftop bar between their places on the boardwalk. It would be perfect to catch the sunset there.

Aubrey danced as she got ready. A night out exploring with a new friend. She didn't want to get too dressed up, but she still wanted to look cute, so she settled on jeans, a tank top, and wedges.

Chapter 6

⚓

Jake looked pretty hot in a blue, fitted V-neck shirt and jeans. He already looked better than all of the guys Aubrey had met at the rooftop bar the weekend before. He looked her age, but he seemed more mature than the guys her age.

"How old are you anyway?" Aubrey asked Jake as the bouncer checked their IDs.

Jake smiled. "Take a guess."

"Twenty-nine."

Jake handed her his ID. "I get that all the time. Check it for yourself. I know you won't believe me."

Aubrey's jaw fell open. He did not look thirty-six.

"You look so young!"

"I know; it's this face. What can I say?" They both laughed.

Everyone looked younger here in San Diego because everyone was tan and in such good shape. Aubrey had never dated someone that old, but this wasn't a date.

They enjoyed tacos and a few vodka sodas at a table by the roof's edge with a perfect view of the sun setting over the ocean. They talked about where they grew up, life in Chicago and Washington, and what they wanted to do in San Diego. They both loved the beach, were active, and enjoyed hiking and biking.

Jake was really easy to talk to, and they were having fun together, but Aubrey still didn't know if this was a date. It seemed like they were flirting with each other, and he kept flashing his ridiculously cute smile, but she didn't want to assume anything. They decided to check out another bar on the boardwalk and headed to Wave Rider. Neither of them had been there before, but the bar was playing old-school hip-hop music so it looked like a fun time.

Aubrey's shoes started sticking to the floor as soon as she walked in. People were dancing and standing around everywhere, at least two-people-deep in front of the bar. It was only eight o'clock, yet people already looked pretty rowdy.

Aubrey blushed as Jake took hold of her hand to lead her through the bar. She had her answer. It definitely felt more like a date now and she couldn't help but smile.

Jake motioned to get the bartender's attention as they made it to another section in the back of the bar.

"Two tequila shots and two frozen Red Bull slushies, please."

Aubrey laughed. She felt like she was back in college on spring break.

"I hope you like tequila. Cheers to San Diego and living our best beach life in our new city!" Jake said with a smile as he raised his shot glass next to hers.

Aubrey licked the salt off her wrist, downed the tequila, and grabbed for the lime slice as the tequila burned in her stomach.

"This has been the year of the tequila shot. I used to organize all my work happy hours in Chicago and was known for throwing epic parties at work. One time, I planned a happy hour where I spent $588 on forty-eight shots of Patrón alone."

Jake laughed as he slapped his hand on the bar. Aubrey smiled, remembering how much fun the happy hour had been. She chose not to tell Jake that she had made it a rule not to drink any more tequila shots because of everything that had happened the past year because of tequila. Jake seemed so fun, and it wasn't like they were going to get wasted. They were casually getting to know each other and exploring their new city. A shot or two wouldn't hurt. Aubrey ordered a water from the bartender to pace herself just in case.

The bar was playing old school '90s hip-hop, including one of her favorites by Akon, which reminded her of her freshman year of college. A circle formed on the dance floor as people started showing off their moves inside the circle. The circle quickly turned into a twerk contest among a few girls.

"Are you a dancer?" Aubrey asked Jake with a smile. She loved to dance; a guy who could dance was such a turnon.

Jake shook his head and laughed.

"Nah, not much of a dancer, unless I'm wasted, and even then, I'm not very good. Typical white guy moves. What about you?"

"I once won a twerk contest on stage at a Jason Derulo concert at the beach. You could say I'm a good dancer." Aubrey grinned as she took a sip of her Red Bull slushie.

Jake's mouth fell open as his eyes grew big.

"Dang, look at you twerking queen. Let's see those moves in action." He gestured to the dance floor.

Aubrey shook her head. "Not tonight. I don't think you could handle it."

Jake smiled and motioned to the bartender for two more tequila shots. After they downed the shots, Jake slammed his shot glass down on the bar.

"I haven't won a dance contest since my honeymoon. Luau contest on the beach." He stared at her, waiting for her reaction as he took another sip of his drink.

Aubrey's stomach was still burning from the shot, and it was now doing flips. She felt sick. Was he married? What was going on?

"Are you married?"

Jake shook his head. "I was. Well, I guess I technically still am. Currently getting a divorce."

Aubrey wanted to know what had happened, but she didn't know how to ask. Some people got all angry talking about their divorce, and she didn't know how Jake would react.

"We've been separated for a while," Jake said, "and we decided things weren't working out. Married for ten years. Ended on good terms. We just realized we didn't want to be together anymore. No kids. Actually, my ex was the one who encouraged me to move to San Diego. I always wanted to live here at some point and it seemed like the right time."

Aubrey was taking it all in. Jake had said all of this so casually, without any hurt or anger in his voice. She didn't have many friends yet who had gotten a divorce. Most of the people she knew had recently gotten married, but Jake was eight years older, so it made sense given his age.

Married for ten years! She couldn't imagine what that must have been like, let alone getting a divorce. She had always said she wouldn't want to date anyone with kids or who was divorced, but she had never been faced with the decision before.

"Oh, well, thanks for sharing. I'm glad things ended on good terms, not like in the movies where they find out someone had been cheating the entire time."

Jake winced. "Yeah, I'm not proud of it, but I did cheat on her in the past. But that's not why it ended. She never found out about it."

So he was a cheater. Just like the guys in all those movies and like her first serious boyfriend who had cheated on her in college. Even though she had just met Jake, he didn't look like someone who would cheat. She didn't know what else to say so she raised her glass in the air for a cheers.

"Well, cheers to a new life, new beginnings, and new friends in San Diego."

Jake smiled as they clinked glasses.

The music seemed to get louder around them. Aubrey surveyed the bar; the twerking circle had expanded. Half the bar was dancing while others ripped shots at the bar and drank their Red Bull slushies. Guys hung out around the dancing, scoping out ladies they wanted to take home that night.

"Well, spring break was fun. Should we go somewhere a little less rowdy and sticky?" Jake suggested as he motioned for the bartender.

Aubrey laughed. "Yes, absolutely. Time to move on."

Instead of listening to the warning bell going off inside her, Aubrey let Jake grab her hand again as they made their way out of the bar.

Chapter 7

⚓

Even in the dark, Aubrey could see the white of the waves crashing along the shore. Her cheeks were flushed from the ocean breeze and the feel of Jake's hand around her waist as they walked along the boardwalk. She couldn't stop smiling.

"That's my place." Aubrey pointed to the condo building a block away.

"Wow, you must make the big bucks! Accounting for the win! Isn't it crazy we get to live here?" Jake laughed.

Aubrey had found her newly renovated, one-bedroom apartment right on the beach only a few weeks before she had to move. She didn't have ocean views; her apartment faced the back alley, but she could be on the cliffs overlooking the beach within minutes of leaving her apartment.

"What are the odds of both of us moving here on the same day and meeting today on the beach while watching dolphins?" Aubrey asked.

Jake laughed. "I know, right? That was my first time swimming in the ocean, too. Well, I have a confession to make."

Oh, gosh. What now? Had he been lying about his job or that he had just moved here?

"I came out to the beach and noticed you standing by the water. I noticed you had a pretty nice butt, so I put my towel down by you, hoping I'd get a chance to talk to you. And then the dolphins were there and it worked out perfectly."

Aubrey pretended to punch his arm.

"So, you did plan that. Well, part of it. And thank you, I guess." She blushed.

They arrived at Barrel Roll, a smaller bar a few blocks from Aubrey's apartment. The bar already felt quieter and more relaxing than Wave Rider. Only a handful of people sat around the bar. No loud music or raunchy dancing.

They ordered a few more vodka sodas at the bar. Even though she was sitting on the barstool, Aubrey started to sway a bit.

"Don't you feel like we can do anything we want now?" Aubrey asked. "That we can finally become who we were created to be here? San Diego is a fresh start for both of us. We can be anyone and do anything we want."

Aubrey looked into Jake's blue eyes.

"Oh, most definitely," Jake said. "It's like we are superheroes in a new city, ready to take on the world."

Aubrey giggled as Jake flexed his muscles over his head.

"But seriously," Aubrey said, "if you could do anything in the world, knowing that you would earn enough money and be successful, what would you do?"

Jake stirred his drink.

"I think about that question a lot actually," Jake said. "If I could do absolutely anything, I would coach high school basketball. I would be your typical family man, going to my kids' games, coaching basketball, and then enjoying dinner with the fam."

Gosh, he is so sweet.

"How adorable. What an amazing dream. You can totally do that, you know. You're still young, well sort of."

Jake punched her arm.

"Very funny," he said. "Enough about me and my dreams that are never going to happen since I'm almost an old man. What about you? What's your dream now that you're out of the Midwest and officially a beach girl?"

"Well," Aubrey said, "in the middle of writing a boring accounting memo last week, I actually googled, 'what to do when you hate your job.' So, I basically decided to become a workout instructor and start a travel blog. I want to start a hip-hop workout class on the beach."

Jake's eyes lit up. "I would totally pay to attend and just watch!"

Aubrey slapped Jake's leg in return. Her cheeks hurt from laughing so much all night. She hadn't had this much fun or felt this way getting to know someone in years. They had an instant attraction and connection where they could talk about everything and anything.

"I'm really glad we met today," Jake said as he stopped laughing and looked at her intently.

Time seemed to move in slow motion as Aubrey's face grew warm from Jake's hand on her leg and the buzz of the alcohol. Before she could respond, Jake leaned in and kissed her.

Aubrey felt like she was floating off the barstool. She forgot where they were and that other people were in the bar. She forgot they had just met, and she forgot Jake was still technically married. She forgot she didn't even know his last name.

They drew apart.

"I'm really glad, too," Aubrey said. "To my first beach friend." She clinked his glass.

Aubrey excused herself to use the restroom. They had been drinking for a solid four hours by now, so she needed to call it a night soon. She was feeling more drunk than she wanted to, and while she'd had an amazing time, she didn't want to ruin things by hooking up with Jake right away.

When Aubrey had moved to San Diego, she had decided she wasn't going to sleep with a guy unless she was in a serious relationship with him. She wanted and knew she deserved more than just a hookup. She was done with the guys who wanted to sleep with her but not date her.

But Jake was amazing. He was what she had always wanted in Chicago—someone to explore and have fun with. But he was also going through a divorce. She couldn't imagine dating someone who had been married for ten years and was getting divorced.

Aubrey shook her head. They weren't going to date. They were just enjoying each other's company in their new city. In the bathroom, Aubrey spent a few extra minutes by the mirror, touching up her makeup. When she got back to their seats, Jake was gone. She looked around the bar, but she didn't see him anywhere.

How could he leave? They were having such a great time together. They had just made out!

Her shoulders slunk as she made her way out of the bar, holding back tears. She barely knew Jake, but she didn't understand why he would leave. Was it something she had said? Was she a bad kisser?

She was used to guys ghosting her and not responding to her texts for no reason, but this was different. She had never had someone straight up leave in the middle of a date. A few tears started to fall as she made her way home. Thankfully, her place was only a block away.

Her phone went off as she closed her apartment door. Jake. She cleared her voice and answered.

"Where did you go?" Jake asked. "You were still in the bathroom, so I decided to pee myself, and when I came out, you were gone. I asked the bouncer which way you went, so I figured you must have gone home."

A sigh of relief washed over her. Aubrey started to laugh.

"I'm back home. I came out of the bathroom and didn't see you, so I thought you left."

"I would never leave without saying goodbye. We were having such a fun time, and I wasn't done kissing you yet. I'm still not done; I'm right by your place actually."

Aubrey wasn't done kissing him either, but she didn't want to hook up with him tonight. She had a few bottles of rosé in the fridge; she could invite him up and they could talk and make out some more. She didn't have to let things go any further than she wanted to. She wasn't going to have sex with him tonight. They were just having fun, getting to know each other.

"Would you like to come inside for a drink?" she asked.

"I thought you'd never ask."

Aubrey made sure her makeup wasn't smeared from her tears before heading down the stairs to let Jake in. They both laughed as she opened the door. He immediately grabbed her face and kissed her.

"I would never leave you without saying goodbye," he said as his hands cupped her face.

After that kiss, she couldn't believe she had thought he had left. They enjoyed a few glasses of rosé while talking and standing on her balcony. It didn't take long before Jake's lips found Aubrey's lips again.

Aubrey broke away from Jake as his kisses started getting more intense.

"We need to stop," she said. "We just met; I'm not hooking up with you. I don't want you to get the wrong idea, but we are not having sex."

"That's fine; we don't have to. I'm just going to enjoy kissing you." He grabbed her waist and went in for another kiss.

Aubrey woke up the next morning in bed with Jake's arms wrapped around her. She smiled as she felt his touch and his chest rising with every breath. Last night felt like a dream. How had she met someone like Jake so soon in San Diego?

She hadn't felt this way in so long. The way he looked at her. The way he smiled at her. The way he kissed her.

Aubrey hadn't wanted to sleep with Jake last night, but she had given in. She missed the comfort of being with someone. She missed the feeling of lying in someone's arms and feeling wanted. She missed feeling adored.

Aubrey fell back asleep and forgot all about her plans to go to church.

Chapter 8

⚓

Aubrey sat on the cliff overlooking the beach by her apartment while sipping a cup of tea. The clouds were already starting to glow a bright pink as the sun made its way closer to the ocean.

She smiled as she gazed at the ocean and the beach scene around her. People going for a run, people walking their dogs. A few toddlers still playing in the waves, not caring that it was getting chilly or that they had sand in their hair.

The past few weeks since moving in and meeting Jake seemed like a dream. Meeting Jake on the beach while watching dolphins and having an instant, crazy connection with him was like being in her own real-life Nicholas Sparks movie. It felt like fate—meeting on the beach and both moving to San Diego on the same day. What were the odds? Meeting a guy like that had never happened to her before.

Over the past few weeks, Aubrey and Jake had spent almost every weekend together. While Aubrey spent her weekdays traveling to Colorado for a new client at work, she spent the weekends with Jake, exploring beaches during the day and hitting up new bars and restaurants in the evenings.

Jake was so different from all the guys she had dated in Chicago. And she didn't have to worry about him ghosting her—they texted each other nonstop every day and even talked on the phone when she was traveling for work. He had already taken her to the zoo, bike riding along Sunset Cliffs, and to a romantic Italian restaurant in Little Italy.

They hadn't officially talked about how they felt about each other, but it was clear they liked each other. Spending the night together wasn't even a question anymore. They quickly fell into the pattern of hanging out together and waking up in each other's arms the next morning. She wanted Jake to be her boyfriend, but she didn't want to freak him out by asking him where things were headed. All the magazines she had read on dating always talked about how you shouldn't have the talk too soon and that you should wait for the guy to initiate the conversation so you don't scare him away. Plus, there was Jake's very recent divorce she had to think about. He wasn't even legally divorced yet; she didn't want to pressure him by asking him if he wanted to be exclusive so soon.

Aubrey checked her phone. Jake was almost there. They were both feeling hungover from the drinks they had had the night before, so they made plans for a movie night at her place.

"Hello stranger. Is this seat taken?"

Jake appeared behind her on the cliff, looking adorable in jeans and a red sweater.

"I'm saving it for a handsome man to watch the sunset with. Are you interested?"

Aubrey stood up and gave him a kiss.

"Very interested. This handsome man would love to watch the sunset with you. And I come with refreshments. It's almost

Christmas; you know what that means. Hot chocolate with peppermint schnapps." Jake held up a thermos and two cups.

"That sounds like exactly what we need. I decided not to drink peppermint schnapps anymore after all the shots I took in college, but I'll make an exception for you." She winked.

They sat on the cliff watching the surfers while the sun glowed a bright orange and dipped into the ocean.

"What are your plans tomorrow? Want to go surfing with me?" Jake slid his arm around Aubrey's waist.

Tomorrow was Sunday and Aubrey hadn't been to church since she had met Jake. She needed to go; she felt guilty about all the alcohol she had been consuming and for missing church.

"I already have plans to go to church tomorrow. I started going to the Freedom Church a few weeks ago. Do you go to church?"

Jake took a drink of his spiked hot chocolate.

"Nah, I'm not really a church-going type of guy. I'm not even sure if God is real to be honest."

Aubrey was caught off guard. She had always believed in God—for her, there was no question he existed. Most of her friends believed in him, even though they didn't go to church or talk about him. But she had never met someone who didn't believe that God existed at all.

She took a sip of her drink. "Oh, well, did you go to church growing up? Did your parents go?"

"I used to go with my grandparents as a kid. My parents split up when I was seven. My mom never went to church. I spent a lot of weekends with my grandparents, so I went with them, but I stopped going as I got older. I just didn't see the point. With so many bad things happening in this world, how could God exist?"

Aubrey didn't know how to respond to that. She was fortunate to have grown up in a family that loved her, with her parents still married. What kinds of bad things had Jake faced that he didn't believe in God?

"I just know God exists," Aubrey replied. "I can't explain it, but I just know. He's always been there."

Jake continued to stare at the ocean. While Aubrey enjoyed going to church and wanted to make God more of a priority, dating someone who didn't believe in God wasn't a deal breaker. Growing up, her mom had always told her how important it was to date someone who also believed in God, but she wasn't going to rule out Jake because he didn't believe in God. Aubrey preferred to be with someone who shared her faith, but if he was a great guy, had a good job, and had his life together, that was good enough. Besides, she never met any guys who actually went to church.

"So where does your dad live? Are you guys close?" She could tell Jake didn't want to talk about God anymore.

"No, we aren't close at all. He currently lives in Arizona. I hadn't seen him in almost ten years, but then he decided to show up to my sister's wedding last year."

Oh, gosh, this wasn't a good subject either. How was she supposed to know he had so much family drama?

"My mom finally told me a few years ago that my dad was a drug addict and had been addicted to meth when I was little. That's why he left, and that's why she let him leave. Figured it was better for me and my sister. He's remarried now, and my mom told me he doesn't do drugs anymore, but I can't have a relationship with someone who wasn't there for me my whole life, you know?"

Aubrey could see the hurt in Jake's eyes. She didn't know how to respond to any of this. She didn't know how anyone could abandon their kids like that. She wrapped her arms around him and rubbed his back.

"Thank you for sharing. I know that wasn't easy to talk about, and I'm sorry for bringing it up. I think you're pretty amazing, and I'm so glad you decided to move to San Diego."

A large Husky ran below them on the beach, running in and out of the waves.

"I miss my dog Kona," Jake said as he pointed at the Husky. "He looked just like him."

"I'm so sorry. Did he pass away?"

Jake shook his head. "He's back with my ex in Washington. We got him together, and we figured it would be best for him to stay with her for now until I get settled here. Plus, she has a bigger condo with more room for him to run around instead of being cramped up in my apartment all day."

Jake pulled out his phone and started scrolling through pictures of a Husky, starting as a puppy until he was full grown.

"What a cutie, just like his dad. He has your eyes."

"I know, he's the best. He's the only kid I may ever have."

"Do you still want kids?" Aubrey asked. "It's not too late, you know. You can still have your dream basketball coach job with a minivan full of kids."

Jake smiled. "I do want kids. That's one of the reasons my ex and I decided to get a divorce. My ex had always wanted kids, and I didn't want them for the longest time. But I turn forty in a few years. I realized she was my last chance because I don't want to be an old dad. But things were already ending for us. She didn't want kids with me anymore. It was too late."

Aubrey didn't know how to process all this information. How did they keep returning to touchy subjects that were awkward to talk about?

"It's never too late," she said. "You could totally still have kids with the right person. Guys have all the time in the world."

"Thanks for being so positive. I know it's not too late; I just never planned on being single again at thirty-six. I don't even know how to be single. All these dating apps didn't exist before I was married. How do you kids put up with this?" Jake laughed.

Aubrey responded with a fake laugh. Was he on the dating apps? Was she someone he would consider dating and having kids with one day? What were they doing together anyway?

She had thought she wanted to be his girlfriend, but the more she learned about Jake, the more she realized he was not ready to be in a relationship. She wasn't about to ask what he wanted or what they were doing together. She knew he needed time to be alone and to figure out life again on his own. But if he was on the dating apps, then he clearly didn't see her as someone he could seriously date and have a future with.

"Are you on the dating apps now? How is that going for you?" She took a sip of her hot cocoa.

"No way. I'm not ready for that yet. I'm just having fun in my new city meeting amazing people like you."

Jake kissed her cheek. She was glad he wasn't on the dating apps, but she couldn't help but feel a tad rejected that they were just having fun. Aubrey couldn't hold it in any longer. Now was her chance to see what his intentions were.

"I know we have been having fun the past few weeks, and I know you haven't been single in over ten years, but I hope you know it's more than just fun for me. I'm starting to really like you and I was wondering, well, if you saw this going anywhere."

Aubrey avoided looking directly at Jake. She could feel her face growing red as she tried to hide behind her cup of hot cocoa.

Jake gently pulled her arms and cup away from her face and turned her chin toward him. Aubrey couldn't avoid looking back into his blue eyes.

"I'm starting to really like you too, but I don't know how to navigate this. I never expected to like someone so soon after moving here. I know I still need more time to process everything, but I don't want to stop hanging out with you. I'm hoping to have more clarity after I go home for Christmas. I know that's probably not the answer you're looking for, but I'm trying to be honest with you."

Aubrey tried to focus on the part where Jake had said that he liked her, but she couldn't help but still feel rejected.

"I understand." She didn't know what else to say. Tonight hadn't gone like Aubrey had planned, but it felt like they had grown closer in a way by talking about Jake's past and the possibility of them being together.

"Come on; let's head in," Jake said. "Time for some popcorn and a movie under a blanket."

As Aubrey got settled in on the couch, Jake took out a rolled piece of paper.

"Want to join me? There's nothing like watching a good movie a little stoned," he said as he took out his lighter.

Jake had smoked weed a few times in front of her already, and she had politely declined every time he had offered it to her. At first, she didn't mind since he didn't get out of control, but she didn't see why he had to smoke when they were watching a movie together. Did he smoke every night, even when they weren't going out?

They ended up falling asleep on the couch after she had set an alarm to get up for church.

Chapter 9

⚓

"The Bible is alive; it is the most powerful weapon you have against the Enemy. As you study the Word of God, it's so important that you pray it back to God and speak it out." Pastor Davis was fired up as he preached about the power of prayer.

"Prayer is talking to God; it's how we communicate. This is why it's so essential to spend time in prayer with God every day. With any relationship, if you never talk to someone, how are you going to get closer to that person? How are you going to know what they are thinking? Prayer is like talking to your best friend. God wants us to be able to talk to him about everything. He already knows everything you are thinking anyway. He is just waiting for you to invite him to be a part of the conversation.

"So how do we pray? Other than speaking God's Word back to him, how else do we pray effectively? This may sting a little bit, but a lot of you pray these weak prayers. You come to God like he's going to scold you for asking for what you want. Like your prayer requests are bugging him or inconveniencing him. As a child of God, you should never feel afraid to ask God for what you want. He's God; he already knows what you want, so you may as well ask him for it."

Cheers erupted from the auditorium.

"So," Pastor Davis continued, "now you know you can come to God boldly and ask for what you want, and you know the power in speaking God's Word. But something is missing."

A Bible verse appeared on the screen behind him.

"Don't worry about anything; instead, pray about everything. Tell God what you need, and thank him for all he has done. Then you will experience God's peace, which exceeds anything we can understand. His peace will guard your hearts and minds as you live in Christ Jesus.

"As we take everything to God in prayer, we need to remember to thank God for all that he has done. These verses from Philippians 4:6-9 tell us that God wants us to approach him first with praise and thanksgiving. When we pray to God with thanksgiving, we experience peace from God. We don't have to worry about what is going on around us. God already sees and knows everything going on, so we can come to him confidently and boldly through prayer and trust that he is in control. If you could bow your heads, it's time to pray."

The worship team started playing a song as people made their way out of the auditorium. Aubrey noticed an information booth in the lobby. She had tried finding more information about the church's small groups online, but she couldn't tell if the groups had just started or if they were open to new people joining. She walked up to the information booth. It couldn't hurt to ask about the small groups and ministries the church had for young professionals.

"Welcome! How did you enjoy the service?" said a woman her age, smiling at her as she approached.

"It was great. I'm really enjoying the messages here. I just moved here about a month ago, and I'm looking to meet some more people. Do you know where I can get more information on small groups?"

The woman's eyes lit up. "Oh, my goodness! Well, welcome to San Diego! I'm Amanda." She gave Aubrey her hand to shake.

"I'm Aubrey. Nice to meet you."

"We are so excited to have you here," Amanda said. "It's a big church, but we have so many small group and fun events to make the church feel small."

Amanda took out a pamphlet that listed several different ministries.

"We have everything from volleyball meetups, hiking, Bible studies, and even a singles ministry; they had a bonfire last weekend. Are you single?"

Was she? Even though she and Jake hadn't talked about what they were, Aubrey wasn't interested in dating anyone else.

"No, no, I'm not. I would like to check out the volleyball ministry, though. That sounds awesome."

Aubrey took the pamphlet. She was about to ask Amanda which groups she went to, but a couple was waving Amanda down from the other end of the information booth.

"See you next Sunday," Amanda said.

"Thanks," Aubrey replied.

If churches had a volleyball ministry when I was growing up, maybe I would never have stopped going to church, Aubrey thought.

Aubrey treated herself to an iced coffee and bagel after church and found a secluded rock to sit on along Sunset Cliffs. Aside from the cliffs right outside her apartment, Sunset Cliffs was becoming her second favorite spot in San Diego. She could walk the cliffs along the ocean's edge for miles and always found new paths to explore that led to more breathtaking rocks above the waves. Sitting on the rock while staring at the waves and the vast ocean in front of her, she was always filled with hope for the plans God had for her.

As Aubrey breathed in the ocean air, Pastor Davis' message about prayer came back to her. She needed to pray more, but she wasn't sure how. She had tried saying quick prayers at night before falling asleep, but she had never really enjoyed it. She didn't know what to say most of the time. She had gotten into the habit of praying more consistently on her runs when training for the Chicago marathon before she moved, and she had always prayed the same prayer in her head.

God, please give me the strength and energy I need to get through the day, the love I need to give others, hope I need for my future, and peace for whatever comes my way.

Whenever Aubrey prayed, she did feel more at peace and that God was with her for the day ahead. But she had stopped praying when she moved to San Diego since her routine was different.

Prayer was going to be one of her New Year's resolutions, along with going to church and getting more involved so she could meet new friends. Aubrey missed having friends she could call up and make plans with on short notice. She missed having friends she could be herself around without worrying about making a good impression. She missed having those kinds of friends she could grab a nice dinner with or stay in with while wearing comfy sweats for a movie night.

While she had been having so much fun with Jake and was enjoying having someone to explore with, she felt like she was moving backward. She was still doing things she promised herself she would leave behind. Drinking every time she hung out with Jake. Having sex even though they weren't in a committed relationship. But the

New Year was a chance to start fresh. She would tell Jake she didn't want to drink as much. And maybe he would want to start dating officially and be ready for a relationship in the New Year. She hadn't had a serious boyfriend in more than six years and both she and God knew it was time.

In addition to a boyfriend, maybe this would also be the year she would quit her job and pursue her true passion, whatever that was. She could leave the accounting world behind her and travel the world as she started a travel blog. Or she could get her fitness instructor certification to teach cardio kickboxing or hip-hop dance classes on the beach.

Aubrey smiled as she remembered Pastor Davis' message. God wanted her to talk to him like he was her best friend. He was waiting to be invited to the conversation. She didn't need to worry what was going to happen with Jake or her job.

Aubrey looked around to make sure she was alone. Then she closed her eyes and bowed her head as she prayed silently.

God, thank you for this new life here. Thank you for letting me live on the beach in San Diego. Thank you for letting me and Jake meet on the beach while watching dolphins.

God, I pray that you show me what I'm supposed to do here and what my purpose is. Show me if I'm meant to do accounting or if I'm meant to do something else. And I pray that you make a way for Jake and me to end up together. Help me have the relationship I've been wanting all these years. It's been so long, God, and I want that with Jake. Please, God, let Jake be my boyfriend who actually wants to date me.

God, help me live a new life here, free from drinking and my past mistakes. Help me meet new friends at church. Help me put you first, God. Amen.

Chapter 10

⚓

Aubrey made it through another work week full of boring technical accounting memos and client presentations on how companies should recognize revenue. It was finally Friday morning—time to head to Newport Beach with Jake for her company holiday party.

She had felt awkward asking him to go since they had only known each other a few weeks, but she wasn't going to go if she didn't have a date. Jake hadn't hesitated, so using her hotel points, Aubrey booked them a suite at a fancy resort overlooking the ocean. Aubrey had never had a date for any of her work holiday parties before. But tonight, she couldn't wait to introduce Jake to her coworkers while she showed off her new red dress.

They made their way to Newport Beach and found a beachfront restaurant for lunch. On the patio overlooking the ocean, they raised their cocktails for a toast.

"Cheers to a beautiful winter weekend by the beach!" Aubrey said.

"Are we going to get lit tonight or what?" Jake replied.

Aubrey needed to be careful. She had gotten too excited at work events like this in the past, and she didn't want to black out or do anything stupid around coworkers that she would regret. She needed to be honest with Jake, especially if they had a future together. He would learn the truth at some point.

The waiter brought over a tray of oysters. After he left, Aubrey said, "I am so excited for tonight, and I am so happy to have you as my hot date." She grabbed Jake's hand. "And I know we always have so much fun together, but I need to be careful not to get too drunk around my boss and coworkers."

"It's a holiday party—everyone gets wasted." Jake swallowed an oyster.

Aubrey hesitated as she moved her finger around the rim of her drink. She needed to make sure he understood where she was coming from. This was different than a night out in Pacific Beach where they could do whatever they wanted. They were getting pretty close, and she felt like she could trust him not to judge her for her past mistakes. Jake seemed to drink a lot himself, and they were going to her work event. It was important for him to know what had happened last year. Maybe he would even think it was funny like some of her friends did.

"I'm totally down with having fun and a few drinks, but I actually want to remember the night. I need to be functioning and can't do anything stupid. I tend to make dumb mistakes when I'm drunk, and last year, I did something at a work-related event that was seriously frowned upon. I thought I was going to get fired." She sipped her Moscow mule as Jake stared at her.

"Go on. I'm listening. What happened?"

Aubrey sighed. What did she have to lose?

"Salt, tequila, lime!" Aubrey took back the shot and wiped her face.

Why did it burn so bad? She looked around her as her coworkers finished their shots. Others were showing off their moves on the dance floor, singing to the piano player's version of Beyonce's "Crazy in Love." A few coworkers were already getting pretty cozy with each other in the corner of the bar.

Aubrey loved these work trainings. She and her coworkers from all around the country had decided to go out to a dueling piano bar for their last night in Tampa together. They only got together once a year, and when they did, they went hard.

"Aubrey, we're ready for another round! More tequila!" an associate from Chicago shouted across the bar.

Aubrey shook her head and laughed. They had already had four rounds of tequila shots, but the night was not over yet. Aubrey motioned for the bartender as she held up ten fingers.

"Ten more, please!"

A few associates standing next to her cheered. She loved bringing everyone together. Nights out like these were a celebration of all the hours they had all been working.

"Aubrey, the bar is about to close. Some of us are going to go swimming at the hotel when we get back. You down?" an associate asked her.

"Sure, why not?" Aubrey didn't hesitate. She was having such a great night, and it wasn't time to end yet. It didn't matter that it was almost 2 a.m. and they were all supposed to be in class for training by eight the next morning.

They found themselves sitting in the hotel's hot tub shortly after, sharing a case of beer. The pool gate was closed, but that didn't stop them; they helped each other hop the fence.

Another epic night out at training. Now this was what networking was all about. They found themselves splashing in the pool shortly after until the pool lights turned on.

"The pool area is closed! What are you guys doing out here?" A loud voice startled them as a security guard appeared out of nowhere.

Aubrey climbed out of the pool and ran to the lounger where she had left her clothes. She hadn't packed a swimsuit coverup with her, so she attempted to put on her skinny jeans.

The security guard started walking a few of her coworkers out of the pool area. A few others started running back to their rooms. She needed to get dressed and get out of there fast.

"Do you need help?" asked her coworker Matt. "Everyone else has already left. Come on; let's get you dressed." He started helping her pull up her jeans.

Aubrey started to laugh.

"We're getting kicked out of the pool, and I can't even put my jeans on! Have you ever tried putting on skinny jeans when you're wet? This is impossible!" She stood up and tried to wiggle the jeans on.

Matt laughed as they finally managed to get her jeans on.

"Do you think we will get in trouble? Where did that security guard go?" Aubrey noticed that the security guard hadn't come back for them.

"We'll be fine; we were just swimming after hours. The lounge area outside the pool area is technically still open, and we have a few beers left. Wanna join me?"

She had always thought Matt was pretty cute. They had exchanged a few hellos back in the Chicago office, but Aubrey really didn't know too much about him. She wasn't ready for the night to end or to miss out on an opportunity to get to know him better.

And it was sweet of him to stay behind to help her get dressed in a moment of panic. He could have easily left her and gone back to his room.

They spent the next few hours talking, drinking the rest of the beer, and making out on the patio furniture. The security guard never came back. At some point, Aubrey started to sober up and checked the time on her phone.

"Oh, my gosh, it's almost 6 a.m.! We've been up almost the entire night!"

"I haven't had this much fun in ages. And definitely not at a work event." Matt pulled her closer.

"Too bad we both have roommates. Otherwise, we could have had a lot more fun," Aubrey said.

Matt yawned. "One day we will each have our own rooms when we get promoted to managers. But in the meantime, we can always go back in the hot tub and have some more fun."

"We can't get kicked out again. Then we would really get in trouble."

"I know, but it's almost 6 a.m. According to that pool sign over there, the pool area opens up at six. That means we can walk in and not get kicked out."

Matt was so smart. Why hadn't she thought of that?

She grinned at him. "Let's do it."

Shortly after, a different security guard came and unlocked the pool gate, and they made their way back to the hot tub.

"Now, where were we?" Matt asked as he went in for a kiss.

It didn't take long for their swimsuits to come off and for another security guard to yell at them.

"Hey! You guys can't be doing that in here. There are families here!"

They managed to put their bathing suits back on as the security guard approached the hot tub.

"Name and room numbers please." The security guard took out his phone as he typed in their information.

"I'm so sorry. We know we shouldn't be in here like this. We didn't mean to cause any harm," Aubrey apologized, hoping to win the security guard's favor.

Would he report them? Would he call the actual police? Was there a hotel jail he would take them to?

"Go back to your rooms and don't do this again."

Aubrey and Matt said their goodbyes and went back to their own rooms. Aubrey was too hungover and too tired to make it to class the next morning, so she slept until she had to pack and leave for her flight back home.

After she had unpacked and settled into her couch back home, she got an email from Firmwide Security, which appeared to be a department similar to Human Resources in her company.

Subject: HR Incident
Hi Aubrey,

You have been scheduled for an interview with Firmwide Security this Monday in Boston. Please book travel arrangements to arrive by noon on Monday and check in on the seventh floor with the receptionist when you arrive.

This is a confidential matter that is not to be discussed with anyone else.

Regards,
Firmwide Security

Aubrey couldn't stop the tears that had already started falling down her face. This couldn't be happening. This had to be a scam. People did dumb stuff all the time at work events. She had never heard of the Firmwide Security department or anyone having to fly to another state for an interview.

Was she getting fired? Should she tell her boss that she would be flying to Boston on Monday instead of her scheduled client trip to California?

This had to be one of those phishing emails. This couldn't be real. She texted Matt to see if he had gotten an email. He had received the same email for an interview, but for a different day.

Aubrey spent the entire weekend freaking out, trying not to cry every time she thought of having to get on a plane to go to Boston. She thought about not going, but she didn't know what else to do. She eventually called her performance manager, Kurt, and told him everything. They had always had a close relationship and she knew he wouldn't judge her for getting drunk and getting kicked out of the hot tub. Even though the email had said not to discuss her interview with anyone else, she had to tell her boss why she wouldn't be in California for work on Monday.

Kurt had tried to reassure Aubrey as she broke down in tears over the phone. "I've never heard of anyone having to fly to another office for an interview investigation, but I don't think they are going to fire you. If they were going to fire you, they would have asked you to come into the Chicago office on Monday to hand in your laptop. Just try and get some sleep and this will be over before you know it."

Aubrey knew she had to face her mistakes by getting on that plane, no matter what the consequences were. On Monday, Aubrey felt like she was in a movie, walking through the airport security line with only her work bag. *Who travels without any luggage? Bad guys and people who get kicked out of the hot tub at work events, that's who.*

Her interviewer in Boston was a representative from Firmwide Security, which the interviewer explained was part of the firm's legal department. She explained that Aubrey had to fly to see her due to the nature of the incident and because there were only two women in the Firmwide Security Department in the country. The interviewer explained that she had to gather the facts for the HR report and that the firm would then decide what action to take.

"Do you understand the risks you put the firm in by your behavior? You violated several of the firm's core values, not to mention breaking the law by indecent exposure. Did you ever consider that the hotel could have pressed charges? How much did you drink that night? What did you have to drink? Did you consent to the sexual behavior the security guard witnessed with your coworker? Did your coworker force you to do anything you did not consent to? Do you understand the firm takes matters like this very seriously?"

Aubrey burned with shame with each question. She felt like she was being treated like a criminal. She was afraid of the consequences, but she grew more and more angry as the interrogation continued. She was angry at herself for letting things get so out of hand. Even though she knew her behavior had been unprofessional, she was also angry at the firm for making such a big deal out of it. People did stuff like this all the time, yet most of them got away with it. Why was she being punished for getting kicked out of the pool area twice? People had done much worse things at her company.

Aubrey answered all the questions honestly and flew back to Chicago the same day. She then flew out to California the next day for her client and focused on preparing more balance sheets and exploring the beaches in Southern California while she waited for the verdict from HR.

Two months went by and Aubrey figured the company must have either forgotten about the whole incident or decided it wasn't serious enough to take action on. But as soon as she was able to get through a work day without remembering what she had done, her national boss, Devon, who was her boss's boss, gave her a call.

"Hi, Aubrey. I'm sure you can guess why I'm calling today. It's to discuss the incident at training in Tampa a few months ago."

Aubrey's stomach dropped. They hadn't forgotten about her after all. Why did they insist on flying her out for an interview immediately after the incident but take months to follow up with her?

Aubrey went into an empty conference room and shut the door. This was it. The moment that decided her future at the company. The moment she had to face whatever consequences the legal team had come up with.

"My admin will be sending you an email containing a verbal warning statement after this call," Devon explained. "The verbal warning is from the legal counsel and explains how your behavior was out of line with the firm's values. As a result of your behavior, you will be on probation for one year. If you violate any of the firm's core values in any way, you will be immediately terminated. In addition, you will not be eligible to receive variable compensation this year. Do you have any questions?"

Aubrey didn't know how to respond. So many emotions rushed through her that she felt like she couldn't speak.

At least she wasn't getting fired, but was she still eligible for her promotion to manager that year? Before the incident, her boss Kurt had already informed her she was on track to get promoted—

she was ranked as one of the top performers among her peers. She couldn't imagine not getting promoted after years of busting her butt, working all those extra hours and traveling on those client trips just to get recognized.

"Um, yes. Thanks for explaining all this. Do you know if I'm still eligible to get promoted?"

"Yes, you are still eligible for a promotion, assuming your performance is in line with the next level's expectations."

Aubrey exhaled. She wasn't getting fired and she was still eligible for a promotion, but how dare they take away her bonus this year? Everyone knew the bonus for getting promoted to manager was one of the highest in public accounting. Her bonus was likely to be at least $10,000, and she had gotten screwed the year before since the firm had experienced a poorer year than expected.

Aubrey didn't know what else to say so she agreed to sign the verbal warning and abide by the firm's core values going forward.

Aubrey continued working after she faced the consequences, but she couldn't pretend everything was normal. What was the point of working so hard if she wasn't going to get her bonus? Why did she have to get caught and get punished when people did stuff like this all the time?

She thought about quitting and working for one of her company's biggest competitors, but she knew that wasn't the solution. She had already put in her paperwork to transfer to California, and it would be too hard to start over at a new firm in a new state.

"So yeah, here we are," Aubrey said, finishing telling Jake her story. "I decided to stick it out and do the bare minimum. I still got promoted and transferred to California to live at the beach. So, it all turned out great, better than I expected really, but I still need to be careful." Aubrey took a long sip of her fresh Moscow Mule that the waiter had brought over.

"Look at you—you're such a rebel! I knew you had a wild side to you." Jake winked. "All joking aside, I'm sorry that happened to you and that you got caught. You're right; people do that kind of stuff all the time but never get caught, but I'm glad you pushed through it. Thank you for telling me."

At least he wasn't judging her for what had happened. Aubrey knew everyone made mistakes, but it was hard talking about it to someone she liked so much. Someone she wanted to impress.

"Have you ever done anything stupid like that?" she asked. "I just shared something very personal—now it's your turn." She smiled.

Jake gazed at the ocean, debating whether he wanted to open up or not.

"Well, yeah, I think we all have. I've gotten two DUIs before. They are on my record now, and it sucks."

Aubrey gasped. She hadn't expected Jake to be the type of guy who got a DUI, let alone two.

"Shocking, I know. I look like such a good guy." Jake gave a cheesy smile. "The first time I was driving home from a buddy's house after a football game and a police car pulled me over for speeding. I vowed never to drink and drive after that, and I was pretty responsible about it. I would even hide my friends' keys when they tried to drive a little tipsy.

"The second time was straight unlucky. I was at my buddy's house for a birthday party, and by that time, I knew my limits. I only had a few beers and drove home because I knew I wasn't drunk.

The drive home was only a few minutes through the neighborhood. A cop pulled me over because my taillight was out. Next thing I know, he asks me to take a breathalyzer because he smelled alcohol on my breath. So I think, 'No problem, I've only had a few beers.' But I ended up blowing a .09, which is just above the legal driving limit in Washington. So, I spent the night in jail and got the second DUI, which is on my record for ten years now."

Aubrey thought she had faced major consequences, but Jake's story was much worse. She couldn't imagine what it must have been like to go to jail and have something on your record.

Jake raised his glass to hers. "Cheers to moving on from past mistakes and to still having fun."

Aubrey's heart swelled as she admired how he had put himself out there and shared something like that from his past.

"You didn't have to tell me that," she said, "but thank you for sharing. I guess we all have a past and things we try to forget and move on from."

"We live in California now," Jake said. "We can do anything we want here, and we don't have to worry about the past."

Aubrey smiled, but something didn't feel right. Could they really both move on from their past mistakes? They had both moved out to California, each trying to leave behind some of their past, but they were still dealing with the consequences. Aubrey shook her head to push aside thoughts of the past. She was going to enjoy this moment and night with Jake—her first actual date to her work holiday party in one of the country's most breathtaking cities.

They flagged their waiter down for the check so they could head to the hotel to get ready.

"So, here's to having the most appropriate amount of fun tonight while not making fools out of ourselves," Jake said as they downed the rest of their drinks.

As expected, the firm had gone all out for the holiday party. It was held in the nicest ballroom at the resort with a walk-out patio overlooking the ocean. The drinks flowed all night at the open bar and food stations were everywhere, filled with prime rib, scallops, and honey-glazed ham.

Aubrey's coworkers and many others she didn't know from other departments occupied the dance floor all night. She and Jake drank too much, thanks to the open bar, but they were still able to function. Jake wasn't the best dancer, but he made her laugh as he spun her around the dance floor. And at least her boss and other coworkers were more drunk than they were, judging by their dance moves that got more colorful as the night went on.

When Aubrey woke up next to Jake the next morning, one thing was certain: She was falling fast, and she didn't know how to stop.

.

Chapter 11

⚓

"Welcome home, sweetheart! We missed you so much."

Aubrey gave her mom a hug as she got into the car at the airport.

"Home sweet home for the holidays!" Aubrey said. "Thanks for picking me up, Mom. Is Dad still at work?"

"Oh, my pleasure. Yes, he's been working some overtime. Things have been picking up again, which is good. He's already planning on bringing you your favorite chicken finger pita sandwich on his way home."

Aubrey smiled as she wrapped her jacket tighter around her. Her dad was so thoughtful. He always went out of his way to make her feel special when she came home.

"I'll turn up the heat for you, in case your body has forgotten how to adjust to the Michigan cold."

Aubrey laughed as her mom started driving on the freeway.

"I've already gotten soft," she replied. "I don't know how I lived in the freezing Midwest for so long."

"So how does it feel to be home? Are you still loving San Diego?" her mom asked.

Aubrey was so happy to be home for Christmas. She had never missed spending a Christmas at home, and she wasn't about to start just because she lived thousands of miles away.

"It still feels like a dream. I miss you guys, but I am enjoying living by the beach and exploring. I'm enjoying going to that new church I told you about, but I still don't know what I'm supposed to do with my life."

"I'm so proud of you for going to church on your own," her mom replied. "It's a big step going by yourself in a new city. I'll keep praying that God will show you the plans he has for you there. He will guide you, don't worry."

Aubrey smiled. Even though she didn't have many new friends yet, she knew she could always count on her mom to pray for her all the way across the country.

"So, have you met any new people yet? How are your neighbors?" her mom asked.

Aubrey had been debating telling her mom about Jake. Growing up, she had never really told her mom much about the guys she dated or was interested in. Her mom had always lectured her about not having sex until she was married and made a big deal about not going on the pill.

They both knew Aubrey had already had sex, so Aubrey chose not to bring it up anymore. Her mom had lectured her enough when Aubrey was eighteen.

As Aubrey got older, though, her mom had seemed more understanding and supportive. She was always there when Aubrey needed her most. Whenever Aubrey went through a breakup or realized a guy wasn't into her, her mom always listened and made her feel better.

Should she tell her about Jake, even though they weren't actually dating? She still wasn't sure how she should describe their relationship.

"Well, I did meet this one guy. His name is Jake and he's super-sweet. We met on the beach while watching dolphins, and we realized we actually moved to San Diego on the same day. We're just friends, but it has been nice having someone to hang out with."

Her mom didn't need to know Jake had been married for ten years and was going through a divorce. Or that he smoked a lot of weed. Or that they were sleeping together.

"Oh, that's lovely! Taking it slow is good; no need to rush anything. Does he go to church?"

Aubrey had known that question would be coming, but she wasn't prepared to give an answer. She didn't want to lie about him already, but she also wasn't in the mood to explain why he didn't go to church.

"He said he went to church occasionally back home with his family. He says he's still getting settled in San Diego and hasn't found a new church yet." The partial truth would have to do for now.

"I'm going to rest my eyes for a bit. I didn't sleep well on the flight," Aubrey said as she reclined her seat and closed her eyes.

As they pulled into the driveway a half hour later, Aubrey's niece and nephew ran outside to greet her.

"We missed you, Bree!" Kyle gave her a big hug. He already seemed a foot taller since she had seen him before she had moved. When Kyle had first started talking, he began calling her Bree and it didn't take long for her new nickname to catch on.

"I missed you too! You guys are growing way too fast. Kate, are you as tall as your dad now? You are getting so big!" Kate laughed as she wrapped her arms around Aubrey's legs. She had just turned four and was the most fearless, adorable kid Aubrey knew.

"I didn't know you guys would be here to greet me," Aubrey said. "I feel so loved. Are your mom and dad here?"

"Surprise, Bree!" Kate cheered.

"Dad is in the house on a work call while Mom finishes their Christmas shopping," Kyle said. "They help Santa get gifts because Santa has so many kids to visit on Christmas Eve."

Kyle was getting so smart. And thank God he still believed in Santa Claus. Every Christmas with Kyle and Kate was so special; Aubrey enjoyed practicing all the Christmas traditions with them that she had enjoyed as a kid. Baking Christmas cookies, making red and green paper chains, watching all the Christmas movies, driving around looking at Christmas lights, gazing at all the Hallmark ornaments her dad put on the tree and watching them move around and light up, and playing with the Nativity set her mom always set out.

"Come on, Bree; time for cookies! Gramma said we could bake when you got home." Kate pulled Aubrey inside the house. As they walked by the office, Aubrey waved to her brother who was still on his work call. Looks like she wasn't the only one who had work to finish before Christmas.

"I can't wait to make cookies with you guys. I'm going to make the best cookies. But I have some work to finish up first, and then we can bake cookies. Why don't you play Pac-Man for a few minutes until I'm done?"

Her dad loved arcade games; they had a basement full of them, and a tabletop Pac-Man machine sat in their living room. Her parents didn't care about decorating or mind having toys out. Aubrey always loved coming home and seeing all the same furniture and games from her childhood.

"Work? What do you do for work?" Kyle asked.

How could she explain accounting to a seven-year-old? Her parents still had a hard time understanding what she did.

"Great question, Kyle. Well, I'm an accountant, and I basically help big companies count their money. I work on a computer with a bunch of numbers, and I help them make sure the numbers are correct."

"I like money, but counting numbers sounds pretty boring. I do enough of that in school." Kyle turned his attention to the Pac-Man game.

Well, he was right. It was boring, but she did like the money and the lifestyle her job provided her, so she hadn't quit yet.

Aubrey opened her laptop to finish sending a few emails before she could take off for the holiday break. One of her old bosses in Chicago had sent her a new email, asking her to take on a few last-minute client requests. Only a few hours of her time? Not likely.

She hung her head in her hands. Would the emails and requests ever end? She was already on personal time off, but she had to finish a few things she had already committed to before she could disconnect for the holidays. She didn't want to keep working. She didn't want to take on any new requests. Why did she feel bad for saying no? She had already been working overtime and spending almost ten hours each week traveling to and from clients.

"Bree, are you done yet? I want to make cookies!" Kate yelled from the kitchen.

Aubrey flipped her hair out of her face. Why was she even thinking about saying yes, only to miss out on baking Christmas cookies with her family? Besides, working a few more hours wouldn't get her anything in the long run. Even if her boss remembered picking up these extra requests for her performance review at year-end, it wasn't worth missing out on spending time with her niece and nephew at Christmas. They were only going to be this age once.

Aubrey quickly responded that she couldn't take on any additional requests and she was already on her personal time off with her family. She didn't feel bad as she told him she wouldn't be available until after the New Year.

"I'm done! Time to make cookies! Who has the cookie cutters?" Aubrey closed her laptop and ran into the kitchen.

The kids were already going through all the shapes on the kitchen table.

"Look, Bree. I have the Santa shape! I'm going to put green sprinkles on his belly," Kyle said.

"And I have an angel!" Kate said, smiling. "I'm going to give her long hair and hang her on top of the Christmas tree."

For the next hour, they rolled, patted, and shook sprinkles on the cookies while eating a good amount of the dough. Flour and sprinkles were everywhere—all over the kids' faces and even in their hair. Aubrey smiled as she took a few photos to capture the moment. The kids' teeth were already stained from the red and green decorating gels they had sampled.

"So, do you know what we are celebrating at Christmas time?" Aubrey's mom asked the kids as they nibbled on their fresh, out-of-the-oven cookies.

"Santa comes and gives us presents! Daddy said I could have a toy horse this year." Kate smiled.

"Yes, that's true; Santa comes and gives you gifts if you've been good, but what else are we celebrating at Christmas? Whose birthday is it?" her mom asked.

"Jesus!" Kyle shouted.

Aubrey's mom pretended to be surprised. "Yes, that's right! Great job! We celebrate the birth of Jesus every Christmas. Jesus is God's son, and God sent him to Earth so we could go to heaven. Jesus was born at Christmas in a manger." As she spoke, Aubrey's mom dunked her angel cookie in a glass of milk.

"Jesus rode in his momma's belly on a donkey," Kate said. "I like the donkey; he's funny. And I love the sheep and horses too."

Of course, Kate would remember all of the animals from the story.

"Can we watch *The Star* again, Grandma?" Kyle asked.

"Yes, of course! You got it." Her mom got up to start the movie.

Aubrey's mom was always trying to teach the kids about Jesus. She made it a point to share a new Bible story with the kids whenever they were over, and the kids loved the prayer song they sang together before dinner. Aubrey's brother, Tyler, and his wife, Marie, didn't go to church much, but they were grateful that her mom taught the kids about God. A few weeks ago, Tyler had found Kyle in bed praying. Kyle told his parents he was praying to God to heal their dog's leg because he had been limping on it. It warmed Aubrey's heart that the kids were learning to pray on their own. If a seven-year-old could pray to God, she could pray more to God too.

While the kids were snuggled up on the couch, watching *The Star*, her dad walked through the front door.

"Welcome home, dear. How was your day?" Aubrey's mom asked, standing up to give him a kiss.

"Dad! I'm home!" Aubrey gave him a hug.

"I can't wait to have dinner with my girl," said her dad. "So glad you are home. Are you ready to come back and buy a house in Michigan?" He set a restaurant to-go bag on the table.

Aubrey shook her head. "Very funny, Dad. You know I'm loving San Diego. I just got there. And you know I'll travel home to see you guys any chance I get with work, especially if you keep buying me my favorite sandwich. They don't have these in California."

Her dad was only half-joking. Even though her dad was proud of her and happy she was doing well in her career, Aubrey knew he still wanted her to move closer to home. But Aubrey still had no idea what she was supposed to do with her life. Moving back to Michigan to buy a house because they were more affordable wasn't the answer. And she had no idea when she would meet her future husband. Could Jake be the one? Would they end up in San Diego together? Only God knew.

Chapter 12

⚓

The next morning, Aubrey was sipping mimosas and eating cinnamon rolls with her four girlfriends from high school. No matter how long it had been, they always picked up right where they had left off.

"Aubrey, have you met anyone in San Diego yet? Do all the guys have six-pack abs?" Alexa asked. She had always been Aubrey's loyal single companion in Chicago, hitting the bars with her on weekends and staying in with her for movie nights when they weren't up to going out.

Aubrey smiled. The other girls had always gushed over their fiancés and now husbands, but now Aubrey finally had someone to talk about as well.

"Actually, I have. I met this guy on the beach while watching dolphins. We both realized we had moved to San Diego on the same day."

"Oh my gosh, talk about a romantic way to meet. Just like a Nicholas Sparks book!" Quinn put her hand on her chest. Quinn and Aubrey had grown up reading romance novels together, dreaming of the day they would have a guy like the ones in the books they read. Quinn had found her guy at work.

"Details please." Tina reached for another cinnamon roll.

"His name is Jake, and he just moved from Washington. He works at this online marketing company so he gets to work from home by the beach. We met on the beach and instantly hit it off. We've had this crazy connection, and we have so much fun together. Hiking, surfing, all the beach-barhopping. He even came to my work holiday party."

"Show us a picture. How old is he?" Alexa asked.

Aubrey pulled up Jake's Instagram on her phone.

"He's thirty-six. Definitely the oldest guy I've ever dated, but he looks our age. He's adorable, and yes, he almost has a six-pack."

"Have you slept together yet? Is he good in bed?" Alexa asked.

"We have. At first, I wanted to do things differently and wait until we were officially dating before having sex, but I couldn't resist."

"So you guys aren't officially dating? Do you think he'll ask you to be his girlfriend?" Courtney asked.

Courtney knew how bad Aubrey wanted to date someone. In college, they had both hooked up with guys like it was no big deal until Courtney had met her future husband at a bar. Things were different with him; she had waited to have sex until they were in a committed relationship, and she wouldn't move in with him until they had gotten married. It hadn't taken him long to propose after they graduated, and they settled down near the lake in northern Michigan.

"Not exactly," Aubrey replied. "It's a bit complicated."

These were her closest friends. They wouldn't judge her if she told them the truth. They stared at her, waiting for her to continue as they drank their mimosas.

"He's going through a divorce. He was married for ten years and moved to San Diego after he realized it wasn't working anymore. But he is such a great guy and things are civil with his ex."

"And there it is. I knew it was too good to be true. Meeting while watching dolphins. There's always a catch." Alexa shook her head.

"That's a big transition for him," Tina said. "How do you feel about his divorce?"

"It's weird," Aubrey replied. "I always thought I wouldn't want to date anyone who was divorced or had kids, but now that we've met and I see how awesome he is, it just feels right. Like it's not an issue or a big deal. He doesn't seem angry or bitter like the people we see getting divorced in the movies. It's weird because I don't actually know anyone who has gotten a divorce. All our friends are either getting married or are recently married."

"I guess it's true then," Alexa said. "We will snag the good guys on their second time around, after their first marriages end. Crazy to think that half of our friends will be divorced by their mid-thirties."

"But not you guys!" Aubrey said after seeing the looks on her married friends' faces. "Anyway, I'll keep you posted, but I'm excited to actually date someone."

"Yes, please keep us posted," Tina said. "I'll be praying for you and that God reveals the perfect guy he has for you. Just be careful—Jake may be going through a lot of stuff with his divorce. Married for ten years—that's a long time and it's a big adjustment. I'm excited for you, but I don't want to see you rush into anything and get hurt."

"I know. He needs more time to learn how to be alone and to figure out what he wants. We won't rush anything." Aubrey turned to Courtney. "Enough about me. Courtney, how are you and the hubby doing after your first year of marriage? How's life by the lake?"

Courtney was beaming. "I've been waiting for the right time to tell you all this, and now that we are all together...." They all looked at her.

"Oh my God, you're pregnant!" Quinn and Alexa shouted.

Courtney laughed. "Yes! We are pregnant! Baby girl coming next May. Get ready to be aunties, ladies!" She started crying.

They all clapped and stood up to give her a hug. Aubrey realized she had been drinking plain orange juice. While getting pregnant was expected after a year of marriage, she couldn't believe one of them would be having a baby. A new season of life. A season that seemed so far away for her. Would she have the fairy tale wedding her friends had had? Would she buy a house in the suburbs, get a dog, and eventually have babies?

She gave Courtney another hug. She was happy for her and the life God had given her. If he could do it for Courtney, he could do it for her too.

God, Aubrey prayed silently as the girls talked about baby names, *thank you for blessing Courtney with a baby. Thank you for preparing her to be a mom. I pray that one day I'll get to experience being a wife and a mom too. Amen.*

Aubrey couldn't stop the thoughts whirling around in her head about Jake. She had just gotten home from the Christmas Eve service at church with her family and was reading a book by the fire, sipping hot cocoa. She was so grateful her entire family had decided to go to church this year; even Tyler and Marie had decided to join them. It was so precious seeing Kyle and Kate sitting on stage with all the other kids as the pastor told them about the birth of Jesus.

Even though she had a family that loved her, Aubrey couldn't help but feel lonely this time of year. And she couldn't stop the doubts and worries that started to creep in.

She checked her phone again, but Jake still hadn't responded to her last text. The past few days, she had texted Jake to see what he was up to, but his responses had been delayed and were pretty short. He wasn't his flirtatious self. No selfies, no emojis.

Would he feel lonely his first Christmas single after having a wife for ten years? Would he see his ex this Christmas back in Washington? Would they get back together?

Aubrey tried reading her romance novel and watching the Christmas movies on the Hallmark channel to take her mind off Jake, but she couldn't stop thinking about what he was doing. And all these couples in the movies and in her book only reminded her of how single she still was. She didn't have a loving relationship with Jake. He hadn't showed up at her doorstep and confessed his love to her like all the guys in these movies. He hadn't even asked her to be his girlfriend yet or given her a cute, romantic Christmas gift.

God, Merry Christmas. Help me not to feel lonely this year. I know you have a plan for me and that you know how I feel about Jake. I'm sick of feeling all alone around the holidays. God, I desperately want someone to share my life with. God, I don't want to feel this way. If Jake is the one, let him want to date me. Amen.

Chapter 13

It was the day before New Year's Eve. Aubrey was looking forward to spending her first New Year's Eve in San Diego with a few of her friends who were coming to visit. She usually wasn't a big New Year's Eve fan, but she felt more hopeful this year in a new city, with the possibility of something happening with Jake.

Jake had gotten back from Washington that morning, and he was on his way over so they could watch the sunset together. They hadn't seen each other in over a week, and Aubrey wouldn't be able to spend much time with him once her friends arrived tomorrow. She secretly hoped Jake would join her and her friends in going out to celebrate the New Year, but she still didn't know what his plans were. She hadn't had a New Year's kiss in so long. Before Christmas, Jake had said he was still confirming his plans for New Year's Eve with a few of his buddies, but he would love to get together if they were all going out to celebrate.

Aubrey's phone buzzed with a text from Jake as she finished curling her hair.

Outside on our cliff. Grab a blanket, it's chilly.

Aubrey grabbed a blanket and a thermos with rosé before heading out the door. She couldn't ignore the familiar feeling of butterflies in her stomach as she ran down the three flights of stairs.

The sky was already lighting up shades of oranges and pinks as the sun started to dip behind the clouds. She saw Jake standing on the cliff outside her apartment, taking in the view and the surfers below him by the pier. Her heart skipped a beat as she gave him a hug from behind. Reunited at last. He felt so warm in her arms.

"Hello, stranger," Jake said. "I'm glad you survived the Michigan cold. Welcome home." He kissed her forehead.

"Yes, this is our home now. How's Kona?"

"He's so good. He was so excited to see me; we spent a lot of quality time together. I miss him already." Jake stared at the dogs walking along the beach below them.

"I'm glad you got to see him. He's one lucky dog to have a dad like you."

Jake smiled. "It's December, and it's beautiful; we live in the best place on Earth." He raised his arms like he was hugging the sky. They sat down and took in the views as they passed the thermos of rosé back and forth.

"So, did you figure out what you're doing for New Year's?" Aubrey asked.

Jake took another sip of the rosé. "Yes, actually, that's what I wanted to talk to you about." He continued to stare at the surfers.

Aubrey's smile started to fade. This didn't sound good. Her stomach started doing backflips. She knew something had been off over Christmas.

"Oh, yeah? What's up?" she asked.

Jake turned toward her so his knees were touching hers. "I've had the best time with you the past few months and have had so much fun getting to know you. You are beautiful, smart, amazing, and funny, and I always appreciate how honest we can be with each other, which is why I wanted to have this conversation."

No. This isn't happening. We are not having this conversation. It is not about to end like this.

"I know if we continue to hang out like this," Jake continued, "we will end up dating and in a relationship, and I'm not ready for that yet. It's not fair to you to lead you that way when I'm just not ready."

She had her answer. He still wasn't ready for a relationship. Aubrey gazed at the ocean. While she appreciated him being honest and she was glad they were finally having this conversation, it still hurt. Was she not good enough to date? Had their time together meant nothing to him?

"I understand and I agree. I don't think either of us are ready to be in a relationship. I know you are still working through things with your divorce, and I'm still figuring out what I want for myself here."

Jake grabbed her hand. "You've been so understanding and patient with me, and you've been such a good friend. I don't want to hurt you, but I want to be honest with you at the same time because I truly appreciate and value our friendship."

Friendship? Sleeping together and going on romantic dates was more than just friendship.

"I haven't been sleeping with anyone else since I met you," Jake said, "but an old friend is coming to visit me for New Year's and we most likely will hook up. That's why I didn't want to make any plans with you for New Year's, and I wanted to tell you the truth."

What? Aubrey felt like the air was sucked out from beneath her. She gazed at the ocean as she tried to breathe and process what he was saying. Not only did Jake not want to date her; he wanted to sleep with other people. It really had been too good to be true. Their Nicholas Sparks romance was over.

Aubrey felt sick. The rosé rushed to her head and she couldn't think. She still had her sunglasses on to hide the tears that were forming. Inside, she was screaming and breaking down, but she continued to stare at the ocean as tears started to fall down her cheeks. Jake saw the tears and put his arm around her as she continued to stare silently at the ocean. She felt numb.

Why was her heart shattering into a million pieces when they had only known each other less than a few months? She knew he wasn't ready to date and that there were major red flags, but she couldn't help the feelings she had for him. She did want to date him. She wanted him to be her boyfriend. She wanted to explore San Diego together and have fun, romantic getaways together.

But now she was crushed, just like she had been by every other guy she had ever liked. It never turned into something real. Why did she think things would be different this time in San Diego? These guys were all the same. The Nicholas Sparks love stories never happened to her in real life.

What kind of person says something like this the day before New Year's Eve? He knew her friends were coming to visit and how excited she was for her first New Year's in San Diego. Why did he have to tell her this before this weekend? How was she not supposed to think of him having sex with another girl on New Year's Eve?

What a jerk. Aubrey had always hated New Year's Eve, but now she really hated it. It was a single girl's worst holiday after Valentine's

Day, and now it was unbearable thinking about Jake spending it with someone else. Aubrey felt her insides starting to shake. She was about to erupt in ugly tears. She needed to get inside. She wasn't going to give him the benefit of seeing her mad or breaking down.

"Thank you for telling me the truth." She exhaled a deep breath as she tried to steady her voice. "I understand you aren't ready for a relationship right now, but I really like you, and I think it's best if we don't talk for a while. Happy New Year."

She grabbed her blanket and thermos and headed toward the door. Jake called her name, but he didn't come after her. Aubrey tried running up the three flights of stairs as fast as her legs would carry her.

Why would an old friend be visiting him on New Year's? A few weeks ago, he had said he didn't have any plans. It took planning for someone to book a flight and visit someone, especially during the holidays when flights were so expensive. Who was this old friend? Had they hooked up before? Had he seen her in Washington during Christmas? Why would he want to sleep with this friend when he could sleep with her? Was she not good enough? What could this other girl give him that she couldn't?

Aubrey had so many questions, but it didn't matter. Knowing the details would only cause more pain. She tried to push all the unanswered questions to the back of her head as she made her way inside. She threw the blanket and thermos on the floor and fell on her couch as she cried into the pillow.

It was over and she had to move on. She had done it before and she could do it again. She couldn't believe she already had a broken heart in San Diego. She had even told her mom and friends about him; she felt so naïve thinking that he would want to date her.

Why, God? Why doesn't he want to date me? Am I not enough for him? Was the sex not good enough for him? Why do I always end up getting hurt like this? Will I ever meet someone who actually wants to be with me, God? What's wrong with me, God?

She cried out to God as she sobbed into the pillow. She cried for what seemed like an hour before she fell asleep on the couch with mascara all over her face.

Chapter 14

⚓

Aubrey glanced at her eyes in the rearview mirror. She was on the way to the airport to pick up her friends, and her eyes were still swollen from the night before.

She wanted to curl up in a ball and stay in bed all weekend. If her friends weren't visiting, she would have skipped New Year's Eve this year. She didn't want to get all dressed up and pretend she was excited. She didn't want to be out at a crowded bar, surrounded by other couples, trying to pretend she didn't feel miserable and lonely. Not only was she single again on New Year's Eve, but she was heartbroken as well. This was the worst holiday ever. At least on Valentine's Day, she and her friends didn't have to go out and see all the couples around them kissing at midnight.

A car blared its horn behind her. Aubrey looked up and saw that she had been sitting at a green light. She needed to stop thinking about how awful tonight was going to be. Her friends were flying all the way across the country to see her, and she didn't want them to join her pity party the entire trip. It was the first time she was having guests visit in San Diego, and it would be fun to show them around. Even though playing tourist was the last thing she felt like doing, it would be good for her to get her mind off Jake.

They hadn't texted each other since their conversation the night before. It already felt weird not texting each other. Jake was probably texting that other girl instead, or maybe he had already picked her up from the airport. They could already be having drinks together on the beach and doing cute, couple-like things on the boardwalk.

Aubrey shook her head. She couldn't think about them being together. She cranked up the song she was listening to, "Giants" by Francesca Battistelli. It was a Christian song that talked about accomplishing anything with God, even with giants in her way.

Yes, God, I can do anything with you. I can get over Jake. Please heal my broken heart, Lord. Please help me not think about Jake this weekend and to have fun with my friends.

She pulled up to the terminal and actually felt a little better. It was amazing how inspired and peaceful she felt listening to Christian music and after prayer. She smiled as her friends walked up to her car.

"Welcome to San Diego!" She got out of the car and gave them each a big hug.

She was grateful that she got to hang out with Alexa again so soon, and that Brittany, their friend from college, had joined her.

"San Diego, we made it!" Alexa exclaimed.

Aubrey put their luggage in the back of her crossover SUV and headed off toward Pacific Beach. Their faces were in awe as they took in the palm trees, the view of the marina by the bay, and the view of downtown San Diego in the distance.

"Wow, I can't believe you actually live here now," Brittany said. "You are so freaking lucky."

Aubrey smiled. She really was lucky to be here, and she wasn't going to let a few months with Jake ruin her time in her new city.

"I know—it still feels like a dream," Aubrey said. "I'm so excited to show you around. We can do whatever your hearts desire. Hiking, biking on the boardwalk, the beach, brunch—there's a cool farmer's market downtown on the weekend—beach workouts, you name it."

"I can't wait! All your photos of doing beach workouts and hiking look amazing. What have you been up to this week? How's the new dolphin guy?" Alexa asked.

Her heart stung. She had known Jake would come up eventually, but she didn't want to talk about it. She had already been replaying what he had said in her mind over and over. Saying it out loud to someone else wasn't going to help. But there was no hiding how she felt. She may as well be honest and get it over with. They were her close friends after all, and they cared about her.

"Yeah, about that; we aren't talking right now. He told me last night he wasn't ready for a serious relationship. I totally understand with his divorce and everything, but he also told me this girl was visiting and they would most likely hook up."

Brittany turned to look at her in the front seat. "Aubrey, I'm so sorry."

"What a douchebag!" Alexa said. "Where does he live? I'll go and light dog poop on fire, leave it on his doorstep, and slash his tires."

Aubrey laughed. "I appreciate the support, but no need to do that. I'm glad he was honest with me, and I knew we weren't serious or exclusive with each other, but it still hurts knowing he wants to sleep with someone else."

"I know you were starting to really like him," Brittany said, "but honestly, this is for the best. He clearly doesn't know what he wants if he is going through a divorce after being married for ten years, and this is another red flag. You can do so much better, Aubrey."

"Yeah, I know all that, but it still sucks. I just need to move on. New Year, new opportunities. Let's find you both a guy on the beach who you can make out with tonight. Shall we start with brunch?" She didn't want to talk about it anymore.

"I need a Bloody Mary," Alexa said.

Aubrey was actually glad they were here. Even though she didn't have a lot of close friends yet in San Diego, she was thankful for the close friends she had back home in the Midwest. Morgan was also in town, and she was glad they would all be meeting up to celebrate New Year's Eve in Pacific Beach.

They spent the afternoon brunching, drinking a few mimosas and Bloody Marys, walking the boardwalk, and watching reruns of *Laguna Beach* while they got ready for the big night out. As they finished the last bottle of rosé, it was time to head to the bar for New Year's.

"All right, ladies, let's do this. Time to have some real fun." Aubrey forced herself to be positive about the night, but she was already feeling like it was going to be a long night.

They finally made it in at a dive bar that had the shortest line. They should have gotten tickets to a nicer bar, but they hated paying a hundred dollars for cheap booze for one night. It didn't take long for all of them to feel very single—and much older than the rest of the people in the bar. They were surrounded by couples already making out with each other and drunk girls who were already grinding on each other.

Well, may as well join them if we're going to make it to midnight, Aubrey thought. Shots would be the only thing to get her going tonight. She needed to have fun. She couldn't go home and crawl into bed, thinking about Jake with someone else tonight.

After a few rounds of shots, it was clear her friends felt the same way about New Year's. Except they just felt very single; they didn't have a broken heart. Deep down, they all wanted someone to spend the New Year with—someone to kiss at midnight and someone to feel hopeful about. Why was it so hard to meet someone these days? They were almost thirty and so many of their friends had already gotten married. Were any good guys left? Would they have to settle for the douchebags they always met in the bars or on the dating apps?

Alexa had recently met a guy on Bumble and had a great first date, getting a few drinks with him. After their date, she found him on Facebook, and it was evident from his photos that he didn't even live in Chicago. When he asked her out for a second date, she confronted him and he admitted that he was just looking for a physical connection while he traveled to Chicago for work.

Morgan managed to meet guys organically in New York, but she still wasn't having the best luck. She had gotten really drunk the other weekend while day drinking and watching football at a bar, and she ended up going home with a guy she had met at the sports bar. When they woke up in the morning, Morgan realized he was much younger than she had originally thought. He had textbooks on his desk and it looked like he and his roommates had set up a permanent beer pong table in their living room. When he got up to use the restroom, she found his wallet on the nightstand and saw that he was only twenty-one on his ID.

Brittany was the least promiscuous among them; she went on a lot of first and second dates and managed to keep it in her pants, but the dates never went anywhere.

Aubrey was mad at herself for thinking Jake was different. She was mad that she had ignored the red flags and gotten involved with someone going through a divorce. She was mad she had brought him to her holiday party. And she was mad at herself for having sex with him too soon. She fought back tears. She was not going to cry. She was not going to let this night bring her down and start the New Year feeling sorry for herself.

She took a few more shots and forced herself to dance. She didn't care how drunk she got tonight or even if she blacked out. She just needed to escape.

What seemed like hours later, the countdown began and they reached midnight. Finally! They could go home. None of them had gotten a New Year's kiss, and nobody had even talked to a decent guy all night. Morgan managed to get a ride on Uber while the rest of them stumbled the few blocks to Aubrey's apartment.

Aubrey still felt so angry and upset. She wanted to break down and cry, but she wanted to be alone. She quickly went into her bedroom and threw on workout clothes and her running shoes. Alexa was helping Brittany get undressed as Brittany rolled around drunkenly on the couch.

"I'm going for a run," Aubrey said. "I'll be back."

"What? No. It's one in the morning. Why are you going to run in the dark in the middle of the night? That's not safe. Stay here." Alexa tried to stop her, but she was also still trying to help Brittany get undressed.

"I need to run. I'm fine. I'll be back soon." Aubrey took her keys and headed to the beach. She knew she was drunk and that she shouldn't be out running in the dark by herself, but she needed to do something. She headed out the door to her building and ran down the steps to the beach. She passed a few homeless people asleep on the boardwalk and she could hear music coming from the bars and laughter in the distance.

Was Jake still out with that girl? Which bar had they gone to? Were they already at his place, in bed together? She started running on the sand toward the ocean, and then started sprinting as soon as she hit harder sand. The ocean waves roared at her as she ran. It was pitch dark on the beach, but the white waves crashing against the shore illuminated her path.

Aubrey wanted to run until she didn't feel the pain anymore. Until she could forget about Jake. Until she could forget about all the other men who had made her feel the same way. Her lungs started to burn. It was difficult running while she was this intoxicated. She stopped running and finally broke down in sobs. She stared at the ocean, sobbing as if the waves could make her feel better. As if the waves saw every tear and could comfort her.

She imagined that Jesus was with her, just beyond the roaring waves. Then she felt oddly at peace.

Why does this always happen, God? Why does this always happen to me while everyone else seems to find their soulmate? Why do I always get treated like crap? Why does my heart always get broken? God, I want things to be different. I need things to be different. I can't do this anymore. Please help me, God.

Aubrey shouted at the waves as she prayed and cried her heart out to God. God knew the answers and could help her feel better. She felt bad she hadn't been going to church lately; she needed to keep going to church now more than ever. She needed to meet other people and make new friends besides Jake.

She checked her Fitbit. Almost 2 a.m. She started laughing out loud. Who goes running while drunk, on the beach in the middle of the night? She jogged back home, imagining Jesus running along-side her the whole way, keeping her company.

Aubrey quietly made her way back inside the apartment. Alexa and Brittany were already asleep. She ate the leftover pizza on the stove before passing out and leaving another lonely New Year's Eve behind her.

Chapter 15

⚓

Aubrey and her friends had spent the rest of the holiday break exploring San Diego's most Instagram-worthy spots. Hiking Torrey Pines, brunch and gawking at the sea lions at La Jolla Cove, lying out on Pacific Beach, sipping cocktails in Little Italy, and the inevitable night out in Gaslamp.

Aubrey had enjoyed herself, but she was relieved the holiday break was over now so she could stop thinking about Jake being with that girl or running into them on the boardwalk.

She was already on a flight for work, headed to Tampa for her annual training. Getting back to work and seeing everyone again at training would help take her mind off things. At least she didn't have to do accounting work this week for clients.

As Aubrey gazed out at the clouds, she decided to journal her goals for the New Year. She set new goals and resolutions every year, but this year was different. This year actually meant something. She was in San Diego now, and she knew God had a plan for her life. She just had to figure out what that was. She started listing her goals in her journal.

<u>New Year Goals</u>

- Go to fitness meetups to make friends
- Join a beach volleyball league
- Go to church more regularly
- Get involved at church by joining a small group or a volunteer team
- Pray
- Learn how to scuba dive
- Travel to Hawaii and the Bahamas
- Rent a lake house with the family up north in Michigan in the summer
- Start a travel blog
- Eat healthier and lose 10 pounds
- Drink less, say no to shots

Aubrey needed to stop taking shots. She had learned her lesson too many times last year. No good came from taking shots, but she was still doing them. Why had she continued to let people and her emotions influence her to continue drinking so much?

She was in control, not anyone else. This year had to be different. This week at training was going to be different.

Aubrey took a deep breath. She felt nervous about going back to work training after what had happened last year, but she knew she could be strong. She wouldn't get wasted and make those mistakes again. She was going to act and drink responsibly. No more tequila shots or hot tubs for her.

At least she didn't have to worry about running into Matt at training this year. The firm had also taken away his bonus last year after the hot tub incident, and a few months after they received their punishment, Aubrey had seen on LinkedIn that he had started a new job at a private equity firm. She felt relieved she didn't have to see him anymore at work; he had been a constant reminder of her drunken mistakes.

Aubrey turned back to her New Year goals. She debated writing "Get over Jake" on her list, but he didn't even deserve to be a part of her goals or the New Year. Her broken heart would heal in time, just like it had all those other times.

As the plane headed into Tampa, Aubrey felt hopeful for the new year ahead. She would pursue her goals, and God would show her what she was really created to do. She would keep trying new things until she figured it out.

In the meantime, she would enjoy all the travel benefits from work and the opportunity to travel to new places. Every year at training, the firm planned something big for the whole group, like a happy hour or fun event at one of the local attractions. Her group had had a really good past year, so they must be going all out this year. She was determined to still have fun while not drinking too much.

"Hey, Aubrey, it's been a while. We miss you in Chicago. The happy hours haven't been the same without you." Her coworker Wyatt gave her a hug.

They had just gotten to their first training class, a training on how to account for business acquisitions and combinations.

"I miss you guys, too. But I'm excited to see what they have planned for us this week. Does anyone know what the plan is?"

Carly, another coworker from Chicago, chimed in. "I confirmed with the partners, and they decided not to have anything this year. Turns out the other groups didn't do so well compared to ours, so they don't have the funds this year for the big events."

"What? No happy hour?" Wyatt said, reading Aubrey's mind. "After all the hours we've worked and revenue we've brought in for the firm this year? Man, that's a load of crap."

Well, this was a first. They had had an event every year for the past five years. Was the firm getting that cheap that it didn't want to throw them a happy hour? It was the only time during the year that everyone got together from all over the country to network; how could there not be a happy hour?

"Interesting," Aubrey said. "Didn't the partners talk about how they had experienced significant growth this year compared to last year on that call before Christmas? And aren't they always going on and on about how important it is for us to network to meet more people? If they had all this growth and want us to network, why can't we still have a happy hour?"

"Exactly," Carly said. "It doesn't make sense. They are just being cheap."

Throughout the day, several people kept asking Aubrey if a happy hour was planned. Everyone knew she had planned happy hours in Chicago, so if there was a happy hour, she would know about it.

"No, no happy hour planned this year. Looks like we will have to plan our own," Aubrey joked to a few coworkers as the day went on.

During the last training of the day, her national boss, the leader of her entire practice, Devon, texted her.

I heard you are planning a happy hour. What type of happy hour do you have in mind?

Why was Devon texting her? She had known Devon for a few years and he was a cool guy, but she was still surprised that he would text her instead of emailing her. Was this some sort of test? Was Devon testing her to see how she would respond after the incident from last year? They both knew she had to be on her best behavior, but he also knew she was capable of planning a pretty good social event for the group. Aubrey replied to his text.

No, I'm not. Do you want me to?

Yes, if you can put something together that would be awesome. Thanks.

Do we have budget?

It was no small task to plan a happy hour for a large group of people. In Chicago, Aubrey had planned happy hours and events for thirty people. Most bars and restaurants charged a minimum to reserve space big enough for that many. At this training, there were probably at least one hundred people who would be invited. Devon texted back.

No budget this year.

Aubrey sighed. Devon didn't understand how many details went into planning an event this big and that you needed a budget to secure space. One hundred people couldn't just show up to a bar and expect to have space. They were in Tampa; there were families and tourists everywhere.

Why wasn't Devon's assistant planning this? It wasn't part of Aubrey's job. She was a manager now, not some associate who didn't have anything better to do. She already had clients emailing her, requesting things get done this week. She would already have to miss some of her training classes to do the client work. Planning a happy hour would only take up more time and energy she didn't have.

A part of her wanted to tell Devon no, but she felt obligated. So many people seemed to be counting on her to plan something, and Devon had even texted her himself. Aubrey texted back.

> I can see what I can do without any budget and the limited advance notice.

She wanted Devon to know this would not be an easy event to plan.

During lunch the next day, Aubrey found a restaurant that would reserve space for them for a $1,000 deposit. She had been there before, but she needed funds to secure the space.

"Good to see you, Aubrey! How are you liking California?" asked Kevin, a partner from one of her first projects, as he sat down at her table.

Kevin! He would be the perfect person to ask for help. He was one of the more fun partners, always supporting team events and boosting team morale. When they had team dinners and happy hours on their project together, Kevin had always picked up the tab on his corporate credit card.

"Great to see you, Kevin! California still feels like a dream. I'm loving the West Coast. I miss seeing everyone, though, so being back at training has been great." She smiled. Now was her chance.

"I'm actually trying to plan a happy hour for the practice; there weren't any firm events planned this year, but I need a credit card to secure the deposit. Do you know how I can get it approved?"

"Here, use mine. We can easily absorb the cost in our regional events fund." He took out his wallet.

Success! Another epic happy hour was about to unfold. After using Kevin's card to make the deposit to reserve the space, Aubrey texted Devon.

I found space. We are all set for Thursday night.

Aubrey felt accomplished, knowing they would have a happy hour after all. But she still resented that she was always the one planning the team events. She remembered all those events she had planned in Chicago. She had always been passionate about people, which was why it was so important to her to bring people together and plan fun events like happy hours. She knew everyone enjoyed getting together, but she had gotten frustrated with the partners and their lack of support for team events. They always said how important it was to network and promote a team culture, yet they barely made any effort to come to the events themselves or get a firm budget for them. And Aubrey had never received the recognition she deserved for taking all the time to plan and coordinate the events.

At least they would all have fun—that was what was most important. If she hadn't agreed to plan the happy hour, one hundred people would miss out on bonding and catching up with each other. She couldn't allow that to happen.

Chapter 16

⚓

"Welcome, everyone! It's that wonderful time of year again. We have a tab open, enjoy!" Aubrey raised Kevin's credit card in the air as cheers erupted around her. Everyone loved free booze on the firm.

Everyone stepped up to the bar to order drinks, and a few groups were already ordering rounds of shots.

Aubrey smiled as she took in her coworkers around her. Already about eighty people were in the room she had reserved. She hadn't seen Devon or the other partners yet, but it was only a matter of time before they showed up.

"Aubrey! Come take this shot with us!" a group of her coworkers from Chicago shouted from across the bar.

Aubrey laughed as she ran over to give them all hugs.

"Glad you guys are already having fun and taking advantage of the free shots. I'll sit this one out, but you enjoy."

"Ah, come on! One shot isn't going to hurt. It's tradition!" her coworker Wyatt encouraged her.

Wyatt had gotten kicked out of the pool with her last year, but he had been smart enough not to get kicked out twice.

Aubrey hesitated. She had been sticking to vodka soda, but shots were part of the team bonding, and she figured a few wouldn't hurt.

She had just started drinking and had been sure to eat a big dinner before heading out to soak up the alcohol about to be consumed.

"Well, it is tradition whenever I'm with you guys. Why not?" she said.

Wyatt motioned for the bartender and ordered six tequila shots.

The next hour flew by as Aubrey made her way around the room, catching up with coworkers she hadn't seen all year.

"I'll take another water, please," Aubrey said, motioning to the bartender. She had already lost count of all the shots she had taken; people kept handing them to her, and she was feeling pretty buzzed.

She finally saw Devon and the other partners make their entrance from across the room. Kevin was the first one to step up to the bar, so she made her way over.

"Hey, Kevin! Thanks for letting us use your credit card. Everyone's already having a lot of fun, and they really appreciated the firm sponsoring this."

"Oh, of course. That's what I'm here for! I'm not sure how long I am staying; I have to review a client report tonight. Would you mind closing the tab out for me and giving my card back tomorrow?" Kevin asked.

"Sure, no problem. Cheers!" Aubrey smiled.

Wow, free rein over his credit card! Now she had to remember to close out his tab and take his credit card at the end of the night.

Aubrey ended up ordering another shot with one of her mentees. She was definitely drunk at this point, but she wasn't worried. A lot of other people were already slurring their words, and she felt confident she wasn't going near the hot tub or taking her clothes off in public this year. She was still in control.

⚓

Aubrey woke up the next morning with a pounding headache. She checked her phone. Already 7 a.m., and she was still wearing her outfit from the night before. She made her way to the bathroom to chug water. She hadn't even taken her contacts out or washed her face before falling asleep. A wave of nausea washed over her, making her feel like she was going to throw up.

Oh, gosh, what happened last night? She groaned as she got back under the covers.

She remembered leaving the bar with Drew, a coworker from Chicago. They had hooked up a few years ago after their work holiday party. She thought he currently had a girlfriend, but she remembered making out in his hotel room before falling asleep there.

How did she get back to her room? Had they had sex?

No, they wouldn't have had sex. She would have remembered it. No matter how drunk she got, she always remembered having sex.

Jake! What would he think? She winced as she remembered that he wouldn't even care. He was hooking up with other people too. She opened her texts in her phone and checked her call log. Thank God she hadn't drunk-texted or called Jake last night. She would have made a fool of herself. What if she had called him when he was in bed with someone else?

More flashbacks came. She vaguely remembered closing out the tab and having a hard time figuring out what to tip.

How much did she tip the bartender on Kevin's credit card? How much was the bill?

She remembered a very long receipt. She sprang up, hoping she still had the receipt and Kevin's credit card. She found her purse on the floor and found the receipt inside wrapped around the credit card. It was about four feet long. She winced as she saw the total and the tip she had left. $3,500 total and an $800 tip.

Should she tell Kevin how much it had been? Technically, he hadn't given her a maximum budget, but this seemed a bit much.

An image of her wearing the receipt as a sash came flashing back to her. The receipt was so long that someone had tied it around her waist like a sash Miss America would wear.

She couldn't believe she had been wearing the receipt at the bar! Aubrey started to panic when she remembered crying while talking to Devon.

No. No. No. What had she said to Devon? Why had she been crying? Had she told him how frustrated she had been that she had to plan the happy hour?

Crying to her main boss in front of everyone at a happy hour. That was not good.

Aubrey barely made it to the toilet before she threw up.

Why had she drank so much again? Why had she cried in front of her boss? What the heck did she say? Why did she take all those shots?

The alarm on her phone went off. At least the drunk version of her had been smart enough to set an alarm. There was no way she was going to make her last training class of the week. She had a flight back home in the afternoon, and she wanted to curl up in a ball, forget last night happened, and go back to sleep.

But she had to give Kevin back his credit card. She checked her email. Kevin had already emailed her saying that he would meet her at breakfast. Breakfast ended in fifteen minutes. Aubrey wiped the mascara from her face, threw back some mouthwash, and quickly put on some clean clothes. She looked and still felt drunk, but she had to get this over with. Her breath reeked of vodka, but she had no choice.

Aubrey made it down to breakfast as the hotel staff started clearing away the food.

Please don't let me see Devon. Please don't let me see Devon.

Luckily, Kevin was still at a table, eating his breakfast with someone she didn't recognize.

"Hey, Kevin. Thanks again for letting us use your card. We really appreciated it." She tried to sound genuine.

"Yes, of course! What was the total damage?" he asked.

Aubrey hesitated. "I think it was around $4,000." She had left the receipt upstairs in her purse. He didn't need to see it. He would see the total damage on his credit card statement.

Kevin started to laugh. "Not too bad for a hundred people. Thanks for planning and organizing."

She winced inside as she smiled. "My pleasure."

At least she hadn't said anything rude to Kevin last night.

Aubrey barely made it upstairs to her hotel room before she got sick again. It was going to be a long day. She forced herself to chug down some water with some aspirin and fell back asleep in a dizzy haze of regret and shame.

Her alarm went off a few hours later. She threw everything into her suitcase, ran downstairs, and sat back in the Uber as she reflected on everything the night before.

She had been so hopeful that this year was going to be different. That she wasn't going to make the same drunken mistakes.

What had she said to Devon? Why was she crying? Why had she hooked up with Drew? She knew he was a player. Who would cheat on his girlfriend and take advantage of someone that drunk like that? Gross.

It wasn't his fault, though. It was hers. She had to start taking full responsibility for her actions. She had tried to do a good thing by planning a happy hour, but she had let her emotions get in the way.

Why had she let everyone pressure her into taking those shots? She already knew tequila had almost been the death of her the year before. She already knew that drinking like that was not the path she wanted to live. And now this had happened when she was trying to be good.

She felt like she wanted to throw up again. Why did she have to keep drinking like this?

God, I don't want drinking to ruin my life. Please help me stop, God. Give me the strength to stop drinking like this. You've already opened my eyes to how destructive a few drunken mistakes can be. God, please help me stop.

Aubrey sat at the gate, waiting for boarding to begin for her flight back to San Diego. She didn't want to text Drew, but she had to figure out what she had said to Devon and why she was crying.

Taking out her phone, she texted Drew.

Hey, sorry, if I was a drunk mess last night. Do you know why I was crying at the bar talking to Devon?

She sent the same text to her close coworker, Paige, who had also been there last night.

Drew responded right away.

You were a drunk mess. You passed out fast as soon as we got back to the hotel. I saw you crying, so I came up to you to see what was going on. You mentioned something about being mad at Devon for having to plan the happy hour, and then we left the bar shortly after that.

Aubrey hoped she hadn't said anything too bad to Devon in her drunken anger. At least she and Drew hadn't slept together. She received a text from Paige.

> Girl! How you feeling? OMG last night was crazy! You were pretty drunk but so was everyone else. You said something about Devon not being grateful after you were talking to him. Then you left with Drew.

Aubrey replied to her text.

> Did a lot of people see me crying at the bar?

> No, most people had already left. Everyone who was still there was pretty drunk. You only cried for a few minutes. You didn't do anything crazy.

Aubrey knew a lot of other people had also been drunk, but she had embarrassed herself in front of Devon. Even though she couldn't remember what she had said, she couldn't pretend like it hadn't happened.

As Aubrey boarded the flight and got settled into her seat, she texted Devon. Normally she would have sent an email, but it felt appropriate since Devon had texted her first originally.

> Hey Devon, thanks for letting us have a happy hour last night. I realize I got too emotional last night and wanted to apologize as that was not very professional of me and I know I was out of line. Have a great flight home.

Short and sweet and to the point. There, she had owned up to her mistakes. Now she had to move on and actually try to drink less. This year could still be different. She could still become who she was created to be without alcohol slowing her down. But how? How was she supposed to drink less when everyone else around her was always drinking?

Aubrey kept checking to see if Devon responded until it was time for her to switch her phone to airplane mode. Maybe he was currently flying back home too and his phone was off. Aubrey convinced herself not to worry and that she had done all she could do before falling asleep with her head on the tray table.

Chapter 17

⚓

Aubrey spent the next few weeks in Chicago for a new client. While she was grateful for the travel to take her mind off Jake and what had happened at training, she was already over the winter cold in Chicago and missed being home at the beach during the week. She had just moved from Chicago, so why did they already have to send her back there in the middle of winter?

"It's a great opportunity and they need a strong manager," Russ, the project's lead director, had told her when she had been assigned. "You'll get a lot of visibility working with the partner, and we need someone who will work directly with the chief financial officer. Plus, you'll rack up travel points while you get to see all your friends again in Chicago."

Russ did have a point. She still hated the work she was doing, but at least she got to see her friends and it helped take her mind off of Jake.

Aubrey was working from her hotel room, wrapping up a memo to send to the client. She had to finish it before she could go meet her friends at her favorite restaurant tonight in Gold Coast. She tried focusing on the memo, but she only felt more frustrated as she stared at the snow falling out the window. She didn't want to be in Chicago. She didn't want to be working fifty-plus hours a week doing accounting and sitting in an office all day.

How did this memo she was working on even matter? How did any of her work on accounting matter? She didn't want to be like the partners who sacrificed so much of their personal lives to sit in an office all day working on accounting. She was already sacrificing so much of her personal time to travel across the country for this project. Was the recognition really worth being away from home and away from the beach all week?

Aubrey shook her head. No, it wasn't. It was never worth it. No matter how much money the partners made, this job would never be worth all the things she had to sacrifice in return. This memo could wait until the morning. Work would always be there the next day. Tonight, she needed to take a break and have some quality time with the girls. At least her dinner would be on the firm since she was traveling.

Aubrey shut her laptop and ordered an Uber. No way was she walking in the freezing tundra. She didn't even have the right shoes for this type of weather anymore.

Alexa and Brittany were already seated at their table, sipping their martinis and glasses of wine.

"Welcome back to Chicago! What are you having to drink? It's still happy hour." Alexa smiled as she raised her wine glass.

Aubrey wanted a few glasses of rosé to unwind, but she promised herself she was going to drink less. It was dinner with a few friends; it wasn't like she was going to get crazy.

"A glass of rosé for me please." She smiled at the waiter.

"So, have you heard anything from Jake?" Alexa asked.

Aubrey shook her head. "Nope. Nothing. I told him not to contact me, but I expected him at least to say he was sorry or something."

"A clean break is for the best. He has too many red flags. You don't need to be dating a guy who is going through a divorce and is technically still married," Brittany said.

"I know, I know. He has other red flags, too, like that he cheated on his wife and that he doesn't believe in God. I still can't help how I feel, though. I thought he was different. I thought things would actually work out this time."

"Everyone cheats. We just have to accept that nowadays." Alexa sighed.

Maybe Alexa was right. Why had she expected anything different from Jake? While it was awful that he had cheated on his wife, had she been expecting too much from him too soon by assuming they had been exclusive?

Aubrey didn't admit how much she missed him. She didn't tell them how hard it was not to think about him, especially on the weekends, wondering what he was up to or who he was hanging out with. She was fine during the week, but she felt so lonely every weekend. She wondered if they would run into each other on the boardwalk or on the beach. She checked her texts constantly, wondering if he had texted to say he was sorry and had made a mistake.

"How did your work training go this year? Did you get kicked out of any hot tubs again?" Alexa laughed.

Most of Aubrey's friends thought her previous hot tub incident was funny, but after what had happened a few weeks ago at training, none of it seemed funny anymore.

Aubrey attempted a smile as she stared into her wine glass.

"No, but I got pretty drunk and was crying in front of my main boss who leads the practice nationally."

The girls stared at her with their mouths open.

"Oh, no, what happened?" Alexa asked.

"I was upset and frustrated that I had to plan a happy hour for a hundred people at the last minute. They usually have one planned, but this year they didn't because they were being cheap, so my boss asked if I was planning one. I didn't want to do it; I was sick of always planning stuff. Fast forward to the happy hour—I ended up taking more shots than I should have and then told my boss how I felt. I don't really remember what I said, but I remember crying. I sent him a text the next morning apologizing, but he never responded. I figured that isn't a good sign."

Aubrey had tried not to worry too much about Devon never texting her back. She had done the right thing by apologizing, and there was nothing else she could do at this point. What had happened had happened, and she couldn't keep dwelling on what she could have said to him.

"Ah, that stuff happens all the time," Brittany said. "Lots of people get too drunk at their work events. I'm sure you didn't say anything too bad. He was probably drunk too."

"I'm not so sure." Aubrey grabbed another bread roll. "I can't believe I did something stupid again at training for the second year in a row. Guys, we are almost thirty! Don't you think I should have my stuff together by now? People make dumb, drunken mistakes like this when they first learn to drink in college, not when they are almost thirty!"

Alexa laughed. "It happens all the time. Your stories are so entertaining and fun. Everyone acts like that at my work, too, and hooks up with each other. It's not a big deal."

"Oh, gosh," Aubrey said. "I totally forgot I hooked up with my coworker, Drew, again. I don't know exactly what happened, but I remembered being in his hotel room making out. At least I woke up in my own bed, though."

"Hey, that's awesome!" Alexa said. "At least you hooked up with somebody besides Jake. That will help you move on."

Aubrey loved her friends and knew they were always there to listen, but she wasn't so sure how helpful their advice was. She definitely did not feel better about herself after getting black-out drunk again and hooking up with a coworker she did not want to hook up with. It only made her miss Jake even more by reminding herself that Drew wasn't Jake. It wasn't the same.

No matter how drunk or upset she was, she didn't want to continue hooking up with guys who only wanted to get some. She didn't want to continue doing dumb, drunken shenanigans at training or hooking up with guys from work. It might have been funny and expected in college, but it needed to stop.

Why do I keep making the same mistakes? When will this cycle ever end? she asked herself. She didn't care if everyone else was doing it. She couldn't do it anymore.

Aubrey tried to be present with her friends the rest of the evening as they shared about their recent Bumble stories, but it only reminded her more of Jake. She didn't want to get back on the dating apps. She didn't want to move on. She just wanted Jake.

As Aubrey made it back to her hotel room, she couldn't help reminiscing about when she and Jake had been together in the hotel room in Newport Beach. She wished he was here to explore Chicago with her. They could have had so much fun together. They could even enjoy the champagne the hotel had put in her room as her free platinum gift.

Aubrey started to run a bath in the jacuzzi tub and uncorked the champagne. She was proud of herself for only having two glasses of rosé at dinner, and she wasn't about to waste some free champagne.

As she waited for the tub to fill, she started scrolling through Jake's Instagram while sipping the champagne on the bed. Jake hadn't posted much since the New Year. A photo of the sunset on New Year's Day and another photo of him and his buddies at a bar downtown watching football. No photos with any girls.

It had been three weeks since they had seen each other. Aubrey missed her beach friend. Why couldn't he still hang out with her as friends and as someone to explore with?

She knew he didn't want to date her, and that was fine because she knew he wasn't ready to. But why couldn't they still hang out casually? Why couldn't they still be friends? They liked each other and had a great time together, and she didn't want to give that up. She needed friends in San Diego. She felt so lonely back home without him.

Aubrey started texting, "I miss you."

Should she text him? Would he even respond? Did he miss her too?

Aubrey was about to hit send when a text came in from Tina.

Hey girl! Miss your face. You've been on my heart today, praying that you are having a great New Year so far and that God is showing you the plans he has for you.

Aubrey shook her head as she threw her phone on her bed. What was she doing? She couldn't text Jake. She knew he wasn't part of the plans God had for her. Texting him would only be moving backward. She needed to keep moving forward, even if it meant feeling lonely without him.

Aubrey dumped the rest of the champagne in the sink before getting into the tub. She didn't need to be texting Jake, and she didn't need to consume any more alcohol. No more Jake and no more alcohol for the night.

Chapter 18

⚓

The following weekend, Aubrey was running on the beach by her apartment. Another sunny, beautiful day in San Diego. Surfers rode the waves by the pier. Little kids looked for snails and other sea creatures in the low tide. Several people walked along the beach, gazing at the ocean and running into the waves.

This morning had been her first time at church in the New Year, and she couldn't stop thinking about how to hear God's voice in her everyday life.

Pastor Davis had talked about how God wants to speak to them and that they are meant to have a relationship with God where they communicate with him. He reminded everyone that prayer is the primary way they communicate with God, where they tell him how they are feeling, they praise him, they give him thanks, and they make their requests known to him.

He had also talked about listening and how important it is to pause and be still to listen for God to speak back.

"Be still, and know that I am God! Psalm 46:10," Pastor Davis read from his Bible on the podium.

"We live in such a busy world, with never-ending to-do lists and appointments, that most of us rarely ever sit in silence with God.

There is already a conversation going on about us in heaven, but a lot of us miss it because we aren't listening to God. We don't take the time to slow down, pause, turn off our cell phones, and sit in silence with God. So, I challenge each one of you to set aside time each day with God to just be silent.

"Be still and listen for his voice. Don't keep rambling on in your prayers, thinking God is going to shout over you so you can hear him. Pray, make your requests, and actually listen to the one who already knows everything about you and who wants to speak to you."

Aubrey sat down on a large rock and gazed at the ocean. Did God really speak to people out loud? What did his voice sound like?

She had started following more Christian people on Instagram. They talked about doing or not doing things because God told them to do something or told them they shouldn't go through with something.

One Christian blogger had posted: "God told me to go to a new coffee shop one day. I almost didn't go, but then I ended up meeting this elderly woman. She was sitting at her table all alone, wiping tears from her face, so I went up to her. She was grieving the loss of her husband, so I was able to comfort her, and I even invited her to church with me, where she surrendered her life to Jesus."

Another influencer had shared: "God told me to move to San Diego one day. I didn't even have a job there, but then someone offered me a job my first time at my new church."

A Christian author had said: "I knew my boyfriend was about to propose, so I kept praying to God, asking if he was the one. I really liked him—he went to church with me, read the Bible, and seemed like the perfect guy. But then God kept telling me no, so I finally broke up with him. I was heartbroken, but I wanted to obey God.

Then a few months later, I found out he had cheated on me and gotten another girl pregnant."

God had never spoken to Aubrey like that, but there was a time in college when she had felt like she had heard a voice from within telling her to turn around. She had been leaving the library at night, and when she turned around, a man was behind her who looked like he was about to grab her. She had startled him by turning around, and he had walked off.

Had God spoken to her then to save her?

Aubrey knew she needed to hear more from God. She was making an effort to pray to God more, but she wasn't getting any answers. She still had doubts about her job, so if she was supposed to be doing something else, she wanted to know.

God knew she wanted to know the plans he had for her life, yet he hadn't told her anything yet. Why wasn't she hearing from God?

She had tried meditating before when she felt stressed out, but she had never meditated to hear God's voice. The pastor was right. She needed to slow down and sit with God.

She had been asking God for the answers, and she knew God wanted to speak to her, but she needed to sit and listen to him.

She sat on the rock with her eyes closed, focusing on taking deep breaths as she felt the ocean breeze on her skin and the warmth of the sun on her face. She heard the waves crashing in and out along the shore and kids laughing in the distance. She pictured God in heaven, clothed in white, sitting on a throne. She prayed silently with her eyes closed.

What do you want me to do, God? I want to pursue my dreams here, but I'm frustrated with work. I spend all this time working at a job I hate and traveling, and I'm exhausted. I want to do something I feel passionate about. Something I actually enjoy. I feel like I'm in a job and a career where I don't belong. I'm stuck in a sea of accountants who only care about making money and getting promoted. I know I have an impact on people, but that's not what gets recognized, and people take advantage of me. All they care about is how many hours you are charging to the client and how much revenue they are earning. God, I know there has to be more to life than doing a job I hate.

Am I supposed to stay here for the money? Am I supposed to pursue something else, like starting a travel blog or becoming a workout instructor? Is this the year I can quit accounting to do something else? What is my purpose, God? How can I pursue my true passions and figure out what I'm supposed to do with my life?

Aubrey breathed in and out. The breeze on her skin started to give her goosebumps as her sweat started to dry.

Call Tina. The thought came vividly out of nowhere. Yes, she would call Tina! Why hadn't she thought of Tina before?

Tina was her only Christian friend. She loved God, and she also worked in business as a consultant. Tina would understand how she felt about not feeling fulfilled and questioning what her purpose was at work. Tina was super-smart and had a great job designing websites. She was very good at what she did, and she also loved people like Aubrey did.

Aubrey took out her phone and called Tina. That was enough meditating for one day.

"Hello, beautiful! How are you doing?" Tina asked.

"Tina! I miss you so much. Oh my gosh, I was meditating, thinking about my purpose at work, and I had this strong thought where I was like, I must call Tina!" They both laughed.

"I can tell this is going to be a deep conversation. What's on your mind?" Tina asked.

"Well, I've been thinking a lot about my purpose at work and how we can pursue our passions in our job. I've been struggling to understand why I work so much, especially if it's a job I feel I don't belong in. I feel different, like my priorities are different from everyone's else, and I don't understand why we spend so much of our lives working if we're in jobs we hate. I'm grateful for the money and benefits my job provides, but a job is such a big part of our life, and there has to be more to work than just a paycheck, right?"

"Mmm. That's a good question. Have you thought about working in a different field, somewhere you could work doing something you were passionate about?"

"Yeah, I've thought a lot about quitting, but it would be like starting over in a whole new area. I wouldn't quit and do accounting somewhere else. I would want to do something with people or something other than business, like becoming a fitness instructor or starting a travel blog, but I know those would be very hard to excel in and make good money."

"I've talked about this with Bryan before," Tina replied, "and we've studied this in our small group at church. God gives each of us certain gifts, talents, and passions to use in our lives and in our work. Bryan feels like he is called to make money for God and to give to others who are in need, and he gets a lot of satisfaction from making a lot of money. I, however, completely agree with you that my purpose at work is more than just the money. I'm there for the people and I've learned that we can focus on the areas we are passionate about at work. I love when I get to meet someone new at work and help them with something during the day, so I feel like my purpose is to encourage those around me. God has also given me opportunities to talk about him and church at work, which is so awesome. I don't purposefully go around talking about God, but most of my coworkers know I'm a Christian and go to church, so sometimes they will come up to me and ask me for prayer or they will have questions about God. At the end of the day, I feel like I'm making a difference with the people around me, and I feel like that is my purpose."

"Yes, that makes total sense!" Aubrey said. "Ah, I love that, Tina. That is so awesome that God is using you at your workplace and you get to pray for people when they need it. At my job, I love bringing people together, and I can see the impact it has, but it's hard when there is so much of my job that I still have to do that I hate. I don't understand why God would want me at a job I don't like. I want to figure out my true calling, something I'm passionate about."

"God has you there for a reason," Tina replied. "You do have purpose there and you are making an impact on his people. He knows your heart, and he will let you know when it's time to leave. I'm so proud of you that you've been going to church and really thinking about what God wants you to do. This is random but I started a new online Bible study; would you want to do it with me?"

"What's an online Bible study?" Aubrey asked. "I've never done a Bible study before."

"It's studying a book called *Discerning the Voice of God* by Priscilla Shirer," Tina said. "There are daily and weekly readings, and there are videos posted for free online. The book talks about how we can hear and discern God's voice when he is speaking to us. Do it with me; it will be so good! Maybe God will even speak to you about your job and purpose at work!"

The voice of God? It was like what the pastor had talked about that morning. Aubrey knew she had to start spending more time with God besides just going to church. She had been praying more, but it wasn't enough. Maybe the Bible study was a good way for her to learn the Bible in a way she could understand so she could actually figure out what God wanted her to do.

"Sure, why not?" Aubrey said. "I've been wanting to prioritize God more, and I actually don't know how to read the Bible so I think this will be good for me."

"Yes! You're going to love it. I'll send you all the details, and we can talk about it after we finish the lessons and video each week."

Before Aubrey hung up, they agreed to chat about what they were learning and how God spoke to them during the Bible study.

Aubrey smiled as she looked out over the ocean. She was so glad she had a friend like Tina. Even though Tina was thousands of miles away back in Michigan, Aubrey appreciated how Tina was always there for her. And Tina never judged her. Tina's drinking and hookup days were behind her, but whenever Aubrey told her about her drunken mistakes and all the hookup stories with guys, Tina always listened and encouraged her.

Aubrey kept staring at the waves, reflecting on how much she was learning about this whole life with God when a familiar arm tattoo walked in front of her by the shore.

Jake! Was that really him? Same height, same arm tattoo, and same smile. Crap. He had seen her and was already walking up to her. There was nowhere to go. What was he doing here? This was her part of the beach.

Jake stopped ten feet in front of her. "Hi. I saw you and wanted to come say hi. It's been a while, and I've missed you. I understand if you don't want to talk to me, but I just wanted to say hi." He fidgeted with the drawstring on his shorts.

Aubrey sighed. She did miss him, and it was good to see his face. He looked adorable as he always did, even in beach shorts and a fitted tank. She had known they would run into each other eventually; it was bound to happen living so close together by the beach.

"Hi, it's good to see you." She smiled back.

He paused and stared at her before sitting down on the sand next to her.

"How have you been?" Jake asked.

So many thoughts whirled through her head. How had she been since the last time they had seen each other? She had been upset and heartbroken that he wanted to sleep with other people. She had been embarrassed and mortified from crying in front of her boss. She had been ashamed for hooking up with a coworker who had a girlfriend. And she had been frustrated that she was traveling back to the freezing cold in Chicago for a job she didn't like.

"I've been better, but I'm good," Aubrey replied. "Currently working in the tundra in Chicago. How about you?"

Jake attempted a smile. "I've also been better. But, hey, we live at the beach, and if we live at the beach, we're lucky enough."

Aubrey didn't know what to say. She wasn't about to ask him how his New Year was with that new girl. And she wasn't going to bring up how hurt she had been by what he had done. They stared at the ocean for a few minutes before Jake broke the silence.

"I understand if you don't want to talk to me again, but I am truly sorry for everything. I never wanted to hurt you, and I wanted to be honest with you. I still care about you, and I miss hanging out together. You're such a great person, and I want you to be happy."

Aubrey tried processing what he had said. Why did she like him so much when she was still hurt by what he did? At least he had been truthful with her from the beginning. They hadn't been exclusive, and he had been honest that he wasn't ready to date.

There wasn't a good solution for either of them. Was it fair for them never to talk or hang out again just because he wasn't ready to date? But they both missed each other. If they both felt the same way, maybe they could still hang out as friends. Having Jake as a friend would be better than not having him at all.

"I appreciate the apology. I wish things were different, too, and I do miss my first beach friend. I'm still upset that you want to sleep with other people, but I'd rather have you as a friend in my life than not have you in my life at all."

Jake smiled. "Then let's be friends. I'd like that."

Aubrey breathed a sigh of relief. She didn't have to miss Jake anymore. They could still be friends and be in each other's lives.

"Okay, we can be friends but on one condition," Aubrey said as Jake's smile faded. "We can be friends, but we can't have sex. You know it's only going to complicate things and I don't want to get hurt again."

She accepted that he had hooked up with another girl over New Year's, and she knew it was time to move forward. She wasn't going to have sex with him anymore. If he wanted to hook up with other people, he wasn't going to get any from her. They had had such an amazing connection, so if he wanted to sleep around with other people, it was his loss. Yes, they could still be friends and not have sex.

Jake started nodding his head. "While I enjoyed our time together, I think that's the right call. I want to respect you and our friendship, and I understand you not wanting to sleep together anymore."

"Thank you for understanding."

Great, so they were on the same page. They could still be friends and enjoy each other's company on the beach.

"So now that we're friends again," Jake said. "I was thinking of going for a bike ride and getting some tacos. Would you care to join me?"

"Let's do it."

Chapter 19

⚓

Aubrey smiled up at the sun with her new Bible study book in her lap. She had spent another week in the cold in Chicago, but now it was time to savor being home. She was looking forward to lying out all day at the beach, and she felt like she was at peace for the first weekend all New Year.

She and Jake were friends again and she didn't need to wonder if he would ask her to hang out this weekend. Jake was visiting his mom back in Washington for the weekend and had already texted her several photos of him and his dog, Kona.

Aubrey smiled as her phone buzzed with another text from Jake.

Brrr it's freezing here. Missing being in your arms. Come keep me warm?

Aubrey sighed, taking herself back to last Sunday when they had gone for a bike ride and gotten tacos together. They had picked up right where things left off; like New Year had never happened at all.

They had ridden their bikes up and down the boardwalk, creating their own mini bar crawl, as they sampled tacos and margaritas at all the restaurants with ocean views. They laughed and seemed to talk about everything except their relationship status and New Year's. As the night went on, Jake suggested a movie back at his place.

"Come on; let's relax a bit. I'm having too much fun catching up with you and I'm not ready for the night to end." Jake had convinced Aubrey to watch a movie.

"Okay, but remember our rule, we aren't hooking up. And I can't stay super-late; I have an early flight in the morning for work and I haven't even packed yet."

As they watched a movie, she kept reminding herself they were just friends, so she wasn't prepared when Jake started kissing her.

We're just friends! We shouldn't be making out! Aubrey thought to herself. But she couldn't stop. She knew that deep down she didn't want him to stop. She couldn't push away the feelings she still had for him that came bubbling back to the surface as they laughed over margaritas and tacos.

She ended up staying the night at Jake's place and getting an Uber at 5 a.m. to go back to her apartment and pack for her flight.

Now, reminiscing on the beach, Aubrey tried justifying that it was okay that they had slept together again. A part of her felt guilty that she had given in so easily, but she couldn't deny how Jake made her feel when they were together. What was wrong with being friends with benefits? At least they were still having fun together.

> The beach misses you too. We will be waiting for you when you get back.

Aubrey sent the text, then turned her phone off. Today wasn't about Jake; it was about God and figuring out what he wanted her to do with her life.

She opened to the first page of the Bible study and laughed to herself; she couldn't believe she was actually excited about doing a Bible study. She prayed silently, *God, please speak to me through this Bible study. I want to learn more about you and how to do your will. Amen.*

Priscilla Shirer was the author and speaker of the Bible study. Aubrey had never heard of her before, but she was quickly drawn to her stories and how she talked about God. She was like the pastors at church—she could talk about God in plain English while also incorporating humor, so Aubrey was instantly hooked.

"Hearing God starts with our commitment to humble obedience. He will not long waste His words on those who aren't postured to obey," Priscilla said. "Obedience is the key that unlocks all of the blessings God intends for us. So I've gotta ask you a tough question right here on the first day we're together in these pages: Do you intend to obey God, to obey His Word? Do you really want to do His will? Or have you already decided to follow your own way despite what God's Spirit will say?"

Interesting. Aubrey had never really thought much about obeying God before. How could she obey God and know his will if he wasn't speaking to her? How could she obey him when he had never told her anything yet?

"We're all prone at times to hold on too tightly to our own ambitions, relationships, expectations, and even our successes, long after God has instructed us to let them go. In the moment, letting go doesn't make sense. Releasing them doesn't seem worth the alternative. But hearing from God and enjoying the freedom that comes from doing what He says often requires us to empty our hands, trusting He will fill them with something better. We must be willing to pay the cost that leads to his best.

"There is sacrifice involved in your commitment to God," Priscilla continued, "but the benefits far outweigh the costs. In disobedience, we miss God's blessings, invite His necessary discipline, and break the intimacy that allows our spiritual ears to hear what He is saying to us. What modifications do you already suspect you'll need to make to be obedient to God's directives?"

Aubrey immediately thought of drinking and all the mistakes she had made recently. She didn't know what the Bible explicitly said about drinking, but she knew that drinking like she had been was definitely out of line with God's will for her life. God didn't want her to get black-out drunk and make stupid mistakes at work happy hours.

After what had happened at her work training, Aubrey felt like God was showing her that she needed to stop getting drunk. God was making it clear she needed to give up drinking and the party scene. God was already opening her eyes and showing her what would happen if she continued drinking like she had in the past. She wanted to surrender getting drunk and partying to God.

Priscilla then started talking about the Holy Spirit.

"Every human being has a spirit. It is the core and inmost essence of a person. The human spirit was designed for relationship with God. If not divinely connected to Him in this way, we're left with a vacuum that can never be properly or completely filled. Like an intricately designed puzzle piece, the only true fit is the one true God. When you became a believer in Jesus, the Spirit of God took up residence in your human spirit. Here, at your core, you were made brand new. The Holy Spirit is the presence of God himself.

"The Holy Spirit reveals God's plan to you as He orchestrates the circumstances of your life. Over time, your Spirit-led conscience becomes remolded into the image of Christ, able to be used like a microphone for the Holy Spirit to speak to you—convicting you, challenging you, and guiding you toward God's will for your life. Conviction refers to a sense of internal discomfort that leads toward a desire to change your behavior.

"After salvation," Priscilla continued, "because of the Holy Spirit, certain kinds of activities, thoughts, or attitudes don't feel comfortable to you anymore, even if they did before. Something you may have done without concern now feels wrong and problematic—increasingly so over time. Participating in certain behaviors, entertaining certain habits, engaging in certain relationships may become awkward and difficult with little apparent reason. Other than this: God's Spirit is infiltrating your soul—influencing you, molding you. Your conscience is being conformed into the image of Christ."

Wow, this was some crazy stuff. How come nobody ever told her this growing up? She thought God was all about going to church and being a part of a religion, and following a bunch of rules in the Bible. She had never really heard much about the Holy Spirit before. She vaguely remembered other churches talking about the Trinity before, consisting of God, Jesus, and the Holy Spirit, but she had never understood what it meant. A part of God was always with her?

Aubrey had always heard the expression that God is always with you, but she hadn't realized that it was an actual thing. She knew Jesus died for her life so she could go to heaven, but she didn't know he also promised to fill her with the Holy Spirit as a promise and reminder that God was with her. She had also never known that God wanted to have a relationship with her. She knew God created everything in the Earth, including her, but she never thought about God as her father who wanted to spend time with her.

The Holy Spirit seemed like a pretty big deal, but she still didn't understand how God would speak to her or conform her into the image of Christ. Would she hear a voice? Would she feel something if God was trying to get her attention? Would she see an actual sign appearing in front of her, telling her what to do? Could God actually change her desires? Could he actually transform her?

Aubrey thought of Tina and how she had started to change when they all lived in Chicago. She used to go out with everyone, and drink and dance and have fun, and she had even hooked up with the occasional random guy every now and then. She wasn't as promiscuous as the rest of them, but she still liked to have her fun and went on a lot of first dates.

But when Tina had started going to church, she had stopped drinking and going out with the girls as much. She would have the occasional glass of wine and still come out with them to dance a little, but she always went home early, and she stopped bringing guys home. And she seemed so happy. Aubrey and the rest of the girls thought it was a phase, but Tina had kept it up until she married Bryan.

Maybe that's what Priscilla meant by being conformed to the image of Christ. Maybe when Tina had begun going to church, God had started to transform her and had changed her desire to drink and go out.

Aubrey wanted to change, but she never knew how before. But with God, it sounded like it was possible to change with him. If the Holy Spirit could change her desires and help her drink less, she was all for it. She had been trying to drink less and be smarter about drinking, but clearly it wasn't working. God was making it pretty clear. She needed to surrender this area to him, and she needed his help to change.

God, please change my desire for alcohol. You've already showed me a path I don't want to live anymore. You've already showed me the consequences of drinking too much. Help me, God. Help change my desires so I don't want to drink as much. I don't want drinking to ruin my life. Amen.

Chapter 20

⚓

Aubrey sat down next to two girls who looked her age. Even though she hated standing during worship for so long, she purposefully made it on time for church to try to meet other people around her.

"Hi, have you guys been coming here long?" Aubrey attempted to be bold as she greeted the girls next to her.

They looked up from their cell phones. "We come occasionally when we're able to get out of bed." The girl who had spoken went back to her phone.

They didn't seem too friendly, but Aubrey didn't want to waste this opportunity.

"I was thinking of joining one of the Bible study groups or going to a singles event. Have you ever been before?"

The same girl chimed in. "Don't waste your time with the singles events. We went to a few in hopes of meeting a decent guy, but it was mostly girls with creepy guys." She went back to her phone.

The worship band started playing. Aubrey tried not to feel defeated; these girls did not seem like they were looking for new friends. This church was huge; there had to be other people here who could potentially be new friends.

She focused on the music and the singers worshiping God on stage. Even though she felt uncomfortable singing, she appreciated how passionate the singers were. She couldn't imagine singing out loud in front of this many people about God, but she admired their confidence. They didn't care about what others thought, and they genuinely looked like this was their favorite place to be on a Sunday morning.

Aubrey closed her eyes as she reflected on the progress she had been making with God. She had only been doing the Bible study for a few weeks, but it was like God was showing her what a life with him really looked like.

Before, she had thought she had been making progress by going to church more, but now she understood there was so much more to God than going to church whenever she felt like it. She was learning what it was like to have a relationship with God. He wanted to spend time with her, and he wanted to speak to her.

Pastor Davis started preaching about the Holy Spirit and how a lot of people complained that God wasn't speaking to them.

"We've already talked a lot about the Holy Spirit's role in our lives and how God wants to speak to us," he said. "As Christians, we know God wants to speak to us, but so many of us run around trying to understand what God wants us to do. We run around, searching for our purpose and life calling, and we get frustrated when we don't hear from God. It's easy to say to God, 'God, I've been praying and listening, but I'm still not hearing anything. Did you hear me?'"

A few chuckles went around the room. Aubrey was hooked; it was like he was talking about her. She had been asking God for months what she was supposed to do, yet she still hadn't heard anything from God.

"Now, we've already talked about the power of prayer and that you should be talking to God through prayer," Pastor Davis continued, "but as we are praying, making our requests known to God, and as we are listening, we cannot forget to obey what God has already told us. Most of the time, when we don't hear God's voice in our life, it's because he has already given us the answer."

Pastor Davis picked up his Bible from the podium.

"The answer is usually in this book. It can be easy to forget that God has already spoken and given us so much information in the Bible. With every question, every request to God, we must see what God has already said about it in the Bible. The Word of God is the standard of truth, and it never changes. God's truth is the standard for all believers, and we are called to obey God's Word out of love for God. God says we show love for him by obeying his commands, and you can apply the Word of God to every situation in your life.

"A lot of you come to God, asking him to answer you and tell you what to do. You ask for direction and guidance on a situation. 'Should I date this person, Lord? Should I take that job? Should I move to that city?' But a lot of us forget that God has already answered us. He's already told you what to do. And it's right here in this Bible. All the answers you are looking for are right here in this book, yet some of you aren't taking the time to read it. And you wonder why you haven't heard from God? He's sitting up there in heaven, saying, 'I already told you the answer!'"

Cheers erupted across the auditorium.

"You tell 'em, Pastor!"

"Preach it; come on!"

"God's Word," Pastor Davis continued, "is actually the primary way God speaks to us through the Holy Spirit. A lot of us wait around for God to speak to us through signs and wonders in our lives, but he only uses those signs and wonders to confirm something he's already told you. So, with every question, every prayer request you ask God, first ask yourself, what does God's Word say about it? Have you taken the time to read the Word to see if God has already given you the answer?"

Aubrey shook her head. She still wasn't reading the Bible yet. She looked up some of the Bible verses she was supposed to read in the Bible study, but she didn't actually read the Bible for herself.

Whenever her mom read from the Bible growing up, it had never made any sense to Aubrey. When the priest read from the Bible at her Catholic church, it always sounded like he was speaking a foreign language. Aubrey had occasionally read the Bible with her mom before bed, but she still struggled to understand it and enjoy reading it. While she had loved the stories of David and Goliath and Noah's Ark, she had never gotten into the routine of reading the Bible on her own.

Aubrey also didn't understand how the Bible could give her answers for her life. How could the Bible answer her questions and prayers?

The Bible was written thousands of years ago and didn't reflect modern times. Back in Jesus' time, people were farmers and didn't have as many options to have a career. Women got married and had lots of babies when they were still teenagers and sometimes even had arranged marriages.

How could the Bible answer her questions about what she was created to do and what she was supposed to do with her life? How could the Bible guide her as she dated and searched for a husband?

Pastor Davis interrupted her thoughts.

"That's why it's so important to spend time in the Word each day and to actually listen for God's voice. As you read the Word, God will reveal the answers to the questions you've been praying about. We have a lot of younger people at our church, and I always realize they aren't reading the Bible when they are struggling to hear from God. And it's crazy when they tell me why they aren't reading the Bible. The most common reason I hear is that the Bible is outdated and isn't relevant to the times we are living in."

A few gasps went around the room, including a loud gasp from Aubrey.

"I know, right? The same commands that God wrote thousands of years ago most certainly still apply today. God talks about anxiety, fear, partying, stealing, sexual sin—he addresses all of the sins and struggles today's generation is dealing with. And just so we're clear, sin still matters to God. Just because the world has accepted casual sex and drunkenness doesn't mean it's not a sin when you disobey God's commands. Any time you are disobeying God's Word, any time you are doing something that is not pleasing to God, whether you realize it or not, you are engaging in sin. And God's Word tells us that there are consequences when we disobey his Word; God is a God of justice and he disciplines his children just like a loving father."

Aubrey was surprised. The Bible talked about partying? She knew getting black-out drunk and getting kicked out of hot tubs was not pleasing to God, but she was curious what the Bible said about parties. She would definitely have to look that up.

And sexual sin? Her mom had always told her not to have sex before marriage, but she had never listened. No one else she knew was waiting for marriage to have sex. That seemed a bit much. Was having sex before marriage actually a sin? Did people actually obey the commands in the Bible?

When she was growing up, she had always heard the priest talking about the Ten Commandments, but none of her friends had ever talked about the Bible, so she hadn't thought it was a big deal.

Pastor Davis ended his sermon with a prayer and encouraged everyone to spend time in God's Word each day.

"No matter what you are going through or what you are facing, God's Word will speak to and encourage you. Go home and open up the Word and get ready for God to open your eyes to what he's already spoken to you. And give him your heart as you listen to what he tells you to do. Just be ready—God may reveal some areas of your life that are not in line with his Word. But you have a choice: You can repent from your sin and you can choose to start doing things God's way, or you can face the consequences as you continue to disobey God. No matter what God reveals to you, just know that no sin is too big for God to forgive. Jesus already paid the price for all your sins and shortcomings, and what matters now is true repentance and that you turn from your sin and start to obey God's ways. Jesus will forgive you, but it's up to you to surrender it to him and choose in your heart to obey him."

Chapter 21

⚓

Obedience. Based on what Aubrey was learning in Bible study and from Pastor Davis, it seemed like obedience was a big deal to God. Growing up, Aubrey had always heard in church about the things you weren't supposed to do, and that you weren't supposed to sin, but she never understood why or what the big deal was. Now, it was clear that sin meant disobeying God's commands and that disobedience was a big deal to God. It was clear she had to start obeying God out of love and respect for him and their relationship. She was understanding that following God's ways would help her live the life and plans God had for her and that there were consequences when she disobeyed God's commands.

She was so focused on figuring out what God wanted her to do with her life that she hadn't thought much about the things he didn't want her to do. Drinking was an obvious one; she knew it was getting in the way of the plans God had for her life, but she was curious what the Bible said about drinking. She grabbed her phone and started typing in Google: What does the Bible say about drinking?

She clicked on the first article that popped up. A Bible verse from 1 Peter 4:3 caught her eye.

"You have had enough in the past of the evil things that godless people enjoy—their immorality and lust, their feasting and drunkenness and wild parties, and their terrible worship of idols."

Aubrey couldn't believe that "wild parties" was actually in the Bible! Pastor Davis was right—the Bible did address modern times. She continued reading another verse from Ephesians 5:15-18.

"So be careful how you live. Don't live like fools, but like those who are wise. Make the most of every opportunity in these evil days. Don't act thoughtlessly, but understand what the Lord wants you to do. Don't be drunk with wine, because that will ruin your life. Instead, be filled with the Holy Spirit…."

Well, she had enough evidence to support her theory that God was not pleased with her drunkenness. She had gotten drunk with more than just wine, and God had already made it clear it was ruining her life. But surely, she didn't have to give up drinking altogether. Wasn't one of Jesus' first miracles turning water into wine? She made a mental note to ask her mom or Tina about it later.

"I hear you, God, loud and clear. Now, how else can I obey you?" Aubrey said out loud.

Aubrey took a sip of tea. Her Bible lay on the couch next to her, but she didn't know how to start looking things up in it or where to start reading. How long was this book anyway?

She started typing again in Google. "Where does the Bible talk about the Ten Commandments?"

Several articles on Google told her the Ten Commandments were found in Exodus 20, so she found the page number for Exodus in the Table of Contents in her Bible.

Don't worship any other gods but God. Don't worship any idols. Don't misuse the name of God. Observe the Sabbath day to rest from all work. Honor your father and mother. Do not murder. Do not commit adultery. Do not steal. Do not give false testimony against your neighbor. Do not covet your neighbor's house or wife.

These commandments didn't seem too unreasonable to follow. And Aubrey was pretty sure she was obeying them already. But what did some of these words actually mean?

Adultery seemed so harsh. Did that mean people weren't supposed to cheat on each other? That should be a given, but it happened all the time. It made total sense that people weren't supposed to cheat on each other.

But what had Pastor Davis said in his sermon about sexual sin? What type of sexual sin was he referring to? Was her mom actually right that you weren't supposed to have sex before marriage? Did the Bible talk about having sex before marriage?

She went back to Google. "What does the Bible say about sex before marriage?"

Articles mentioning adultery, purity, lust, and sexual immorality popped up.

What was up with all these big words? She knew what lust meant, but she felt like she needed a Christian dictionary to decipher all these words. Why couldn't the Bible just tell it like it is?

She went back to Google. "What does adultery mean?" "What does sexual immorality mean?" "What does the Bible say about purity?"

She stumbled across a blog for women, *Girl Defined*, founded by two sisters, Kristen Clark and Bethany Beal, who were passionate about helping modern girls understand and live out God's timeless truth for womanhood. They had a lot of blog posts and even YouTube videos discussing what the Bible said about sex and used all the big words from the Bible, except they broke it down in plain English.

Aubrey clicked on a blog post titled "Why Premarital Sex Isn't an Expression of True Biblical Love" by Kristen Clark.

From the beginning of creation in Genesis 1 to the end of the New Testament, we see God's beautiful design for sex and the parameters in which it is to be enjoyed. The Bible reveals to us over and over again that sex is an expression of love to be enjoyed within the context of marriage.

"Therefore a man shall leave his father and his mother and hold fast to his wife, and they shall become one flesh" (Genesis 2:24).

Despite what modern society teaches, God designed sex for marriage only. Sex is an expression of love within the marriage covenant.

According to God's word, having sex outside of this covenant is not considered an expression of love, but an outworking of sin and lust (Gal. 5:19, 2 Tim. 2:22, Eph. 5:3, etc). Throughout the Bible, we see glimpses into the lives of individuals who blatantly disobeyed God's design for sex...and with passion. (think of Judah, David, Amnon, etc). These examples remind us that passion doesn't equate to biblical love.

Aubrey reread the blog post twice. So she was actually supposed to wait until marriage to have sex? This was absolutely absurd! Everyone had sex before marriage. Nobody Aubrey knew had waited until marriage. All her friends had sex with men they were dating, and it wasn't a big deal.

Aubrey knew there must be a few virgins who grew up in church and potentially a few pastors who waited until marriage. But not having sex until marriage seemed completely unrealistic. People didn't actually wait until marriage to have sex. Aubrey had lost her virginity her senior year of high school because everyone else around her was doing it, and she wanted to lose her virginity before college.

Over the past few years, she had tried not to sleep with guys right away because she wanted a serious boyfriend. She wanted someone who wanted to date her, not a guy who just wanted to sleep with her. She wanted to wait until she was in an actual relationship before sleeping with them. But waiting until marriage? That was insane.

What did it matter if she gave up sex since she had already had sex before? She was no longer a virgin and it was too late. People would think it was weird if she stopped having sex and waited until marriage. How would she meet someone who would understand this and still want to date her? No guy would want to wait until marriage to have sex.

And how was she supposed to know if the person was good in bed if she waited until marriage? Everyone knew it was like test-driving a car; you didn't buy a car without test-driving it first. How could you tell if you had good chemistry with someone if you didn't have sex until marriage? What if they had a small penis? What if the sex was bad and then you were screwed?

No, waiting until marriage to have sex didn't sound good at all. Aubrey knew she could do some of this stuff like going to church, praying more, and drinking less to get closer to God, but she couldn't commit to not having sex.

She knew she shouldn't be having sex with Jake because he didn't want to date her and she didn't want to get hurt again, but she couldn't even say no when they were together. How was she supposed to give up sex until she was married? She couldn't do it. It was impossible.

She was glad she had found the *Girl Defined* blog because it helped the Bible make more sense, but she still didn't know of anyone who had waited to have sex. Maybe Tina would be able to help her understand some of this.

Chapter 22

⚓

"Oh my gosh, girl, we have to talk," Aubrey said as soon as Tina picked up the phone. "What happened when you started going to church? Did you decide to stop having sex? Did you wait to have sex again with Bryan until you were married?"

Aubrey was power-walking along the beach. She needed to get some fresh air after everything she was learning about sex.

Tina laughed. "Wow, someone has really been digging into God's Word! I like it!"

Aubrey laughed. "Yes, I have. I've been loving the Bible study, and it's like the pastor has been speaking directly to me at church. But seriously, I want to know more about what happened when you started going to church. You changed. I realized it back then, but I just thought you were weird, and I judged you for not wanting to do the same things we always did anymore. I'm sorry for judging you, but that's just how I was back then—I didn't understand what was happening. Did you give up drinking and hooking up with people for God?"

There was so much Aubrey needed to know. She needed to understand how someone could change and give up parts of their life, like sex, to God.

"I can tell God has really been speaking to you," Tina said. "I'm so proud of you for seeking him and continuing to study his Word. And yes, I did change. I told you before that God changed my life, and I am so grateful for the life I have now and the person I've become. I wouldn't be who I am today without God."

"Go on—I'm listening. Tell me everything, and don't leave anything out about how you changed."

Tina kept laughing. "You are too much. Well, I started going to church, and at some point, I realized I needed to go all in with God. I had always believed in him growing up, but over time, I knew something was missing and there had to be more to God besides just casually going to church every now and then. I really loved the messages at Soul City Church in Chicago, and I started getting more plugged in by joining a small group and volunteering in the kids' church. In my small group—it was a group of women—we talked about how to have an intimate relationship with God and that prayer and spending time in his Word by reading the Bible every day was foundational to this relationship with God. We started praying more together, and I learned how to read the Bible. God started to reveal to me that his Word was the truth and the way to live, and I didn't want to live the life of casual hookups and drunk nights out anymore. It was like he fully opened my eyes to who he was and to what being a Christian really meant. So, I surrendered my life to him and accepted Jesus as my savior, and I have never looked back."

Aubrey nodded as Tina described her transformation. It was crazy thinking about it now because she could actually understand what Tina had gone through now that she was seeking God herself and learning more about how to obey his Word. At the time, Aubrey had thought Tina was crazy. She hadn't understood why anyone would just change like that, especially when all their friends were still going out partying every weekend and hooking up with guys.

"Such an amazing transformation. I remember how you started going to church more, and I noticed how you had changed. But what about sex? Did you stop having sex because of God?"

"Yes, of course, the big question on your heart," Tina said. "I did decide to stop having sex except it wasn't because of God; it was for God. The more I read the Bible, the more I realized parts of my life were not in line with how God wanted me to live. Like getting drunk and hooking up with people. So, when I made the decision to go all in for God, I also made the decision to change my ways, which included waiting to have sex until I got married. God showed me that there are consequences when we sin, when we don't follow his ways in the Bible. So, I decided to give up sex out of my love for God and for what Jesus had done for me on the cross."

"Wow, good for you. That's pretty brave that you made that decision and gave that part of your life to God. But what about Bryan? You guys had had sex in high school; did you wait until marriage to have sex again when you got back together?"

Aubrey had always thought Tina and Bryan had the cutest love story. Now that she was learning about God, she realized it really was a miracle from God how they had ended up back together and gotten married. They had started dating their senior year of high school and really hit things off at a party at their friend's house.

They went to prom together and dated their first year of college while Tina attended Michigan State and Bryan went to Yale. But long distance wasn't working, so they had eventually broken up. But they had always stayed in touch throughout college and would randomly see each other at Michigan State or back in their hometown when Bryan was home visiting. They dated other people throughout college, but nothing stuck, and they always somehow started talking again.

After college, they started their adult lives in the real world, Tina living in Chicago and Bryan in New York. After a few years had gone by with no contact, Bryan had called Tina one night out of the blue. They had talked for hours, and Bryan had admitted that he missed her and felt the need to call her. They ended up seeing each other in New York, and it was clear they wanted to get back together. So, they got back together, he moved to Chicago, they got married, and now they were living happily ever after.

"When Bryan and I first started talking again," Tina explained, "I told him that church and God were a big part of my life and I wanted to wait until marriage to have sex. I also asked him if he was open to going to church with me and pursuing a relationship with God. I knew he hadn't grown up going to church and that God wasn't a part of his life before."

Aubrey's eyes got big as she took in how bold and courageous Tina was. She was so proud of her for speaking up for herself.

"Wow, Tina. Way to be bold. What did Bryan say?"

"He said he was open to going to church with me, and he was excited to learn more about God. He knew it was a big part of my life and that it was important to me. He also respected my decision not to hook up or have sex until we were married. He was really sweet about it."

So this kind of stuff really did happen! People could actually wait until marriage to have sex again. Tina and Bryan were proof of it. And even after they had already had sex with each other before, they still decided to wait out of their love for God. So with God, it does still count. It does matter, even if you've already slept with the person.

"Wow! That is crazy," Aubrey said. "Oh my gosh, no wonder you were so excited about all the lingerie you got at your bachelorette party! You could finally put it to good use and have all the sex you wanted!" They both laughed.

"Exactly! I still dress up for Bryan all the time. He loves it!"

"But how did you do it? How did you actually stop having sex?" Aubrey asked.

"It was hard, definitely wasn't easy," Tina said, "but God helped me along the way. He gave me strength, and over time, it got easier to resist. Bryan and I established firm boundaries where we wouldn't put ourselves in situations where we could be tempted. We wouldn't share the same bed, and we wouldn't be alone too late by ourselves, which is why we always loved hanging out with you and Alexa and watching movies. And we set limits with how much alcohol we drank so we weren't even more tempted."

"I always thought you guys were so weird for not sharing the same bed. I'm sorry for judging you at the time, but it's all making sense now. I get how important those boundaries must have been. And the drinking! I actually was wondering about that, and wanted to get your thoughts on whether it's okay to drink any alcohol at all since drunkenness is a sin in the Bible."

"Such a great question! I wondered about that too actually. I asked a few of my mentors at church about it when God was transforming me and, basically, it's a personal decision between you and God. It's clear that we should not be getting drunk, but the Bible also talks about people drinking wine, so I think it's okay for people to drink as long as they don't get drunk."

"Yeah, that makes a lot of sense. It would be pretty hard to avoid alcohol altogether."

Aubrey felt relieved. She was so happy to have Tina to talk about this with. None of her other friends would understand what she was going through.

"Tina, I'm so glad God put you in my life. Thank you for being so open and sharing with me. This was exactly what I needed to hear—things are making much more sense now."

They said their goodbyes. Aubrey stared at the ocean, processing Tina's story.

Aubrey had never understood before that Tina had given up sex for God and waited until marriage to have sex again. She appreciated how bold Tina had been to tell Bryan that waiting until marriage and God was important to her. And look what had happened. She had found a guy who respected her decision to love God and to wait until marriage to have sex, and now they were married.

Aubrey wanted that kind of love story. She wanted a man who would love her for her, not because of sex or her body. She wanted a man who only wanted to sleep with her and nobody else. Finding a man like that would be the ultimate miracle from God. Aubrey knew she needed God in her life and to go to heaven, but she also needed God so she could find a man like that.

Even though Tina had proved it was possible to wait until marriage to have sex, Aubrey didn't know if she could do it. Even if she wanted to obey God in this area, how would she find a guy who would respect her decision to wait until marriage?

Aubrey needed to learn more. She pulled out Google again and started searching for books on purity. A few weeks ago, she hadn't even understood what purity meant. She still didn't like the word; it sounded way too formal and old school Christian, but if it was in the Bible, she needed to learn why it was important.

She purchased a book by *Girl Defined* called *Love Defined* that talked about purity and dating in a way that honors God. She purchased another book called *The Wait* by the actress Meagan Good and her husband about how they had waited until marriage to have sex after they started dating.

If a celebrity like Meagan Good could decide to wait until marriage to have sex and God brought her a gorgeous husband like he did, maybe she could learn how they did it and trust God too.

Even though giving up sex until marriage seemed crazy, what did she have to lose? Yes, sex felt good, but regardless of her decision to obey God, sleeping with people clearly wasn't getting her anywhere and didn't lead to genuine relationships. She had given up the milk for free for far too long, and she was sick of sleeping with the same guys she met at bars who didn't want a real relationship.

Who cares if they liked her butt or wanted to sleep with her? None of those guys wanted to take her on a real date. She wanted and knew she deserved more. She deserved more than someone who wanted to sleep with other people.

Trusting God with dating and her future husband also seemed like a good idea if it meant meeting a Christian guy who would be less likely to cheat on her. The Bible clearly said cheating was wrong. Aubrey wanted someone who wouldn't cheat on her, and if Christian men were less likely to cheat, then she was all for it.

Was it too much to ask to want someone who only wanted to date her? Who wanted to date her and pursue an actual relationship? Tina and Bryan had their fairy tale, their God-written love story, but could that really happen to people like her? Their story was definitely not the norm since Aubrey and all her other friends were subject to the same kind of men that they met at the bars and on the dating apps.

As Aubrey walked back into her apartment, she knew what God wanted her to do. So she closed her eyes and bowed her head.

Okay, God, I am going to at least try. I'm going to try to stop having sex to obey your Word. Lord, please help me at least try.

Chapter 23

⚓

"Let me know what you want for dinner in an email. A few of us are staying late again to recheck the accounting schedules." The intern walked away before Aubrey had a chance to respond.

Staying late again? It was already 7 p.m.—Aubrey was starving.

"Looks like it's time for another Red Bull," Max, an associate working across from her, said as he headed toward the client's kitchen area.

Aubrey hung her head in her hands. Why was she even here? Why was she working so much in a job she didn't even like?

She should have already been on a plane back to California, but the partner had asked her to stay another night; they had a deadline coming up for the client the following week. She knew they were almost done with the first part of their work, but she didn't know how much longer she could do this.

Her main contact at the client had been moody and unresponsive to her emails and requests all week. Her team was trying to track down accounting information from thirty different business units across the country, and they were still missing half of the responses. When Aubrey had asked the client to send out a reminder to the business units, emphasizing how important it was to send in the data, the client had responded, "Isn't that your job? I'm paying you to manage this for me." Aubrey tried explaining how important it was to get management's support behind all their requests, but the client still had not sent the follow-up email they needed. How were they supposed to meet their deadline if they were still missing half of the responses?

She wiped away a stray tear that had escaped. She needed a break. It was her sixth week in a row back in Chicago, and she felt like she was trapped in an accounting world she didn't want to be in anymore. She couldn't pretend to care about numbers or financial statements much longer, but she still had no idea what she was supposed to do instead.

Was she supposed to quit? Would this be her last assignment with the firm? Aubrey wished she had more time to pursue her other dreams, but she was nowhere close to becoming a workout instructor or having a travel blog set up. How could she quit when she didn't even know how to get certified or build a website?

God, why aren't you answering me? Why am I here? I don't know how much more I can take of this job. God, show me what you created me to do. Show me if it's time to leave Assets & Beyond Consulting.

A Bible verse she had seen on Instagram the day before came back to her. "Come to me, all of you who are weary and carry heavy burdens, and I will give you rest."

Rest. That was exactly what she needed. She was getting burned out and needed to take a break before making any huge decisions, like quitting her job. She had a ton of personal time off stored up and it was time to use it. She had been saving it for tropical vacations to Hawaii or Belize, but she didn't have anyone to go on those trips with except her mom.

Taking a staycation in San Diego sounded like exactly what she needed. Aubrey sent an email to her performance manager, mentioning that they needed to talk as soon as he was free. He called her within a few minutes.

"How's it going? Are you enjoying being back in Chicago?" Kurt sounded too cheery for this conversation, but she didn't care. She needed to be honest.

"Actually, that's what I wanted to talk to you about. I need to take a few weeks off. I'm getting burned out, and I need to take some time off to reset." Aubrey didn't mention she was going to quit if she didn't get a break.

"I see. Thanks for telling me how you feel. What's been going on?"

"I need to be home in San Diego, and I need to stop traveling so much. It's been nonstop since I moved and I need time off." Aubrey fought back more tears that were threatening to escape. She got so emotional when she was tired.

"Yes, I was worried about that actually," Kurt said. "I appreciate you being honest with me. I think that sounds like a great idea, and it seems like perfect timing since your current project is almost wrapping up."

They agreed to catch up after her time off, and he agreed to help her find local projects where she could work in Southern California.

It was getting late so Aubrey shut down her laptop. She was done for the day. She would wake up early in the morning to finish what she had to get done before her flight back home in the evening. She couldn't stay in the conference room any longer. She knew she was supposed to stay with the team as the manager, but she needed to leave before she said anything she would regret later.

"Did you place your dinner order yet?" Max asked as he returned to his computer. "We're getting deep dish tonight. We all need some carb motivation."

"No, I need to head out," Aubrey replied. "I have something personal to take care of tonight and it can't wait. I'll review the numbers you sent me at my hotel and will send you any comments I have first thing in the morning." She put her laptop in her work bag.

"Thanks for working so hard this week," Aubrey said, turning to face Max. "I know it hasn't been easy trying to finish the report while we are still missing half the responses, but you've been doing a great job." She felt bad for the team. They were all in this together, and she knew Max wasn't having the time of his life at work either.

"Yeah, yeah, thanks for acknowledging it. We will get it done, and then we will celebrate with a big team dinner downtown on the firm."

Aubrey laughed. "Oh, you can count on it. Steaks on the firm for sure."

The work perks were always the silver lining. No matter how long the day had been or how tired she was, the free points from traveling and all the paid travel expenses always boosted her spirits.

Aubrey was about to order an Uber when she got a text from her coworker Paige. She was working on a different project downtown and was taking her team out.

Hola chica come dance with us! It's going to be a twerking kind of night. Tequila on the firm!

Paige had added three dancing emojis. Aubrey smiled and shook her head. Paige was truly one of a kind. They had always had a blast going out together and tearing up the dance floor. Aubrey did want to relax and let go of some steam from work, but she knew going out with them wasn't the answer. She needed to get a lot done tomorrow morning, and she didn't want to fly home hungover.

Aubrey shuddered thinking about all the times she had flown hungover. It was the worst. She shook her head as she texted Paige back.

Have fun, not going to make it! Still have work to do. Will miss you guys.

Instead of drinking, she would get in a good workout in the hotel gym to relieve some stress. As she stood up to leave, her coworker Austin swung by the conference room.

"I'm hitting the road. Anyone need a ride back to the city?"

Austin was pretty cute; they had gotten to know each other better since working on the project together. He was only a few inches taller than Aubrey, but he was still pretty athletic and had adorable dimples. They had been working at one of the client's locations an hour away from downtown where her hotel was, and she would enjoy his company instead of sitting in an Uber with a stranger for an hour.

"Sure, that would be great." She put on her coat.

Chapter 24

⚓

As Aubrey got in Austin's car, she noticed a few Nike shoeboxes in his backseat.

"Did you treat yourself to some new workout gear for the New Year?"

Austin laughed. "Nah, I was just cleaning out my trunk and forgot to recycle those. Those were from running the Chicago marathon last year."

Aubrey turned to face him. "Seriously? I ran the marathon last year too! I had no idea you ran it; we could have been running next to each other the whole 26.2 miles without even realizing it."

"You're a runner too? I knew I liked you for a reason—I have a thing for runners."

Those dimples. Aubrey was glad it was dark out to hide her cheeks that were blushing a bright pink. She hadn't heard from Jake all week and it felt nice to be flirting with someone else.

"I love running, especially on the beach in warm weather. But the marathon was a commitment. Was it your first time?"

"I've run a few half-marathons so this was my first full marathon. It was hard to train with the demands of this job, but we gotta do something to take our mind off work, especially after sitting in a conference room all day. I can't wait until this project is over."

"Tell me about it," Aubrey replied. "I didn't move to the best place on Earth just to fly back to the freezing tundra every week."

Austin laughed. "Are you enjoying the West Coast? Do you miss us at all, freezing back here in Chicago?"

"Yeah, of course, I miss all my friends and sweet coworkers who offer to drive me home." She smiled at Austin as he glanced over at her. "But San Diego feels like where I'm supposed to be and I miss being home. I miss sleeping in my own bed and taking walks on the beach after work. And I miss being able to cook my own meals and eating something that doesn't come from a restaurant takeout box. And I'm convinced I'll figure out what I'm supposed to be doing by the beach. There has to be more out there than doing accounting, you know?"

Austin laughed. "Oh, trust me, there's much more out there besides doing lease accounting schedules for a month straight. I already applied at a few other places."

Obviously she wasn't the only one who wanted to leave. It was public accounting after all. Who did actually enjoy working in accounting?

They were a few blocks away from her hotel in the River North neighborhood.

"Thanks for keeping me company on the commute home," Austin said. "Would you like to grab a drink somewhere nearby?"

Aubrey hesitated. He was so easy to talk to, and she would love to spend more time with him. They definitely had a spark between them, and it would be so nice to hang out with someone other than Jake.

Aubrey imagined Austin's arm around her as they sat at a bar. Maybe a few intense make-out sessions. She could even invite him back to her hotel room like they did in the movies.

A taxi blew its horn in the distance, bringing her back to reality. As cute as Austin was and as possible as her daydream could be, she knew grabbing a drink with him wasn't a good idea. She still wasn't completely convinced she could give up the whole having sex thing for God, but she at least had to try.

Despite Austin's adorable, dimpled smile, Aubrey mustered the inner strength she had to shake her head no.

"I would love to, but I have to get some more work done before I fly out tomorrow. Maybe another time."

Their eyes locked before she grabbed her bag and shut the door. She felt a sense of accomplishment as she watched him drive away. She was not about to be tempted to do anything she would regret.

As tired as she was, Aubrey did her usual sprint interval workout on the treadmill before heading down to the lobby bar for some dinner. The hotel had one of the nicest lobby bars she had been to in a while, and she wanted to enjoy it. She didn't care that she was still in her workout clothes. She was not in the mood to talk or try to impress anyone. She usually grabbed something quick for dinner and took it back to her room, but tonight, she needed to unwind and not be stuck in her hotel room.

A handful of people were at the bar, sipping cocktails and sharing appetizers. Aubrey inhaled the smell of someone's beer as she walked by and shuddered. She used to love beer, but for some reason, lately she couldn't stand it. Same with whiskey. She exhaled forcefully as she walked by a few older guys who looked like they were drinking whiskey on the rocks.

"Care for anything to drink?" the bartender asked Aubrey as she sat down at the end of the bar.

Even after the long day she'd had, she wasn't craving a drink. Aubrey skimmed the menu.

"Can I get a chicken Caesar salad with the dressing on the side? And do you happen to have chocolate milk by any chance?"

Chocolate milk was one of her favorite travel snacks.

The bartender smiled at her. "Haven't heard that one in a long time. Salad and a chocolate milk coming right up. Sounds like great post-workout fuel."

The bartender seemed friendly, and he was pretty attractive, but Aubrey wasn't in the mood for conversation. She took out her new book, *The Wait* by DeVon Franklin and Meagan Good, so she didn't have to make small talk.

When her chocolate milk arrived, Aubrey shook her head as she laughed to herself. Last year in Chicago, she would have been the type of woman to order a dirty martini after a long day at work while reading a trashy romance novel at the bar or flirting with the bartender. Now, here she was, drinking a chocolate milk while reading a purity book. Perhaps God really did transform lives.

Why hadn't she known about all these Christian books and blogs growing up? They would have helped her understand what God was really all about. They would have helped her actually understand what the Bible was saying. All these people actually made God seem cool.

Aubrey was instantly hooked by Meagan and DeVon's story of how they fell in love and waited until their wedding night to have sex. They had both had sex previously in other relationships, but they had decided to surrender this area to God. Sex had caused so much pain, confusion, and heartbreak, but doing it God's way by waiting until marriage to have sex had eliminated so much chaos in their lives. They had both been born-again Christians when they surrendered their lives to Jesus and made a commitment to purity for their future marriage and for God. They ended up getting married and proved that trusting God with their love story and saving sex until marriage was worth the wait.

It was so uplifting to see other people were actually out there who were also waiting to have sex until marriage—and not just other people, but celebrities in the entertainment industry. Their love story had the fairy tale ending all girls dreamed of, yet it was way better than all the love stories Aubrey had read about and seen in romantic comedies. God was their matchmaker. They didn't have to resort to spending hours on the dating apps swiping or getting drunk at bars to meet someone. If these two celebrities could stop having sex, and if God could write their love story, could God write her love story too?

Aubrey finished her chocolate milk and made her way back to her room. Her mind was spinning from everything she was learning about purity and God's design for sex. She knew she needed to call it a night, but she couldn't resist flipping through her new *Love Defined* book once she got into bed. She still had so many questions and couldn't wait to hear more about how other girls actually obeyed God's design for sex.

A chapter titled "Is It Okay to Date a Non-Christian?" caught her eye. She started reading.

When it comes to dating a non-Christian, God's Word offers some helpful wisdom. As John Piper wisely points out, "The key text is in 1 Corinthians 7:39 where it says that a woman is 'free to be married to whom she wishes, only in the Lord.'

Basically, this verse is a direct exhortation to marry someone who is in the Lord (i.e., a true Christian). And since dating should lead to marriage, it wouldn't be wise to date a guy who isn't a Christian….

Here's another key verse that addresses this issue: "Do not be unequally yoked with unbelievers. For what partnership has righteousness with lawlessness? Or what fellowship has light with darkness?" (2 Cor. 6:14)

When it comes to dating or marrying a nonbeliever, the Bible says you will become like an unequally yoked pair of oxen. Basically, you're not a good match. You will encounter major spiritual differences….

The command in this verse makes it painfully clear that marrying a nonbeliever would be disobedient to God.

Aubrey grabbed her Bible from the nightstand. Was this really true? Did God actually talk about dating other people who didn't share the same faith? Growing up, she had thought that was just a suggestion or strongly encouraged.

As Aubrey read 2 Corinthians 6:14, tears started to fall down her face. "Don't team up with those who are unbelievers. How can righteousness be a partner with wickedness? How can light live with darkness?"

The verse in her Bible was slightly different from the one in the book, but she couldn't avoid what God was telling her. If she wanted to do this whole thing with God, if she wanted to obey what he actually wanted her to do, she would never end up with Jake. God was speaking to her. This verse was jumping off the page. She couldn't pretend like she didn't understand what this verse meant.

Even if Jake wanted to date and be in a relationship with her, they wouldn't be able to end up together unless he also believed in God. If she ignored what God was telling her in this verse, she would not only be disobeying God, but she would essentially be choosing to date someone who lived in darkness. How would their kids end up if Jake thought following God wasn't important?

She felt something inside of her break. Hope that she had been holding on to for so long. Hope that Jake would call her up and confess how much he loved her. Hope that he would change his mind and they would end up together.

But now, that wasn't going to happen. She couldn't date Jake if she wanted to obey and respect God's design for dating. She had been holding on to the hope of them ending up together, but now it was shattered. She needed to move on. She needed to let Jake go if she wanted to trust God's plan for her.

Why, God? Why do I like him so much when we can't even be together? Why does it hurt so bad, God? Why is it so hard following your Word? Please take away my pain. Please help me move on, Lord.

Aubrey prayed and cried silently as she fell asleep in the king-size bed.

Chapter 25

⚓

"Cheers to Morgan and her promotion! May there be many more trips back to San Diego in your future!" Morgan's coworker Claire exclaimed as they all clinked glasses.

Morgan was in town visiting for work. She had just been promoted to director and wanted to celebrate downtown at her favorite bar in Gaslamp. So far, she was doing a good job celebrating by buying everyone rounds of shots.

"No, thanks. I can't do shots tonight." Aubrey shook her head as Morgan placed a shot in front of her.

"Ah, come on, girl. One shot isn't going to kill ya. Do it with us!" Morgan squealed. Yup, she was definitely already drunk.

Aubrey shook her head even harder. "No way, girl—just looking at them makes me nauseous. I can't do them anymore like I used to. It's all yours, but you should drink this water after—you've had a lot already."

She did feel nauseous just looking at them. God was definitely starting to change her desires not to take shots anymore or to go out to bars like this. Aubrey tried not to go out in Gaslamp as much anymore since it was full of rowdy people who wanted to get drunk, but she made an exception for Morgan. While this wasn't the type of bar she wanted to be in, Aubrey was actually relieved to be out again and have plans on the weekends. It was nice to get all dressed up and go out—especially after the long week she had had in Chicago.

Aubrey checked her phone to see if Jake had texted her back. She had finally heard from him earlier that afternoon, asking what she was up to for the weekend. He was going out with his buddies that night, but they didn't know where yet. She mentioned she was going to some country bar in Gaslamp, and he said they would try to meet up by the end of the night.

She didn't want to get her hopes up. She hadn't seen Jake since she had slept over after tacos and margaritas, and she kept reminding herself they were just friends. He was just a friend, and she needed to keep making an effort to meet more new friends.

Aubrey gazed around the bar. It was full of people having a good time; a handful of people were even starting to dance on the dance floor. Shots were being thrown back at the bar. Guys were posted up along the wall, checking out the girls who were dancing.

Were there any people in this bar she could be friends with? People who wanted to have fun but also do productive things on the weekends? People who even went to church?

Out of the corner of her eye, Aubrey spotted a familiar head of brown hair and an arm tattoo standing behind the bar. Was that Jake?

When he turned around, they instantly made eye contact. It was him. Her stomach started doing back flips. Jake cracked a huge smile and made his way over to her table.

"Well, look who it is—the best thing I've seen all night," he said as he wrapped her in a big hug with a kiss on the cheek. He smelled like a mix of his cologne and tequila.

"What are you up to?" she asked, trying to sound casual.

"Just here with a few of my buddies for my friend's birthday. I'm glad I could see you tonight because I've been thinking a lot about you. I miss you." He gazed into her eyes.

Crap. Why did he always have this effect on her? She was still mad at him for sleeping with someone else, and she was mad at herself for caving and sleeping with him again. But he genuinely seemed like he had missed her. He seemed like he did care about her when they hung out.

"I missed you too." She blushed as she took a sip of her vodka soda. It was true. She did miss him.

"Want to join us, ladies?" Jake asked her friends. "My buddies are single and looking to have a good time tonight. Shots on us!"

"Sounds good to us!" Morgan said as Jake walked her and her coworkers over to his table.

Aubrey exhaled a deep breath as Jake put his arm around her. Nothing was going to happen. They would just have fun tonight as friends, and she would take an Uber back to her place before it got too late.

A few hours later, they were all having a good time. Despite all the free shots being passed around, Aubrey successfully turned them all down and had already cut herself off for the night. She had given all the shots handed to her to Morgan's friends, and they had gladly accepted the free alcohol.

A few of Morgan's friends were getting pretty cozy with Jake's friends on the dance floor, and Aubrey was having fun with Jake. He wouldn't stop kissing her. She knew she should make him stop, but it felt so nice to be around him again. It felt nice to have someone to be affectionate with, almost as if they were a couple on a date.

When Jake got up to use the restroom, Aubrey smiled as she surveyed the bar. She was proud of herself for standing her ground and passing on all those shots. Looked like she still could have fun without getting drunk.

Suddenly, a loud crash sounded from the bar. All she could see were guys rushing in, with punches being thrown.

"Fight!" someone yelled.

The fight was getting closer to their table, so they grabbed their drinks and headed to the back of the bar. Jake still hadn't come back, and Aubrey couldn't find him anywhere in the sea of punches and ladies running for cover. She spotted one of Jake's friends in the middle of the fight, punching another guy. The bouncers finally broke it up, and once again, she recognized the arm tattoo—on the guy lying on the floor. He was lying on the floor right where the fight had started.

"Jake!" She ran over to him. He was mumbling and had his eyes closed.

"Jake! Look at me. It's Aubrey. It's going to be okay. You're going to be fine."

She held his head in her lap as she stroked his forehead. He had some blood coming from his lip, and it looked like his eye was swelling up.

He finally came to and looked at her.

"What happened?" he asked.

His friend came up and helped stand Jake on his feet.

"Yo, Jake, we got to get out of here before the cops come." His friend supported Jake as he hobbled toward the exit. "This guy started going after you when we were at the bar trying to get a drink."

Aubrey looked around. She couldn't find Morgan or her co-workers anywhere. Jake was now managing to walk on his own, but he was in rough shape. Morgan's friend, Claire, came up to them.

"Oh my gosh, is he okay?"

"Yeah, yeah, he will be fine," Jake's friend said. "I've seen him get knocked out before in wrestling back in the day. Once a fighter, always a fighter." His friend shook his head.

Aubrey could tell Claire was hoping to go home with Jake's friend from the way she had her arm on him. They had been flirting and dancing together all night.

"I can take him home," Aubrey said. "We live right by each other. I'll make sure he's okay."

They managed to get an Uber among the crowd of everyone exiting the bar. Thankfully, the Uber driver didn't kick them out because of the way Jake looked. But Aubrey could say goodbye to her five-star rating; she definitely wasn't going to be rated as an exceptional passenger after this ride.

By the time they made it back to his place, Jake was starting to sound like himself, but he still seemed like he was in a lot of pain.

"Drink some water and take these. You'll be glad you did," Aubrey said, placing a glass of water and some pain relievers in his hand.

Jake lay on the couch as she cleaned him up with a washcloth. He started to smile.

"You're the best nurse I've ever had. And the most beautiful." He cupped her face as he leaned up to kiss her.

"Easy there, tiger; you need to take it easy. You just got knocked out."

"I'm fine. Thank you for taking care of me. It means a lot. I don't know what I would do without you. I'm so glad we ran into each other tonight." He had the look in his eyes, the same look he always got before things went too far.

"I missed you so much," Jake continued. "I know you just want to be friends, which is why I have been giving you space, but it's hard. I miss having you around. We have so much fun together, and I still care about you."

Aubrey sighed. It was always the same conversation. They still liked each other and enjoyed each other's company, but she knew they couldn't be together. He still didn't want to date her, and she couldn't date him because he didn't believe in God.

"I've missed you too, but I wish it wasn't so complicated." She gazed back into his eyes as he stroked her hair.

Before she could stop him, they were kissing. Her body wanted it too much, and she didn't know how to stop him. She felt like she was floating; it felt so good to be kissing him again.

Stop.

She drew back from him. Something inside of her had told her to stop. Was this a conviction? She had been so caught up in the moment, yet it felt like something inside of her had gotten her attention.

What were they doing? She had to leave before things went any further.

"We can't do this," Aubrey said. "We can't hook up anymore. I don't want to keep doing this, and it's too painful." She stood up from the couch.

"You're right," Jake said. "I know we both want to, but I'm proud of you for being honest and sticking up for what you want or don't want to do. That's very tough to do."

Why did he always have to be so sweet about everything? She liked him and hated him at the same time for how he made her feel.

"Don't go yet," he said. "Please. Let's just watch a movie and cuddle." He looked so vulnerable. She knew she should leave, but she felt bad leaving him after he had been knocked out. She could tell he didn't want to be alone tonight.

"Fine, but I get to pick the movie." She smiled as she made herself comfortable under the blanket.

Aubrey felt numb. Hopeless. Guilty. She had been making so much progress, but it was like it didn't matter anymore.

It was the following afternoon, and she was sitting in her favorite place outside her apartment on the cliff overlooking the ocean. Watching the surfers by the pier. Watching all the dogs walking down below. Watching the kids jumping in the waves.

She had thought she could try to obey God's will for sex, but she couldn't. Last night, she had slept at Jake's, and she had woken up instantly regretting what they had done. How many more times was she going to hook up with him after she had told herself she was going to stop? She felt so empty inside, and she didn't know what to do. She knew Jake still didn't want to date her and that they couldn't end up together.

Why was this so hard? Why hadn't she listened to God when he had tried to get her to stop before it was too late? It was the craziest feeling last night, feeling that voice from within that told her to stop. She knew God was speaking to her, convicting her to stop kissing Jake.

Aubrey thought back to several of her other drunken mistakes. She had heard that voice before. Time had a way of standing still for a moment, and she remembered something inside of her always telling her she had a decision to make. That she could either call it a night, stop drinking, and go home, or she could see where the night would take her after one more drink with a guy.

Why did she never listen to that voice inside her? Why did she always think she could stop things before the night got out of hand?

Aubrey shook her head. She was being too hard on herself. She wasn't a terrible person just because she had hooked up with Jake again. At least she hadn't gotten drunk like she always had in the past. The old her would have downed all those free shots and wouldn't have thought twice about hooking up with Jake. One night wasn't going to ruin all the progress she had made. She was still making positive steps in the right direction. Just because she had hooked up with Jake didn't mean she couldn't follow God and the life he had for her.

Did she really have to obey all of God's commands to follow him? Was it really possible to stop having sex in order to obey God's will for her life? How did people just stop having sex?

Maybe she didn't have to stop since it was so hard. God obviously saw how hard it was to stop. She had tried, but she couldn't do it. At least God saw that she had tried. Maybe it would be okay if she still had sex once in a while as long as she gave up everything else for him.

She was already changing her drinking habits and spending time with God every morning. Maybe that was good enough for now.

Everything would be okay. She was just being too hard on herself for hooking up with Jake again. She would go to church tomorrow morning and everything would be fine. Tomorrow would be a new day to see what God had in store for her.

Chapter 26

⚓

Pastor Davis talked about the Holy Spirit and how they needed to be listening to him in every area of their lives for guidance and convictions. He seemed to be talking about the exact same things Aubrey was learning in the Bible study. This Holy Spirit sure seemed like a big deal.

"Now a lot of you want this beautiful, abundant life that God promises," Pastor Davis said. "You desire a close, intimate relationship with God, and you desire to hear his voice more in your life. A lot of you come to church, say you love God, give your tithe each week, worship your heart out, and think you're ready to receive God's blessings in your life. But it's not that easy. It's not as simple as doing all those things.

"The key to receiving that intimate relationship with God that you want and his blessings on your life is surrendering all areas of your life to him. Not just parts of your life, but *all*. Not just the parts that are convenient or easy for you to give up, but every single area of your life."

A few people started clapping.

"Amen!"

"Yes, go there!"

"Preach, pastor!"

Pastor Davis continued. "Now, I know this may be cutting a little deep for some of you, so I'm going to give you an easy example to digest."

Heads nodded in agreement around the auditorium.

"A lot of you already know my testimony and my past. I was a big sinner, a hot mess before I came to know God. Before I became a pastor, I was caught up in the party scene, drinking, doing cocaine on the regular, and sleeping with women on the weekends. I thought I was king of the world, having fun with my buddies, making lots of money. Until God woke me up one day after a party to find my best friend dead on the couch from an overdose."

A few gasps went around the room.

"That was the beginning of my journey seeking God, and as you can see, he's radically changed my life. I never would have imagined I'd become a pastor one day. But that's just how God works. God started to transform me through the power of the Holy Spirit. As my relationship with God grew stronger, I started to pray and ask God to convict me of areas of my life that were not pleasing to him or not in line with his Word. And it didn't take long for God to talk back to me. Be careful when you pray that prayer. Make sure you are ready to hear what God has to say because sometimes you are not going to like it. God revealed to me that he really didn't like how much I was swearing."

A few people started to laugh.

"I thought it was funny, too! Like God, really? You care about swearing? But God showed me that he wants to transform and change every sin and area in our lives, no matter how small it seems to us. Sin is sin to God, and he wants us to repent and surrender it to him. Now, at this point, I had already given up my partying days for God, so when God told me to stop swearing, I said, 'Fine, God. You've started changing everything in my life already; you can have swearing too.' So, I prayed and asked the Holy Spirit to convict me and to help stop me from swearing."

More laughs around the room. Aubrey smiled. She loved how relatable he was. And how honest he was in talking about his past.

"And then the craziest thing happened. Any time I felt like I was about to swear, in conversation or even when I was by myself, it was like I couldn't speak. It was like the Holy Spirit was shutting my mouth so I wouldn't swear. And, eventually, the urge to swear was gone, and it was like I had eliminated all those swear words from my vocabulary."

People clapped around the auditorium.

"Now, it doesn't matter what you are struggling with today," Pastor Davis continued. "It doesn't matter if it's something that feels as small as swearing or something bigger, because God promises to help us overcome our sin through the power of the Holy Spirit inside of us. When we surrender it over to him and ask for his help, God gives us the strength through our Holy Spirit to resist temptation. The Holy Spirit is the one who transforms our desires from the inside. The Holy Spirit gives us the strength to stop whatever sin we are struggling with.

"But we can't overcome the sin if we don't surrender it to God. We won't overcome it if we don't pray and ask for God's help. The first step is surrendering the sin to God. Now, some of you are sitting here, and you know you are holding on to certain things— people or activities that you know are not in line with God's Word and will for your life. You're holding on to them because they are comfortable and convenient. You may know something is not what you are supposed to be doing, but it feels too hard to stop or the cost of surrendering this to God seems too great. In case you forgot, Jesus already gave up his life for you. His blood and body were given up for your life. Do you think whatever you're afraid to give up is greater than the blood of Jesus? Do you think whatever you're holding on to is greater than the blessings God has for you?"

"Heck, no!"

"Preach, pastor! Preach!"

"Praise Jesus!"

"The Bible is clear," Pastor Davis continued. "Jesus calls us to lay down our cross, our life, to follow him, and that means all areas of your life. Not just the bits and pieces that are convenient. If you still aren't convinced that God wants every part of your life and not just some, let me put it another way. With every part or area of your life that you refuse to surrender to God, you essentially have an agreement or contract with the Devil for that area of your life."

More gasps around the auditorium.

"When we allow the Devil to control a part of our life, it prevents us from fully knowing and experiencing the life God has for us. Surrendering almost our entire life is not good enough for God. He wants our entire life, and as long as we still have those agreements or contracts in place with the Devil, we will not be able to experience the fullness of God or the plans he has for us. When we allow the Devil to control those certain areas of our life, he will eventually influence and cause havoc on other parts of our lives because his intent is to steal, kill, and destroy our lives. Are you going to let the Devil steal, kill, and destroy your life?"

"Heck, no!"

"Not today, Satan. Not today!"

Several people were standing up now, all fired up and shouting and clapping.

"Come on, Church!" Pastor Davis exclaimed. "It's time to rip up those contracts you've had with the Devil. It's time to surrender all areas of your life to God!"

Pastor Davis then asked people to write down those areas of their lives they needed to surrender to God. He asked people to come up to the altar for prayer and to rip up those contracts they had with the Devil.

Aubrey sat there in shock. She hadn't realized she had had all these contracts with the Devil for so long. She always knew the Devil was real, but she had no idea the Devil could control her life like that. Why hadn't anyone told her? Why hadn't anyone warned her?

Her mom had always told her not to do certain things, but she had never understood why. She didn't want to have any type of agreement or contract with the Devil. She didn't want him to control any part of her life.

"Are you okay?" The guy sitting a few seats down from Aubrey got her attention.

Tears had started to fall down her face.

"Um, yes, of course. I'm fine, thanks." She wiped the tears from her face as she tried to smile. She couldn't be crying in the middle of church in front of a bunch of strangers. She needed to pull herself together, but this was all too much.

"Do you want to go down to the altar for prayer?" The guy nodded to the front of the auditorium.

Hundreds of people were making their way down to the altar, lining up for prayer. Some at the front were ripping up pieces of paper—the contracts they had made with the Devil. A few people were crying, raising their arms in the air, as people prayed for them.

Aubrey felt like she couldn't move. She felt like for the first time she was awakened to the truth all around her. To this whole world with God, a world of good and evil that she didn't know existed. She thought she was doing a good job, learning about God and reading her Bible, but there was so much she didn't know. No matter how much good she did, it wasn't going to cut it if she didn't fully surrender everything to God. If she didn't rip up those contracts with the Devil. She had already surrendered drinking to God, but it was clear she had to surrender everything to God. She had to surrender sex to God.

But there was no way she was going up to the altar in front of everyone. She needed to get out of there. She needed to process this alone.

"No, I'm fine, thank you. Have a great day." She grabbed her purse and quickly moved past the guy before he could say anything else.

The tears kept falling as she made her way to her car. She didn't know how to process this. She didn't know how to surrender everything to God, including sex. It was clear God had spoken to her today. She couldn't pretend sex wasn't a big deal to God. She couldn't ignore what she had just heard—that she had been letting the Devil control her life for so long and she hadn't even known.

She had already tried to stop sleeping with Jake, but it hadn't worked. How was she supposed to stop? She closed her eyes and prayed silently as she made it to her car.

How am I supposed to stop, God? How do I just give up sex? How do I stop the Devil from controlling this area of my life?

Chapter 27

⚓

Aubrey lay on her beach blanket, listening to worship music to drown out the noise of the beach-goers around her. She was exhausted. She felt numb from all the emotions and thoughts that had been whirling around in her head since church that morning. She wanted to keep reading her new purity book, *Love Defined*, but her head was still trying to process what she had heard that morning.

Aubrey had so many questions, but she felt like nobody around her would understand. How had Tina given up everything for God? She would know what to do. Aubrey texted Tina.

Are you free to talk? I have some questions about God.

Her phone buzzed a few minutes later.

"Hey, girl, how are you? What's on your mind, my friend?" Tina was so upbeat, but it only caused Aubrey's tears to fall again. Aubrey couldn't control her crying, but she didn't care anymore. She needed to figure out how to get through this.

"Tina, how come nobody told me? How come nobody told me I had been letting the Devil control my life?" Aubrey sobbed into the phone.

"Woah, there. Slow down. It's going to be okay. Let's talk about it. What happened?"

"I just realized I can't keep pretending that sex isn't a big deal. I know I need to surrender it to God and also surrender my whole life, but I just don't know how. I don't want the Devil in my life anymore. And I'm scared. I don't know how to change my life. I don't know how to have a relationship without sex. How do I just give it all to God like everyone keeps talking about?"

The girls next to her on the beach were staring at her, but she didn't care. They wouldn't understand how she felt. They were taking photos of each other in their thong bikinis; they clearly weren't too concerned about giving up sex for God.

"Wow, Aubrey," Tina said. "Thank you for calling. I'm so glad you have been really thinking about this whole God thing and what it's like to follow him. I had so many questions when I was learning about God, and we need to support each other."

"Thank you. I don't know how I could do this without you. I still don't have any friends here, and none of our other friends understand."

"Yes, that's what I'm here for, girl," Tina replied. "Okay, start from the beginning. What has God been speaking to you, and how is the Devil in your life?"

Aubrey told Tina everything. How she had tried to stop having sex, but then had sex with Jake again. How she felt hopeless because she almost didn't think it was possible to stop. And she shared the message from Pastor Davis and how it had spoken right to her.

"I know I have a choice to make," Aubrey said. "I want to go all in for God, but I just don't know how. I don't know how to surrender my entire life to him, including sex. And even if I did, I don't know how I can stop having sex." She was still crying, but she felt better getting everything off her chest to Tina.

Tina clapped her hands. "Aubrey, this is huge! I've been waiting for this moment. I'm so proud of you. Ah, praise God! You don't need to worry about anything; God will show you how to give up sex. You've already made the decision to go all in for him, so you just have to tell him how you feel. Aubrey, have you accepted Jesus into your life?"

Aubrey smiled. Tina's words and encouragement were giving her the hope she needed.

"I've been praying to God, but I don't know what that means." She remembered Pastor Davis always talking about giving your life to Jesus and accepting him as your savior, but she had never understood it.

"Aubrey, you are ready. I've been praying and waiting for this moment. It's time to give your life to Christ. You've already made a decision to follow him; you've made a decision to surrender all areas of your life to him and to obey God's will for your life. Now, you just have to pray and give it to God. Surrender your life and ask for forgiveness for all your sins. And accept Jesus as your savior, the one who died on the cross for you. When you surrender your sins to God, he takes over from there. He promises to fill us with the Holy Spirit and to give us the strength we need to overcome our past sin. You can stop having sex when you let God into your life. He will make it possible, Aubrey, so you don't have to worry."

More tears fell down Aubrey's face. Except these were happy tears. Something inside Aubrey had shifted. She finally understood what everyone was talking about. What it was like to go all in for

God. And now she just had to pray and tell God she had made the decision to go all in.

Aubrey laughed. "Oh my gosh, Tina, I get it now. I finally get it! I'm ready to give my life to God!"

Tina cheered and clapped over the phone. "Yes, you are ready! Praise God! I am so happy for you. This is the best decision you will ever make in your life."

Aubrey nodded. "Yes, it's time. I'm going to do it. I'm going to rip up my contracts with the Devil and give my entire life to God."

"Get it, girl!" More laughing. "Do you want me to walk you through the prayer?"

"No, I need to do this alone," Aubrey said. "I know what I need to do. Thank you so much, Tina. Thank you for always believing in me all those years in Chicago and always inviting me to church. And now this, I don't know how I could have done this without you. I love you so much."

Now Tina was crying. "I love you too. Ah, I'm just so proud of you and I can't believe this is finally happening. Aubrey, do you remember the prayer walls at our old church in Chicago? The walls where we would write prayer requests?"

Aubrey vaguely remembered seeing people writing on a wall after church, but she had never understood what it was for. "Yes, I remember, but I had no idea they were prayer walls."

"Girl, I wrote your name on the prayer wall at Soul City almost three years ago. I've been praying and believing for this moment when you would surrender your life to Jesus."

They couldn't stop crying and laughing with joy. Aubrey felt like her whole body was buzzing with electricity. Aubrey had had no idea Tina had been praying for her this whole time. And now she finally understood why it was such a big deal. She was about to give her life to Jesus, not just parts of it, but all of it. She was going to follow God and do things his way from now on.

Back in her apartment, Aubrey put on worship music and lit some candles. She rolled out her workout mat and sat on the floor. She grabbed the paper from church and wrote "SEX" in big letters. It was time.

She reflected back on her life in Chicago and the past few months. All the mistakes she had made. All the nights she had drank too much alcohol and all the men she had slept with. She didn't have to live that life anymore. Jesus would forgive her when she surrendered her life to him. She didn't have to carry the shame and guilt she had been carrying for so long. She didn't have to worry about her past holding her back anymore. God was going to change all of that. She could finally be free from that life, the life of partying, hoping to fit in and meet people. Hoping to meet true friends and her future husband. She no longer had to give up her body in hopes of having a boyfriend. She didn't care if she was all alone; she would rather be alone with God than spend time in a bar just to meet people who were bad influences. Yes, she was done with that life. It was time.

Her chest was pounding. It was like a fire was burning inside of her, waiting to get out. The tears started streaming down her face again as she clasped her hands and bowed her head. And instead of praying silently in her head, she cried out loud to God.

God, I can't do this anymore. I don't want to live a life like this anymore. I'm sorry for all the mistakes I made. I'm sorry for ignoring you for so long. God, you've made it clear I can't keep living like that. I want to live the life you have for me.

God, I surrender my life to you. I surrender sex to you. I'm all in for you, God. I rip up any contracts with the Devil. I give you control over 100 percent of my life.

Please forgive me, Lord. Thank you, Jesus, for dying on the cross for my sins. I am forgiven and can be wiped clean because of you. It doesn't matter that I've had sex before. With you, Jesus, I am forgiven and can start again.

God, please give me the strength to stop having sex. I need you, Lord. I want the plans you have for me, plans for hope and a future. Please, God, change my life.

Aubrey ripped up the piece of paper from church. Her contract with the Devil. She thought about burning it in the candle, but she didn't want to start any fires.

She couldn't stop crying, yet she felt a wave of peace wash over her. The anxiety and shame she had felt that morning at church was gone. She felt like she had just jumped off the edge of a boat into the ocean. She had been sitting on the edge, learning about God for so long, and she had finally jumped in. She was swimming in the deep ocean, but she wasn't afraid. She was excited for the life God had for her.

She was all in for God, and there was no looking back. She was about to live the crazy, Christian lifestyle that everyone was talking about. Yes, she was a Jesus freak now, living all out for God.

She texted Tina.

I did it. I surrendered my whole life to God!

Aubrey felt like celebrating, but there was nobody to celebrate with. So she did what she always did when she didn't want to be alone. She walked the beach as she prayed silently to God, daydreaming about the future he had for her.

God, thank you for friends like Tina. Please allow me to meet new people who will be good friends. Please bring me new friends who are Christians. I need good influences in my life. Show me the friends you have for me, Lord.

Chapter 28

⚓

As Aubrey ran on the beach, she felt so much lighter from her decision to follow Jesus and from her time off from work. She had already been off the entire week and was glad she still had an additional two weeks of vacation. She hadn't felt this relaxed and at peace in months. Her job, all the traveling, the drunken happy hour at work training, worrying about Jake—she finally felt like it was all behind her.

Instead of waking up to check her emails every morning, she woke up and read the Bible. She was in a new routine of waking up and spending time with God every day on her couch, reading and praying. Some mornings, Aubrey spent hours reading the Bible and in her Bible study. She was learning so much. The more she learned about God, the more she was learning about herself—who she was as a child of God as a born-again Christian.

And she loved that she could run on the beach in the middle of the day. As she passed a boy running around with a "Happy Birthday" balloon, she started thinking of her birthday the following week. She didn't mind not having anyone to spend it with. She had God this year. She had spent almost twenty-nine years without him, and now, she was about to live the rest of her life with God, pursuing the life he had intended for her.

As she listened to the latest worship album by Hillsong, a guy started waving and walking toward her.

"Hi! Excuse me; sorry to interrupt your run. I'm in town visiting and noticed you were really cute. Would you like to hang out tonight?"

Had he just asked her out? She didn't even know him.

"Um, no, no thank you." She didn't know what else to say, so she kept running.

Gross. Who does that? You can't just go up to people running on the beach and ask them out. He wasn't even cute.

How was she supposed to meet other Christian guys? Where were they? What did they do for fun? While she wanted to stay positive about meeting people at church, she still wasn't meeting anyone at Freedom Church. She loved the messages, but was she at the right church?

Aubrey thought of the dating apps still on her phone. Were Christian men on these apps? What was the name of the dating app for Christians that she had seen on TV?

Aubrey shook her head. She was not ready to be on a Christian dating site yet. She barely knew what this life with God was about, and she had just committed to purity. Would other guys judge her for her sexual past? Would they judge her for all those nights she spent drunk at the bar?

Her Fitbit buzzed, informing her she had received a text. Her heart skipped a beat. A text from Jake.

She hadn't heard from him in a few weeks. Based on his Instagram, he had some friends in town visiting, so she hadn't reached out to him either. She felt a mix of emotions. She was trying to move on, but she missed him so much. She stopped running to open his text.

Someone has a birthday coming up. What are you doing to celebrate? PS – I miss your gorgeous face.

Why did he always have to be so sweet? They had briefly talked about their birthdays when they first met, but Aubrey hadn't expected him to remember all these months later. Her birthday was a few days after Easter this year, and she had already decided she wasn't going to spend her birthday with Jake. She didn't want to start a new birthday year with someone she was trying to move on from.

What was she supposed to say back? Aubrey kept running as she thought of the appropriate response. Should she admit that she didn't have any plans? Should she lie and make something up? What if he wanted to join her in whatever her made-up plans were?

Aubrey wanted to tell him of her decision to go all in for God, but she wasn't sure how he would react. He wouldn't understand. Should she tell him they couldn't hang out because she was a Christian now?

She stopped running. She knew the solution that would fix everything between them.

It was clear God wanted her to date only other believers in Christ, other Christians. And God knew she still had feelings for Jake. And she knew God wanted Jake to pursue a relationship with him as well since God wanted everyone to have a relationship with him. So if both she and God wanted Jake to change his mind, why couldn't she be in Jake's life and help show him what life with God was all about? And then after Jake saw what God was all about, he would change his mind about God and they could end up together.

Aubrey felt a surge of hope. Why hadn't she thought of this before?

God, I want to respect your ways to only date other believers. You know my heart, God. Soften Jake's heart to know you, God. Heal him from anything in his past that is holding him back from seeking you. Show him who you really are, Lord.

Aubrey finished her run by skipping before she responded to Jake.

> Hey! Great to hear from you. For my birthday, I'm going to treat myself to a spa day and enjoy this beautiful weather we've been having at the beach.

Jake texted back within a minute.

> Look at you! You deserve it. That sounds awesome. Wish I could give you a massage as well. I would love to take you out to dinner and celebrate with you if you don't already have plans.

Aubrey wasn't about to give in too soon. She didn't want to seem desperate. And, of course, he would make her spa reference dirty. Typical. She wasn't going to acknowledge the massage comment. She didn't want to encourage those kinds of remarks anymore.

> Yes it's going to be so relaxing! And that's okay, I'm just going to lay low.

He texted back almost immediately.

> Let me take you out to dinner. I want to. You deserve to be celebrated, your first birthday in San Diego, and I want to be there as your best friend that you met on the beach while watching dolphins. Besides, I miss hanging out with you.

Why did he have to mention the dolphins and remind her of their own Nicholas Sparks movie? She couldn't help how she felt, but she wanted to stand firm. She wanted to show Jake what God was all about, but she couldn't give in to her feelings.

They were just friends. She would make it clear they really couldn't have sex again, and she would keep praying, trusting God to change Jake's mind in the meantime. And it would be nice to have dinner with someone instead of eating takeout alone on her birthday. She texted him back.

> I would love that. We can celebrate with the dolphins, it will be special.

Aubrey felt excited to have birthday plans, but she didn't want to get her hopes up. They would have dinner as friends, nothing more, unless Jake also decided to follow Jesus. And she was determined not to sleep with him, even if he did end up going to church with her.

Chapter 29

⚓

Aubrey felt different going to church this Sunday. Not only because it was Easter Sunday and the Sunday before her birthday, but it was her first Sunday at church after she had surrendered her entire life to God.

She felt like she was on a mission, a new mission as a Christian, figuring out what she was supposed to do in this world. She had been on the wrong path for far too long, a path pursuing partying and the wrong kind of men. But none of that mattered now. She was finally on the right path, seeking God and the plans he had for her.

And she finally understood why Easter was so important. She wasn't going to church because it was a big holiday and because her whole family went to church on Easter. She was going because Jesus had personally died on the cross for her. Not only so she could go to heaven, but so her sins could be forgiven and so she could become a new creation.

Aubrey smiled as she parked and got out of her car. She no longer had to worry about how to leave the old life behind. Jesus was already helping her and showing her the way. As she got closer to the church, she took in the swarms of people all making their way to the church. The service started in ten minutes, and she'd had a feeling it would be busy on Easter Sunday, but she'd had no idea it would be this crazy.

The pastor had encouraged everyone to invite new people to church for Easter because people are more likely to attend church on Easter and Christmas than any other time of the year. She hadn't invited anyone—she knew Jake would turn her down again, and she felt awkward inviting strangers to church. But she had never seen a line like this before. She had never seen a line to get into a church before, period. This was insane, yet so beautiful. All these people in line to celebrate Jesus.

Aubrey suddenly felt very alone as she surveyed all the families and couples around her. Should she wait in line? Should she just go home and watch the service online later?

She shook her head as she stood in the back of the line. She couldn't leave. She had just surrendered her whole life to God—it didn't matter that she was at church all alone. God was with her. And she needed to be around other Christians to continue learning more about how to be a Christian.

Was her future husband in this line? Where were all the young, single people? Meeting an attractive, loving, funny guy on Easter would be a great way to meet. They could hang out in the church bookstore afterward, sipping coffee and getting to know each other as they shared their favorite books. Then they could walk along Sunset Cliffs, talking about their dreams and their favorite things to do in San Diego.

Aubrey shook her head. She couldn't get ahead of herself. Besides, she wasn't here to meet someone. She was here for Jesus and to celebrate his resurrection from the cross.

Aubrey finally made it through the church doors only to be led through the lobby, outside to a large tent behind the church. How was the main church auditorium full? This was absurd. There must have been thousands of people at church. She did not want to sit outside in a tent for Easter—she had never watched church in a tent before. Pastor Davis was broadcast on a projector screen in the front of the tent. She wanted to leave, but she decided to forget about her frustrations and focus on the worship and Pastor Davis' message.

He preached the gospel of Jesus and his resurrection on Easter, similar to the messages Aubrey had always heard growing up. Except this year, she finally understood. It felt more real. She understood the sacrifice Jesus had made on the cross, and she felt the love God had for her, despite all of her sins and past mistakes.

"As we celebrate Jesus and all that he's done for us today," Pastor Davis said, "it's time to bow our heads in prayer. Jesus died on the cross for each one of you, and you all have a decision to make. Are you going to continue trying to carry your own cross, or are you going to lay down your cross and follow Jesus?

"One day, Jesus went away to pray, and his disciples headed out in a boat to go to the next town. The water started to get a bit rocky when Jesus headed out to meet his disciples. Jesus didn't need to borrow another boat or swim over—he decided to walk on water over to them. But when the disciples saw him, they thought he was a ghost. Being brave, Peter asked Jesus to confirm it was really him, so Jesus commanded Peter to walk out of the boat on the water toward him.

"Life with Jesus is like that," Pastor Davis continued. "Jesus is waiting for each one of us on the water; he is calling each one of us to step out of the boat and walk to him—to trust him that we won't sink. Jesus is waiting for you to get out of the boat. He is waiting for you to choose him and to go all in for him, to surrender your life to him. Some of you have been stuck in that boat for far too long, afraid or making excuses. But it's time to get out of the boat. The question is: Are you ready? Are you ready to get out of the boat, walk on water, and trust the plans Jesus has for you? Do you want to live a life stuck in the boat, or do you want to live a life of faith with Jesus? If you're ready to get out of the boat today, if you're ready to walk with Jesus, raise your hand."

Aubrey raised her hand, her eyes still closed and head bowed.

Yes, it was time for her to get out of the boat. She had been stuck in the boat for far too long, and she was finally brave enough to give everything to God. She was ready to jump out of the boat into the life and plans God had for her.

Pastor Davis continued speaking. "Lord, I thank you for all these people with their hands raised, and I thank you for their salvation today, in Jesus' name. Amen."

People started to clap. As Aubrey opened her eyes, she quickly realized nobody else around her had raised their hands.

Wait, what? Why didn't they want to walk on water with Jesus? Who wouldn't want to get out of the boat? What's wrong with these people? Why did they want to stay in the boat?

"Praise God," Pastor Davis continued, "for everyone who has decided to surrender their life to Jesus today. If you would be so brave, come up to the front of the altar so we can pray over you."

Oh, my gosh. Oh, my gosh. Crap. Everyone around her was staring and smiling at her. Some people started to clap. At the back of the tent, a few church volunteers were gesturing to her to leave the tent to head to the main auditorium where Pastor Davis was.

Shoot! She had been so into the message and so excited to get out of the boat that she hadn't realized this was the awkward part of the service where they ask people to come up to the front to pray in front of everyone.

Aubrey didn't want to go. She didn't want to walk through thousands of people to the altar. She felt so awkward, but she couldn't ignore the commitment she had just made. She had decided to get out of the boat, and she had already decided last week to go all in for God.

Oh, what the heck? Why not go to the front? She was all in for God; people would find out eventually. This was church; people wouldn't judge her for being all in with God. They were already celebrating her. At least she didn't know anybody here.

Aubrey smiled shyly as she made her way out of the tent and into the main auditorium, along with the few other brave souls who had also raised their hands. The applause got louder as thousands of people cheered them on in the auditorium. She had never seen so many people at church in her life. Thank God she had decided to get more dressed up today, wearing one of her work dresses instead of her usual jeans that she wore on Sundays.

She laughed to herself, finally standing at the front of the altar. She couldn't believe she had just gotten tricked into this altar call thing! And on Easter of all Sundays. *Only for you, Jesus; only for you.*

She stood there awkwardly along with thirty other people as the pastor led them in prayer.

"Heavenly Father, thank you for sending your only son to die for my life and for my sins. Today, I accept Jesus into my life. Thank you, Jesus, for dying on the cross for me. Thank you for forgiving my sins.

Today, I declare I have been set free and I am a child of God. In Jesus' Name, Amen."

Finally, it was over and Aubrey could leave. The people seemed to be clapping and cheering even louder as she made her way out. She was walking on water with Jesus, but she couldn't wait to walk out of this embarrassment and the church.

Aubrey was headed toward the side door exit when an older gentleman stopped her in her path.

"Hi, there. I'm Bruce. Congrats on your decision to follow Jesus today! What's your name, dear?"

"Aubrey. Nice to meet you." She shook his hand.

"Do you have a few minutes to stop by our prayer lounge? We would like to sit down with you and give you a few resources to help you follow Jesus."

Aubrey hesitated. She wanted to leave and get to the beach as fast as possible, but she was interested in any resources she could get to help her with her new life with God.

"Um, sure. I have a few minutes. Thanks." She smiled at Bruce.

It took a few minutes for them to make their way through the crowd, but Bruce finally led her to a seat in the prayer lounge, which was a room off the church lobby. The room was already packed with the other people who had decided to give their lives to Jesus, along with several volunteers who appeared to be praying with each new Christ follower individually.

"Congrats again on your decision to follow Jesus! The angels are celebrating up in heaven as we speak. How can I pray for you and your new walk with Jesus?"

This man wanted to pray with her? But she didn't even know him. How would he understand what she was going through?

"Well, this is all new to me," Aubrey said, "but I've been hoping to hear God's voice more in my life to understand what my purpose is."

Bruce threw up his hands in excitement. "That's wonderful, my dear! Yes, we can definitely pray for that. You are a child of God now. God will show you your purpose as his daughter as you learn to serve the Lord in all you do. Loving God and loving others— that's our purpose we all share as Christians."

Loving God and loving others? That sounded nice, but how was she supposed to do that as an accountant?

Bruce started praying. "Father God, we thank you for this beautiful Easter Sunday, and we thank you for the gift of salvation for your daughter Aubrey today. Thank you for filling Aubrey with the Holy Spirit and for making your home in her heart. God, we thank you that you have a plan and purpose for each one of our lives, and we thank you for revealing that plan to Aubrey. She is a new creation, and you know the plans you have for her, plans for hope and a future. I also thank you for bringing new friends into her life. I see Aubrey walking through a meadow, and at first there aren't many flowers, but then I see her coming to an opening, where lots of flowers are springing up, flowers that you planted just for Aubrey. Thank you for this harvest of new friends for Aubrey. In Jesus' name. Amen."

Aubrey hadn't realized she was crying. How could a prayer from an old man she had just met speak to her soul like that? How did he know she needed new friends? Where was this meadow that he talked about?

Bruce handed her a tissue. "There you go. Let it all out—happens to all of us when God comes into our life."

"Thanks so much. I really needed that prayer. Well, happy Easter." Aubrey stood up to leave. She had experienced enough uncomfortable situations for one day and would do anything to be sipping a latte while lying on the beach right now.

"Wait, these are for you." Bruce handed her a Bible and another book. "You get your very own Bible and a book that talks more about how to have a relationship with God. Congrats again. See you next Sunday!"

Aubrey laughed at herself as she walked back to her car. Surrendering her life to Jesus twice in one week? Not a bad way to start the week.

Chapter 30

⚓

Aubrey called her mom after she parked her car at Sunset Cliffs. She had already told her mom she was going to church regularly and she was learning a lot from doing a Bible study with Tina. But she hadn't told her yet that she had decided to go all in for God.

Aubrey didn't want to tell anyone about her decision until she was 100 percent sure about giving her life to God. And after today, she understood more of why it was a big deal. Walking with Jesus was something to be celebrated, not kept hidden. While it was a personal decision, it was something that should be shared with others.

"Happy Easter, Mom!" Aubrey said as her mom answered the phone.

"Happy Easter, Aubrey! Praise God, this is the day that the Lord has risen!"

Aubrey laughed. Her mom was always so full of joy and made her feel so special when she called. Even though they were thousands of miles away, she could always feel in her voice how much her mom loved her and how much she supported her in San Diego.

"Yes, indeed, praise God! How was church?" Aubrey asked.

"It went well! Your dad and Tyler were on their best behavior, and Kyle and Kate really enjoyed the Easter eggs and candy that everyone passed out. Kyle was even singing along with the worship team, it was so precious. Then we enjoyed Easter brunch together; they all loved my stuffed cinnamon French toast."

Aubrey smiled as she pictured her family together, Kyle singing along and Kate running up and down the church, getting all the candy she could get her hands on.

"That sounds awesome. I'm glad you could convince everyone to join you at church. I miss you guys so much." Aubrey wiped away a stray tear that appeared out of nowhere.

"We miss you too, sweetie. We can't wait for you to come back in a few months. So what are you up to today for Easter? Did you go to church?"

Aubrey started to giggle. "Yes, I went to church. And you'll never believe it, but I got tricked into going up for the altar call!"

Her mom gasped. "What! Oh, my goodness, how did you get tricked? What happened?"

"At the end of the message, the pastor was praying and he asked if anyone was ready to get out of the boat and walk with Jesus. I was really into it and I was thinking, 'Well, yeah, who wouldn't want to get out of the boat and walk with Jesus?' So I raised my hand, thinking everyone would raise their hand, but then I realized it was the part of the service where they ask people to come up to the front of the altar for prayer to give their life to Jesus!"

"Who wouldn't want to get out of the boat? They should have all had their hands raised!" Her mom laughed.

"I know, right? I figured I couldn't back down, and I felt like it was the right thing to do, so I went to the front and I prayed to surrender my life to Jesus."

"Wow, you actually prayed the salvation prayer? Aubrey, do you know what surrendering your life to Jesus means?"

Aubrey smiled as she nodded her head. "Yes, I finally do. I've been learning so much doing this Bible study and through church, and it's like God finally opened my eyes and showed me what a life with him is all about. He showed me that my life of drinking and doing things my way wasn't working and it was against his will for my life. I actually prayed and surrendered it all to God last week; I was finally ready, and today was just like making that commitment in front of everyone by accident."

Her mom was laughing and squealing sounds of joy through the phone.

"Ah, Aubrey! I'm so happy for you! Praise God, what a special Easter indeed! I've been praying for you to turn to God for so long, and I am so proud of you for all the effort you've been making with this Bible study and going to church. Back in Chicago, I could tell you were searching for something to fill the void in your life, but the void can only be filled by God. How do you feel?"

Aubrey gazed at the turquoise waves crashing below her along the cliffs. How did she feel? She felt a peace and confidence she hadn't felt before, and even though she still had no idea what she was supposed to do with her life, she felt like she was exactly where she was supposed to be.

"I'm excited and I'm ready to do things differently. God has been teaching me so much about what it means to be a Christian. I feel like I finally understand what it means to live for him and to represent him. I want to make an impact in this world and not just do the things I did before, like working and drinking with people who don't want to do anything else." Aubrey smiled proudly.

"Yes, you are a new creation, my daughter. I've already noticed the change in you with how you talk about life and God, and I'm so happy this is finally happening! This is the beginning of a beautiful journey with God in San Diego. I'm so proud of you, Aubrey." Aubrey could tell from her mom's voice that her mom was shedding more tears.

Aubrey started crying tears of joy too. She felt so grateful to have a mom who had been praying for her her whole life. Her mom never gave up. She kept praying, kept supporting her, and kept being there for Aubrey when she needed it most.

Her mom had always told her about God, but she had never listened. But now all her mom talked about before was starting to make sense. Aubrey understood why her mom didn't want her to drink so much. She understood why her mom told her not to have sex until marriage and to wear clothes that were less form-fitting. She understood why her mom would always tell her to read the Bible instead of the trash she had watched on TV at the time.

Now, it was like they were finally speaking the same language. And thanks to the new church her mom had gone to in the past few years, they both now understood that God wasn't about following a bunch of rules or a religion. It was about a relationship with him, their loving Father. Someone they could always turn to and someone who was always with them. Someone who wanted an intimate relationship with them. Who loved them no matter what they had done in the past and would continue to love them no matter what.

Aubrey got goosebumps and felt electricity again throughout her whole body just thinking about her new life with God.

She wiped the tears from her face. "Thank you, Mom. Thank you for always praying for me and for never giving up on me. I love you so much." They continued crying tears of joy over the phone as they broke out in laughter.

"I love you too, Aubrey. Now that you have surrendered your life to God, what are you planning to do for your birthday next week?"

Aubrey wasn't in the mood to talk about Jake. She didn't want to make a big deal out of them hanging out.

"I'm not sure yet. I may just go to the beach and treat myself to a spa day and relax. And spend time with God and read my Bible."

"That sounds lovely. I'll keep praying for God to bring friends into your life there. Are you still seeing Jake?" her mom asked.

Aubrey sighed. Her mom was only looking out for her. She knew her mom didn't want her to get hurt or to feel lonely on her birthday.

"No, not really. I'm trying to move on, but it's hard because he's still my only new friend in San Diego."

"I know it's hard. God will bring you new friends there that also love him, and I'm praying that he will also bring you someone who completely adores and cherishes you just like he does."

"Thanks, Mom." Aubrey smiled at her encouragement. "I love you. I'll talk to you later. Happy Easter. Give dad a kiss for me."

After Aubrey disconnected her call, she remained sitting on the edge of the cliff. The ocean always filled her with hope that she could pursue her dreams and find her purpose. And now that she had surrendered her life to God, she knew that hope was true because God had had a plan for her before she was even born.

Aubrey didn't know what that plan was yet, but she trusted that if she kept pursuing God, he would reveal himself to her and reveal those plans. Each day was another day to make positive steps in the right direction, one step closer to the plans God had for her.

Happy Easter, God, Aubrey prayed. *Thank you for an amazing day, an amazing week. I'm excited to live the rest of my life for you, God. Thank you for showing me the way. I trust you, Lord. I trust you. Thank you for this new life I get to live here in San Diego as a child of God. Thank you for making me a new creation with Jesus. I love you, God. Amen.*

Chapter 31

⚓

Aubrey was officially twenty-nine—her last year in her twenties. And she wasn't scared or worried that she should have more accomplished by now.

All of her other friends back in the Midwest were complaining about how old they were getting and that they were almost thirty. They complained that they hadn't accomplished nearly as much as they had wanted to by this age. Most of them had wanted to be married by now, maybe have their first baby, and have a successful career. Own a house. Have traveled through Europe and Asia by now. They complained that time was running out. What would happen if they weren't married by thirty? What would happen if they didn't have kids soon?

A few years ago, Aubrey had felt the same way. She wasn't where she had planned to be at twenty-nine, but God was revealing that she had been living out the wrong plan all along. Even if she had gotten all those things she had wanted while living in Chicago, what would it have mattered if they really weren't God's plan for her life? After learning about God and who she was as a daughter of God, she realized she would still feel unfulfilled with all those things if God wasn't a part of her life.

Aubrey was actually grateful she had never met someone serious in Chicago. She couldn't imagine what would have happened if she had settled down with someone, living the same life in the party scene she was used to living, thinking she was happy but realizing later on that something was still missing. Would she have ever moved to San Diego and pursued a relationship with God?

As Aubrey lay on the beach lounger at her favorite local resort, sipping an iced coffee with her journal in her lap, she felt peace and reassurance about entering her last year of her twenties. She had never imagined that living in San Diego was part of the plan, but this was part of God's plan. She was exactly where she needed to be, and she didn't need to worry about not having a husband, a baby, or a house by now.

She had God, she had the beach in front of her, and she had an open heart that was seeking a relationship with God and the plans he had for her. That was all she needed for her last year in her twenties.

Aubrey smiled as she soaked up the warmth of the sun on her skin. Yup, exactly where she needed to be.

After she dozed off in the sun, she turned on her phone to check her messages. She felt more relaxed and able to enjoy her spa day and the beach with her phone off, but she knew people would be wishing her a happy birthday.

She had a text from Tina.

Happy Birthday girl! Can't wait to see the plans God has in store for you this year! May you feel his joy and love all day today. You are going to be so blessed this year my friend. The angels are celebrating with you in heaven!

Amen! She was already feeling so much joy and love, and the day had just begun. She had just spent the morning at the resort's spa in a full spa ritual. A steam shower, body scrub, body soak, and a full body massage. Now on the beach, God's blessings were indeed all around her.

Next, she read a text from Morgan.

> Aubrey, happy birthday! Hope you are already celebrating and getting drunk somewhere. Take a shot for me.

Aubrey shook her head. Nope, no shots and no getting drunk today. No thank you.

Her mom had also texted her.

> Today is a day I'll treasure forever, the day God brought you into this world. I still remember the day you were born. Grandma looked down at you and just knew you would be smart. Love you so much my beautiful daughter.

People made birthdays all about the person being born, but they should also be celebrating the moms who had brought them into this world on this day! Her mom (and dad) were the ones who had given her life and brought her into this world, with God's hand all around her as she was born. Today was a celebration for all of them.

Earlier that morning, she had woken up to a text from Jake, wishing her a happy birthday. She had told him she would text him after the spa, but she already had another text from him.

> Hope you enjoyed pampering yourself today! Where would you like to go tonight? My treat :)

Aubrey was looking forward to celebrating with Jake, but she was trying to manage all the emotions she felt about him. She kept reminding herself they were just friends who enjoyed each other's company and that they would just have fun tonight. But she also didn't want to get her hopes up or end up disappointed, especially on her birthday.

They were just friends; she shouldn't expect Jake to treat her like his girlfriend or to make tonight extra special. It wasn't a date. It was just dinner between two friends. There would be no flowers, no making out, and no sleeping together.

Aubrey couldn't ignore the feelings she still had for Jake or the effect he always had on her when they hung out. It left her always wanting more from him. But tonight was going to be different. She had already made a commitment to God not to have sex anymore, and she was going to keep that promise. They would only have a few drinks together and then go their separate ways at the end of the night. She wasn't about to start her last year in her twenties feeling hungover or doing something she would regret the next day. She had a plan and she was going to stick with it. She texted him back.

> So relaxing! How about the Fish Shop around 7? I've driven by it. It looks super cute. It's BYOB.

Jake quickly responded.

> I love oysters! Let's go. I'll bring the rosé. I'll meet you at your place at 7, birthday girl.

Aubrey smiled as she gazed out over Mission Bay. It was sweet of Jake to remember that she loved rosé. It was going to be a great birthday. Spa, beach, and a casual dinner with Jake.

God, thank you for bringing me into this world. Thank you for letting me live on the beach in San Diego. Thank you for revealing the plans you have for me this year. Just like you say in Jeremiah 29:11, you already know the plans you have for me, plans for hope and a future.

God, show me what my future looks like here. Show me what I'm supposed to do in San Diego and if Jake is supposed to be a part of it. God, I ask that you soften Jake's heart toward you. Show him who you are, Lord. Show him who he is and who you created him to be. Give me the words to talk about you, God, and give him the courage to accept you into his life. In Jesus' name. Amen.

Chapter 32

⚓

Aubrey decided to wear a striped, off-the-shoulder romper that showed off her tanned shoulders and toned legs. Nothing was going to happen between her and Jake, but she still wanted to show him what he was missing out on. If he wanted a piece of what she had to offer, he would have to go to church with her and he would have to put a ring on it.

A part of her wanted to tell Jake about her commitment to God and her decision to give up sex until she was married, but she didn't know how he would react. She still didn't know how to talk about her decision with others, especially if they weren't passionate about God themselves.

Would Jake think she was weird for surrendering her life to Jesus? What about her other friends back home in Chicago? It seemed so easy for those passionate Christians to talk about Jesus on Instagram and on their blogs, but the people around her in real life didn't talk like that.

She also didn't want Jake to think she was weird by giving up sex until she was married. He wouldn't understand. He already knew they couldn't have sex because she didn't want to get hurt, so what was the point of explaining her actual reasoning? How would she explain to someone who wanted to have sex with multiple people that she wanted to wait until her wedding night to have sex again? She didn't need to tell him the details, and she didn't have to explain anything to him. She had already decided and made the commitment to God, and that's what mattered.

Jake arrived right on time as she finished curling her hair. The Fish Shop was close enough to walk, so they walked arm in arm as they watched the sun set over the ocean. It already felt like a date. Just like it always had felt in the past. The way he would put his arm around her. How he made her smile and laugh with his charm and flirtatious jokes.

As they took their seats at their table, Aubrey knew she needed to set the expectation for the night. She didn't want to fall for Jake's moves again. And she didn't want to get drunk.

"I'm glad you are here to celebrate my birthday with me, but I want to make two things clear." She sat up straighter in her chair.

"First, we are not sleeping together tonight. We've already talked about this and we both know it's not a good idea."

"Right, we are just friends. Got it." Jake nodded.

"And second, I'm not getting drunk tonight. I don't want to start my last year of my twenties being hungover."

Jake slapped the table. "Ah, come on; it's your birthday! Live a little. You have your thirties to recover from all the hangovers from your twenties."

Aubrey raised her eyebrows. Jake's passion for drinking was becoming more and more of a turnoff. *In addition to his salvation, looks like I need to start praying for him to stop drinking so much too,* she thought.

"Here, just enjoy your rosé and relax." Jake placed a wine glass into Aubrey's hand. "Happy birthday, my beautiful beach friend. May this be the year all your dreams come true." They clinked their glasses.

Yes, she needed to relax and enjoy the moment. She had already surrendered everything to God; surely she could still enjoy a few glasses of wine on her birthday.

"So, what have you and the dolphins been up to the past few weeks?" Aubrey knew he had had friends visiting from his Instagram stories, but she really wanted to know why she hadn't heard from him as much after the night he got knocked out from the fight.

"I had some friends in town visiting from Washington, and then another friend came and visited me the weekend after that. I'm thinking of turning my place into a bed and breakfast by the beach. I even started putting chocolates on their pillows." Jake laughed as he took a sip of his rosé.

Did that girl from New Year's visit him again? *No, he wouldn't have offered to take me out for my birthday if he was still hanging out with her. He wouldn't do that.*

"That's great you've been able to see so many of your old friends. Have you spent much time by yourself on weekends, exploring and getting to know people here?"

Was he going on any dates with people here? What did he do during the week? Aubrey had told him she would be home for a few weeks during her time off, so she was surprised she hadn't heard from him during the week.

"Yeah, of course, I have been checking out a lot of new bars during the week. I've been meeting lots of locals just by sitting at the bar and getting to know the bartenders. And I've met a few people who live right next door. It's starting to feel more like home now."

"Ah, that's awesome. I'm glad you've been able to meet people." Aubrey was hoping he would ask her what she had been up to, but Jake continued talking about his neighbors.

"I ended up meeting this one neighbor at the bar down the street, and I had no idea he was this self-made millionaire. He lives in this tiny place by the beach, but he invented a part that goes in every iPhone. Anyway, we meet at the bar, and the next thing I know, we end up at this massive party on his yacht. It was a full-on rager—people were dancing, doing coke, having the greatest time all on a Tuesday night! I love this place more and more every day."

Jake was hanging out with people who did cocaine during the week? Aubrey took a sip of her rosé. She had missed hanging out with him, but it felt like they had less and less in common.

Jake saw the look on Aubrey's face. "Don't worry. I didn't get as crazy as everyone on the yacht. I only did a little coke, but it was still one hell of a good time."

Aubrey set her glass down as the waiter brought over their oysters and fish tacos. She wanted to leave. She didn't know if it was because she was reading the Bible more, but it was like God was putting a big neon sign above Jake that kept flashing "Red Flag. Red Flag."

Remember why you're in his life. He needs to know God, and you can be a good influence in his life.

"So, did you do anything to celebrate Easter?" Aubrey changed the subject as they dug into their food.

Jake tried not to roll his eyes. "What do you think? I told you I don't believe in that kind of stuff."

"Well, lots of people still celebrate the holidays with traditions with friends and family. I wasn't sure if you still participated." She bit into her taco. She wasn't expecting him to sound so defensive about Easter.

"If you must know, I celebrated all alone after my friend flew back home by getting really high and eating half of the food in my fridge. So, yes, I had a great Easter."

She knew Jake didn't want to talk about God or church, but she couldn't help herself. She couldn't let him continue talking about how drunk and high he got without mentioning how important God was to her now. She could tell he was lost; he didn't know how to be alone, and he was trying to find his identity in the wrong kinds of things and people. She wasn't about to tell him she had surrendered her life to Jesus and had decided to wait to have sex until she was married, but he needed to know there was another option. He didn't have to live this way.

"Look, I know it's not your thing, but God is a big deal to me, and he's already starting to change my life. I care about you as my friend and I want to see you happy, and I've seen the difference God has been making in my life. I want that for you, too. I went to church on Easter and things just feel different. I know God has a plan for my life and he has one for you too. I know you don't want to talk about it, but I hope you know the invitation is always open if you want to join me for church, and I'll continue to pray that you figure out what you want to do here."

Jake's face softened. "I know you only want me to be happy, and I appreciate your prayers. You've been a great friend, and it means a lot that you would even call me out like that. Can we just start over? Let's have fun and enjoy your birthday." He finished his drink and reached into the bag to take out the next bottle of rosé.

"Yes, I'd like that. Let's enjoy the night and each other's company." Aubrey said a silent prayer for God to move in Jake's heart as he started talking about his recent project at work.

As they continued to share oysters, fish tacos, and rosé, Aubrey started to realize Jake was only talking about himself. They hadn't seen each other in weeks; they had plenty to catch up on, but Jake only seemed interested in what he had been up to. He didn't ask her too many questions, and he still hadn't asked her what she had been up to over the past few weeks on her time off from work.

It was her birthday; the night was supposed to be about her. She was determined not to let him get to her or make her emotional on her birthday, so she kept sipping her rosé. Jake kept refilling her glass; they were almost through the second bottle of rosé, and she was trying to count the number of glasses she had had so far. She had probably had about three glasses and was already feeling a little buzzed. Between the rosé and the annoyance she felt, Aubrey decided it would be time to call it a night after they finished their last glass.

"All right, that was delicious, but I'm ready to call it a night," Aubrey said as she yawned. She was already used to going to bed early. She loved the feeling of waking up early and not feeling rushed to start her day as she spent time with God on the couch.

"What?" Jake said. "It's your birthday! You can't call it a night yet. Want to start taking shots and see what happens?"

Aubrey punched his shoulder. "No, thank you. I told you I don't want to get drunk, and we both know what will happen if we do."

"Let me buy you one more drink. There's a cute tapas bar a block away that you'll like." He smiled.

She didn't know why she didn't listen to the fact that she was already annoyed with him and that she was already buzzed and should go home. She knew she should go home, but a part of her didn't want to go home and be alone.

"Fine; you can buy me one more drink," she said as she flipped her hair over her shoulder.

Two drinks later, Aubrey and Jake were sitting together at the bar of the tapas place and Jake was still annoying her. Aubrey was also getting upset because he didn't touch her or kiss her like he used to. She knew she had reminded him that they weren't going to sleep together, but she couldn't help but feel rejected.

She missed those days when they couldn't keep their hands off each other and when he would grab her hand. She was supposed to be the one turning him down, not the other way around. Did he not want her anymore? Was he not attracted to her anymore? Why wasn't he paying her more attention?

Aubrey's eyes felt hot as she held back tears. She shook her head. She was not going to cry over him anymore. He was proving over and over again that he wasn't worth it. He clearly only cared about himself and obviously didn't want to date her.

She couldn't hold back the tears anymore. "I'm ready to go home." Aubrey tried to hide the few tears that had slipped out by looking toward the door.

Jake seemed surprised that she was upset and put his hand on her knee. "What's wrong? Are you crying?"

"No," she said as a few more tears rolled down her cheeks.

Why did she always get so emotional on her birthday? The alcohol probably didn't help. She had already had more to drink than she had wanted. And now she was upset. Screw it; it was her birthday, and she was already past her tipping point. She grabbed her vodka soda and took a long, big gulp as the vodka burned her throat.

"What's wrong? Tell me." Jake reached out to hold her hands in his. He rubbed his thumb in the palm of her hand.

"I'm fine. Everything is fine," Aubrey said, sniffling. "I'm glad we are still friends and I have you in my life. I know we are just friends, but it's still hard being around you when you don't treat me like you used to when we would hang out. It's still hard when all the feelings come back when I'm around you. And you don't seem to care about what's going on in my life. You hardly ask me any questions."

At least she was honest, and now he knew how she felt. She felt naïve that she had actually thought they could still hang out as friends. She felt stupid for having thought she wouldn't get her hopes up or that the feelings wouldn't come back. Even with how much he had talked about himself and the drugs that he had done, the feelings had still resurfaced.

Why did she like him so much when he didn't even seem that interested in her?

"I'm sorry," Jake said. "It's not easy for me either. I don't know how to navigate this. You know I care about you, and I want to respect your wishes not to hook up anymore. I love hanging out with you, and I miss the old times, too, but I know that's not going to fix anything when things still haven't changed. I'm still not ready for a relationship. And I'm sorry if you feel like I haven't been asking about you. I do care about you and what's going on in your life. I miss you a lot when I don't see you, and I always think about what you're up to. I've been trying to give you space because I thought that's what you wanted."

A fresh wave of emotions came over Aubrey. He was being honest and sweet, but it still hurt. Things still hadn't changed. He still didn't want to date her, so they were left in this complicated situation where they both still had feelings for each other.

Aubrey shook her head as she took another big sip of her drink.

"I know. I know," she said sadly as she looked down at her lap. She didn't know what else to say. They had already talked about this numerous times before. She had already prayed so many prayers that God would change his mind or that God would help her move on.

"I don't know what else to say either, so I'm just going to say this." Jake tilted up her chin and kissed her.

Chapter 33

⚓

Aubrey slowly opened her eyes as the sun streamed through the window. Her head was pounding and her mouth was dry. She felt awful.

Why had she drunk so much? She knew better. She hadn't wanted to get drunk and be hungover after her birthday. She wasn't supposed to start her last year in her twenties like this.

She felt the bed empty next to her. Jake had already gotten out of bed. She stumbled into the kitchen to grab some water as Jake greeted her with a cheerful hello.

"Well, good morning, birthday girl. How are you feeling?" Jake smiled from the couch where he was eating a bowl of cereal while watching Animal Planet.

"Ugh. Don't ask," she said as she found a blue Gatorade in the back of the fridge.

What was she doing here in Jake's apartment? Why hadn't she just gone home when she wanted to last night? Waves of guilt and shame washed over her.

As Aubrey chugged her Gatorade, she looked up and noticed a new picture on Jake's bulletin board. It was a close-up picture of a woman, smiling as she sat on the beach. Aubrey was used to seeing pictures of his dog, his family, and a few of his buddies on his board, but this was a new picture.

"Who's this girl on your board?" she asked.

Jake looked up and gazed at the bulletin board. "Oh, just a friend from back home," he said, expressionless as he returned to the TV.

Jake did have lots of friends. His place really was a bed and breakfast with the number of friends who had visited since he moved. But still, who was this chick? And why did she get a spot on his bulletin board?

"Why would you hang up a picture of a girl who's only a friend?" Aubrey needed to know more details.

Jake looked back at Aubrey and shrugged. "She gave it to me, so I hung it up. It's not a big deal."

Jake clearly wasn't going to give her any more information about who this girl was. Aubrey didn't want to accuse him of anything, but she had a feeling that something wasn't right.

She was still thinking about it as she went to the restroom. As she returned to the kitchen, she stared at the picture again, getting a closer view. How had she not noticed before that Jake was also in the picture? What had looked like the girl's arm before was actually Jake's arm—his arm tattoo was peeking out. It looked like the girl was taking a selfie, but Aubrey could see that Jake was half cut out of the picture. And she noticed he was actually kissing the girl's cheek.

Aubrey's stomach dropped. Her face went hot. Why would Jake have a picture of himself kissing some girl's cheek, and why would he hang it up on his bulletin board? People didn't hang up pictures of people they casually hooked up with. Jake and she didn't even have any pictures like this together!

People only printed pictures of people who were important to them. Pictures that meant something. Was Jake lying to her? Was he dating someone else? They hadn't talked about whether he was sleeping with anyone else since New Year's. She was always too afraid to ask. They hadn't been spending that much time together anymore, so he definitely could have been sleeping with other people. But still. Why was he also sleeping with her then? Why would he want to take her out to dinner on her birthday if he was sleeping with other people?

Aubrey grabbed the picture off the bulletin board and stood in front of the TV.

"Jake, why are you kissing this girl's cheek if she's just a friend?"

Jake stared at her. Then he sighed and dropped his head in his hands. He knew there was no way out of this one.

Aubrey's stomach started to do somersaults as she braced herself for what was coming.

"She's a friend from back home," Jake explained. "We used to date back in college and ran into each other at my friend's birthday a few months ago. We always had a thing for each other and kind of picked up where things left off."

"Is this the girl who visited you on New Year's?"

"No, that's not her. We ran into each other after that." Jake shook his head.

Anger pulsed through Aubrey's body. Her head pounded as she processed what he had just said. Not only had he slept with someone else; he had slept with two other people. While he was still sleeping with her.

All the hurt and anger she had felt on New Year's bubbled back to the surface. She was so sick of his games. She was sick of his sweet words and cute texts. But he was anything but cute. He was a player, a cheater, and a liar. He was just like the wicked people the Bible talked about who only wanted to do evil.

"I thought you said you weren't ready to date anyone!" Aubrey yelled. "Yet here you are dating someone who doesn't even live here!"

"I'm not ready to date anyone!" he replied. "I told you the truth—I'm not ready for a relationship. We have just been casually hanging out."

"Casually hanging out? Like how we've been hanging out? How do you casually hang out with someone who doesn't even live in the same state?"

Jake hung his head. He couldn't deny it, but he couldn't admit he had been casually hanging out with both of them.

Aubrey was seething by now. How could he be casually hanging out and hooking up with both of them? How could he have let this go on for months? He was leading a double life. He was dating two different women, in two different states, yet he wasn't officially dating either of them. He was playing them both.

She hated him. She hated him for lying to her. She hated him for sleeping with other people. She hated him for making her feel wanted while talking to other girls behind her back. She hated him for not wanting to date her. And she hated him for how he made her feel and for breaking her heart.

She no longer felt sorry for him. She no longer felt enough compassion for him to be in his life as a good friend. Clearly, God hadn't moved in his heart.

Aubrey ran into Jake's room and threw on her romper from the night before. She grabbed her wedges and purse as the tears started to flow. She needed to get out of there. She was not okay.

Jake sat on the couch, looking like a dog with his tail between his legs who had done something he knew he wasn't supposed to do.

He stood up. "I'm sorry. I never intended to hurt you. I told you I wasn't ready to date, and I thought I was being honest with you."

She wanted to throw her shoe at him, but something held her back. Honest? He thought he had been honest?

"You're a liar and a cheat," she said. "If you cared about me, you wouldn't have slept with someone else, two other someone elses! You knew how I felt about you. You knew I didn't want to keep getting hurt." She didn't know how she found the strength to speak. "We are done. Don't text or call me. I never want to speak to you again."

Aubrey slammed his door behind her as she ran out of his apartment. She wanted to get as far away from Jake and last night as possible.

In a blur of tears, she ran as fast as she could down the beach. The sun was already high up in the sky, and she started to sweat. Her hair was a mess, and she felt her makeup running down her face along with her tears. This was the worst walk of shame she had ever done. It was Wednesday, and she was doing a run of shame in the middle of the day while people met up for coffee and kids played on the beach.

She didn't care that she looked like a hot mess. Each step she took, she was running away from the guy who didn't want her. The guy who didn't care about her. The guy who didn't love her.

She felt like she couldn't breathe, so she sat down on the sand. Tears continued to fall down her face. She felt like she wanted to throw up.

Why, God? Why? Why doesn't he love me? Why doesn't he want to be with me? What's wrong with me, God? Why do I care so much about someone who doesn't even want to date me? Why do all guys end up hooking up with someone else? Will I ever be enough so that someone actually wants to date me and only me? Will I ever be enough, God?

She sat there on the beach, letting the tears fall. People walking on the beach just stared at her, but she didn't care. She felt completely hopeless. She was moving backward. She had moved to San Diego for a fresh start and a new beginning, but it had only led to more drunken mistakes and a broken heart.

When would things ever change? Why was figuring out life so hard? Weren't things supposed to be easier now with God in her life? Doing things God's way was too hard. How did people actually do it? Giving up sex still seemed impossible.

Aubrey felt guilty and ashamed for sleeping with Jake again last night. She was mad at Jake for letting her drink so much, but she was also mad at herself. She had made the decision not to have sex with Jake anymore. She had promised God she would wait until marriage. She had made a commitment to God that she would stop, and here she was, only a few weeks later, having sex again. Even in her drunken state last night, she was still aware of what she was doing. Jake hadn't forced her to do anything; she had let him kiss her and bring her back to his place.

And look where it had gotten her. Hungover with a broken heart. Jake had been dating and hooking up with someone else. She had known she would end up getting hurt if she continued hooking up with Jake, but she hadn't seen this coming. She felt blindsided. She felt like she was in one of those movies where you find out someone was having an affair all along.

As she watched the surfers ride the waves, she noticed a few fins bobbing up and down in the water. Dolphins. Just like the dolphins she had seen when she first met Jake. Aubrey had thought it was fate—their own Nicholas Sparks love story. That they would fall in love and live happily ever after on the beach.

But none of that would happen now. The dolphins had always reminded her of Jake before. But now, she felt this weird feeling of hope. And she felt the familiar feeling she had when she sensed God was with her.

As the beach-goers passed by, they didn't even notice the sea creatures jumping through the waves. God was like the dolphins. He was always with her, even when she couldn't see him or wasn't looking. She knew she had to be seeking him to find him, but he was always out there. And just like with the dolphins, once in a while, God showed himself to give her hope, to remind her he was there.

Aubrey felt a wave of peace wash over her. She had God now, and he was always with her. And she knew he had promised to work all things for good for those who loved him. All things. Even her mistakes and a broken heart.

Chapter 34

⚓

As awful as she felt, Aubrey woke up the next morning and went for a run. She had been through breakups before, so she knew she would get through this. Her heart would heal eventually. She would heal and life would move on.

But now she had to deal with the pain and loss she felt over Jake. She had been tempted to stay in bed all morning, but she needed to do something to get her mind off Jake. And she needed to work off all the calories from demolishing an entire box of mac n' cheese the night before.

Working out always helped her feel better. When her college boyfriend had cheated on her, she had thrown herself into working out and fitness and had gotten into the best shape of her life. But now she also had God. God would help her heal. All the books and blogs she had been reading talked about how God was the ultimate healer. Only God could heal a broken heart or a wound from the past.

God was close to the brokenhearted and those crushed in spirit. She didn't have to figure out how to heal by herself. God would heal her broken heart, but there was something she needed to do first.

When she got back from her run, she knelt on her workout mat on her knees.

God, please forgive me. I know I've sinned by sleeping with Jake and getting drunk again. Forgive me, God. Help me change. Give me the strength to stop having sex. Give me the strength to drink less and make better decisions. Please forgive me for having sex with Jake. I'm sorry, God. I surrender this area to you, God. I need your help. I can't do this without you, God. Change me, God. Please give me the strength to change and move forward. And heal my broken heart, Lord. Heal my heart. Amen.

Aubrey started crying again. She had hope that God would help her get through this, but she didn't understand why it hurt so bad. Even though it hurt, finding out this way was a blessing. She had tried over and over again to stop sleeping with Jake, yet she had always failed. But now, it was like God had allowed this to happen so she would finally stop hanging out with him.

But why did it have to hurt so much? Why did it hurt so much when they hadn't even been in an actual relationship? She felt like she had gotten dumped, but they hadn't even been in a committed, exclusive relationship.

Why couldn't God have given Jake the desire to go to church with her? Why didn't God soften his heart to pursue a relationship with God?

Aubrey felt naïve. She had actually thought Jake would go to church with her eventually. She felt stupid for believing he needed a good friend like her in his life and that they could just be friends. They clearly couldn't be friends. Every time they hung out, she always hoped for something more to happen, but she had never been able to change his mind.

She started replaying the events of the past few months with Jake. All those nights, she should have gone home. All those nights, she should have told him no. If she had broken things off with him the first time after New Year's, she wouldn't be so heartbroken now. She had wasted months trying to make something happen with Jake, and it had only made things worse.

Aubrey pulled up Jake's Instagram pictures. She knew she shouldn't be stalking his social media, but she couldn't help it. She needed to know who this other girl was. She needed to know when it had all started.

After some scrolling and digging, she found the girl in a few of his tagged photos. Pictures of them together at sunset on Mission Beach. Bike riding along the boardwalk. Drinking giant cocktails at a bar in Gaslamp.

How had she missed this? She always forgot to look at the tagged photos. She clicked on the girl's profile. It was public. Her name was Beth. She lived in Washington and loved yoga, dogs, and the beach.

Aubrey skimmed her page. There were several more photos of them together. Photos in San Diego and in Washington. She clicked on a photo of them together, standing with a small boy. They were at Legoland. The caption of one of her photos read, "So thankful for you this year. We love you." With three red heart emojis.

Did she have a son? Jake had been sleeping with someone else who had a son!

Aubrey threw her phone on the couch. This was too much. How could Jake do that to a little boy? What kind of person would casually sleep around with someone who had a son? A boy who needed a father, not a guy who slept around and was afraid to commit.

She sat on the floor in shock. She was caught off guard yesterday, but now seeing all Jake's photos for herself, it was real. All the evidence had been there all along. How could she have been so stupid? Jake and Beth must have visited each other several times in the past few months.

Aubrey shook her head and grabbed her phone. She needed to stop thinking about them together. She needed to talk to someone who would understand.

Aubrey retrieved her phone from the couch and quickly called Tina.

"Hello, beautiful. How are you?" Tina answered on the first ring.

"Tina, I've been such a fool," Aubrey said. "I've been so stupid. You were right about Jake. I just found out that he's been sleeping with someone else the whole time. And I had sex with him again. I feel awful, Tina; it hurts so bad, and we weren't even actually dating. How could I have been so stupid?"

Aubrey started crying again. She knew she needed to stop thinking about it, but she needed a good friend right now.

Tina sighed. "I'm so sorry, Aubrey. I know you really liked him and that he was your first real friend in San Diego. I'm just glad you found out when you did before things went any further. Could you imagine finding this out if you were actually dating?"

"No, no, I can't. Thank God we weren't in an actual relationship even after how much I prayed for him to change his mind. I knew he was a bad influence and that we weren't supposed to date since he doesn't believe in God, but I had always hoped and prayed that God would change his mind. I feel so stupid."

"You aren't stupid," Tina replied. "You liked him and only wanted the best for him—to know God. I think that's beautiful that you prayed for his salvation."

Aubrey sniffled. Yeah, at least she had prayed for him. He clearly needed prayer if he was going to sleep around like that with multiple women, especially when a boy was in the picture.

"I just don't know what to do. I know God will heal my broken heart, but I don't know what to do in the meantime. I don't know how to move on from Jake."

"Okay, well, first things first, have you asked God for forgiveness? To forgive you for sleeping with Jake?"

"Yes, I did this morning. It felt good to get it off my chest."

"That's great! Good job. Okay, so now the hard part—moving on. So, you may already know that Jesus gives us the strength and power to walk in freedom from sin, but we must continuously surrender our lives to him. We must continuously surrender our desires, our struggles, and our sin."

Aubrey nodded. "Yes, I'm learning that. He gives us the strength to overcome the sin in our life."

"Yes, he does. But we can help him in the process by intentionally getting rid of things that are holding us back. The Bible tells us in Hebrews 12:1 that we must throw off the weight that holds us back, especially the sin that so easily entangles us. This means we have to give up certain things or people who are holding us back. The Bible talks about repentance, which happens when we throw off these things that are bad for us and we choose to run in the opposite direction. Does this make sense?"

That Bible verse spoke to Aubrey's heart. Jake had been holding her back for months now. He was a bad influence, and he kept causing her to sin even when she hadn't wanted to. She had tried to stop having sex with him and to drink less, but she continued to put herself in the same situation they had always been in. They hung out, drank alcohol, and ended up having sex. Why had she thought things would be any different hanging out together? She had wanted to stop having sex and surrender this area of her life to God, but she hadn't fully turned the other way. She continued to put herself in the same situation that had always tempted her.

Aubrey closed her eyes. "It makes total sense. I never fully repented. I kept putting myself in the same situation that always led to us drinking and having sex. I never threw off the weight that was holding me back. I thought I was doing a good thing by being his friend, but he was weighing me down the whole time."

"Wow. I'm glad God revealed that to you, girl. That's pretty deep."

"I know, it is. So how do I repent? How do I make sure he doesn't hold me back anymore?"

"That is the ultimate question, my friend," Tina said. "I think you already know. It's time to cut him out of your life. It's time to block all contact and communication. Get rid of anything that reminds you of him."

Aubrey knew that was the only way. But did she have to do that so soon? Should she get more closure first? She shook her head. Tina was right. It was time to throw off the weight. It was time to cut Jake out of her life.

Tina and Aubrey hung up. Then Aubrey opened Jake's Instagram again. Stalking his social media was like pouring salt on a wound. She stared at his profile photo one last time before she clicked "unfollow."

She opened her contacts. Did she really have to delete his number? What if she had to get in touch with him? She wasn't worried about texting him so she deleted all their messages instead. All those flirty, meaningless texts. All the sexy photos they had sent each other. Gone.

Then she threw out the dolphin figure he had given her for her birthday, along with a sock he had left under her bed. And she dumped the leftover bottle of peppermint schnapps down the sink.

Next, Aubrey reread the Christmas card he had given her before her holiday party, letting her know how grateful he was to have met her, how much he enjoyed their time together, and how much he valued their friendship.

Aubrey hesitated. Did she really have to give up her only friend in San Diego? Did she really have to cut him out of her life like he no longer existed?

Yes. It's time. It's for your own good. Trust me, beloved.

She ripped up the card and threw it in the trash. Then she went out to the beach to watch the sunset.

Chapter 35

⚓

Aubrey smiled as she took in the view of the ocean beside her while she drove to work. She had gotten up extra early that morning to read and spend time with God before she had to get ready. God's Word and his presence during worship filled her with unexpected hope for her first day back to work after her time off. She was glad she had had a few days off after her birthday to process everything that had happened with Jake, and she was actually looking forward to going back to work to help her think about something else.

While reading her Bible that morning, 1 Corinthians 7:20 had spoken to her. "Each of you should remain as you were when God called you." Aubrey had written the verse on an index card and taped it to the dashboard of her car. Every time she spoke it out loud, it gave her confidence to trust that God would show her what her purpose was at work and when it was time for her to leave.

God had her there for a reason, and she would continue working there as if she were working for God himself. She made the mistake of turning her emails on again on her phone while she was stopped at a red light; her boss had already sent her several emails that morning before she had even got to work. But demanding bosses and an inbox full of emails weren't going to bother her. They would all get taken care of eventually, and she had focused on her number-one priority that morning, which would affect her entire day.

"Well, look who it is. Welcome back!" Her coworker Adam smiled at her as she reached her cubicle.

"Did you miss us? You were gone, what, three whole weeks? How did you manage that one, Aubrey?" asked her other coworker, Brett, sticking his head over the cubicle.

Aubrey smiled. "Hey, the firm gives us plenty of personal time off; vacation days are there for a reason. I encourage you to do the same." She looked at Adam, who always sent emails even when he was supposed to be on vacation.

"I honestly don't know what I would do with that much time off," Adam said. "I would get bored and be ready to come back to work within a week."

"Well, there's your first problem," Aubrey replied. "You don't take enough time off work to actually have hobbies and enjoy doing other things outside of work."

Adam threw a stress ball at her. "Hobbies?" he said. "Who has time for hobbies? Tell us, how did you spend your time not working for three weeks? Tell us all about your hobbies." He grinned.

Aubrey's heart started racing. Should she tell them she had decided to go all in for God? That she had surrendered her entire life to him and had gotten tricked into an altar call? That she had a broken heart and wasn't having sex again until marriage?

"Oh, you know, I kept myself busy with the usual. Exploring new beaches, watching the dolphins, working out in the middle of the day, and reading—lots of reading."

"I can picture you reading those trashy romance novels on the beach, not having a care in the world," Brett said. He knew her old self so well from the time they had worked on a project together before she had moved.

Aubrey felt her heart race again. "Actually, no. I started a new morning routine where I read the Bible and pray after I wake up. It's been such a game-changer. I now wake up stress-free, without feeling the need to check emails right away, and I love having that time to myself to start my day."

Her coworkers stared at her.

"Oh, well, that sounds awesome. Good for you," Adam said. He returned to typing on his computer.

"Oh, really?" Brett said. "I didn't know that kind of stuff was important to you. Have you found a church here?"

Aubrey nodded. "Yes, it's called Freedom Church. It's pretty awesome, great worship and messages." Her heart raced again as she found the courage to ask Brett, "Do you go to church?"

She had never talked about church with her coworkers. She never would have mentioned it before, but things were different now. She was part of this new world with God, and maybe there were others at her work who were part of this world too.

"I used to go, growing up with my parents, but I don't really go anymore," he replied. "We don't have much time on the weekends with the kids and everything."

"Well, if you ever change your mind and want to check it out, just let me know."

Aubrey couldn't stop smiling as she opened her laptop. She hadn't responded to a single email, yet she already felt like she had made a difference for the day.

She spent hours catching up on all the emails in her inbox and setting up calls with new clients and team members. Thankfully, she had been assigned to a few smaller, local clients so she wouldn't need to travel as much.

After taking one of her mentees out for a much-needed afternoon coffee break, Aubrey returned to her inbox. There was a new calendar invite from someone she hadn't met before. Outlook informed her the person was an HR representative from the San Diego office. The subject read "HR Incident Discussion" and the invite told her she was supposed to meet in the conference room at 8 a.m. on Friday for a meeting with the local HR representative.

Aubrey's stomach dropped. HR Incident? This could not be happening again. Was she under another HR investigation?

Aubrey stared at the invite on her computer screen. Her eyesight started to blur and then go black. She couldn't breathe.

Maybe this was a mistake? Was this about the expense fraud that was going on around the company? She had heard of a few employees getting fired from running through personal expenses on the company credit card, but she hadn't submitted any expenses that were personal.

She hung her head in her hands. It must be about the happy hour at training. Devon had never texted her back. This was her own fault. She had drank too much at the happy hour at training and mouthed off to Devon. She had cried and acted unprofessionally.

But another HR investigation? Seriously? Who would have reported this? It wasn't like she had gotten kicked out of the hot tub again or committed expense fraud. Why did she always have to get caught? How could she possibly be going through another HR investigation?

God, why is this happening again? You've already showed me I need to stop drinking as much. And you've already started changing my desires for alcohol.

What-ifs swirled in her head as she imagined what would happen this time. Would they take away her bonus again? Would she get fired this time? What had Devon told them? Who would report this to HR?

As Aubrey continued to stare at the wall in her cubicle, her computer dinged with a new email notification. An updated calendar invite from the HR person.

Oh, crap. Crap. Crap. Crap. Crap. This was not good. The HR person had added Stacey to the invite, who was one of the top leaders in her company. She was Devon's boss's boss, super-high up in the company.

Aubrey and Stacey had met years ago when Aubrey was recruited to join the company since Stacey used to have Devon's position. But this was not good. If she was on this call, then all of the firm's leadership must know what had happened. If she was having a call with Stacey, the firm was taking this very seriously.

She was going to get fired. There was no way around it. Tears started to fall down her face. *So, this is what happens when you drink too much at work events and make two really big drunken mistakes.* She was going to get fired from her job for drinking.

Aubrey wanted to throw up. She closed her laptop as fast as she could and managed to put everything else in her workbag.

"Heading out already? Got an early spin class?" Adam turned in his chair as Aubrey left her cubicle.

She kept walking. "Something came up. Family matter!" she shouted over the cubicle. Her boss had been at a client all day.

Thankfully, she didn't have to come up with an excuse for leaving so early.

Don't cry. Don't cry. Almost there.

This couldn't be happening. She had just made manager, the coveted milestone in public accounting that many people don't stick around to make. She had just moved across the country to live at the beach. She lived in San Diego, the best city in America, and some days, she even got to work from home from the beach.

And now it was all about to be thrown away because of a few nights of drinking. Things like this didn't happen to her. She was a fully functioning adult, not some wild college girl who couldn't handle her liquor.

Aubrey slammed her car door as the tears started to fall harder. She quickly pulled out of the parking lot before anyone could see her.

She knew she had made some big, drunken mistakes in the past few years, but all her old friends always got as drunk as her. And things like this did happen all the time at work events—it was a given that people got too drunk and did dumb stuff. The firm provided the free alcohol. What did they expect? People got hammered all the time at work functions. So why did she have to face the consequences? Why was the firm making this such a big deal?

Her contacts started to get blurry. She couldn't stop sobbing, and her hands began to shake as she gripped the wheel. Was she having a panic attack?

She pulled over at a gas station. She sobbed into the steering wheel until she felt a voice from within.

Pray. Give it to God.

Aubrey sat up. Of course, God would fix it. He was in control. He already knew what was going to happen.

God, please forgive me. You've already shown me the consequences of my drinking and that I need to change. God, I don't want to get fired. Please don't let me get fired, God. I'm sorry for complaining about my job. You've blessed me with so much here in San Diego and through this job. I'm not ready to leave yet, God. Please forgive me, Father. Please don't let me get fired. Please don't make me leave San Diego, God.

Thank you for your grace, God. Thank you for forgiving me and my actions even when I don't deserve it. I know Jesus already died for my life and for all my sins, all my mistakes. You already showed me so much grace, Lord. Please give me grace with this, God. Please don't let me get fired.

Chapter 36

⚓

Aubrey struggled to open her eyes. Her head pounded as she sat up. It was all a dream. She wasn't about to lose her job; it was just a bad dream, confirming that alcohol had almost ruined her life. Waking her up so she would stop getting drunk and be thankful for her job.

She checked her email on her phone. The calendar invite from HR was still there. She fell back on the pillows. There was nothing she could do. She would have to wait until Friday morning before it was all over. When she handed in her laptop and employee ID badge.

She chugged the water on her nightstand and found the aspirin in her bathroom. If she was going to get fired, she would be prepared. She sent a quick email to her team: "Working from home today. Not feeling well. Will reschedule the kickoff to tomorrow." Postponing their kickoff wasn't going to matter; someone would be replacing her once they found out the news anyway.

Aubrey poured herself a cup of coffee and opened her laptop. How did she prepare to get fired? Shouldn't they have some type of checklist: "What to do when you screw up and are going to get fired?"

Would all her coworkers find out what had happened? Most of them would probably just laugh and agree that the firm was taking this too seriously. She shook her head. It was time to focus.

It took hours to make sure all her phone contacts and photos were backed up and to save her personal files on her computer. She processed all her work expenses on her company credit card and traded in all the reward points from her credit card.

At least she was walking away with more than 1 million in Marriott Bonvoy points. The firm couldn't take those away from her. She had worked her butt off to earn those over the past four years—all those nights away from home, away from her friends and her own bed. No matter what happened, she would still save these points for her dream honeymoon, a villa on top of the ocean in the Maldives, that she would enjoy with her husband, whoever he was.

But now all the travels around the world and points would come to an end. She would never be able to travel for free like this again. All her free trips back home. All the trips she had taken to California. The trips abroad to Singapore, Thailand, and Europe.

The flexibility of working from home would also come to an end. Lunchtime walks on the beach. The tears fell on her keyboard. She wasn't ready to leave this job yet. She still needed this job while she figured out what she was really supposed to be doing with her life.

What would she tell her parents? They had already thought she had a drinking problem back in college. Would she have to move back in with them in Michigan? How else was she supposed to make money? None of the other public accounting firms would hire her. She would have to explain why she left Assets & Beyond Consulting, and there must be a way for other firms to know when an employee had been terminated. It was too late to start a travel blog or become a spin instructor now. It would take months just to get certified and finish training, let alone earn enough money to afford her beach rent.

She found Jake's name in her phone. He would understand after everything he had been through. He would tell her that everything would be okay and that she could get another job and still live at the beach. But she hated him. He was a liar and a cheat. Even though she had told him not to contact her before she had stormed out of his apartment, it still hurt that he hadn't texted her. If he had broken her heart, why would he care if she lost her job?

She struggled to breathe as she dialed Tina. She would know what to do. Aubrey started chewing on her nails. The call kept ringing and then went to voicemail. She hung her head. What would Tina say to her right now?

Aubrey closed her eyes and tried focusing on her breath. In and out. In and out. Picturing Jesus sitting with her at the kitchen table.

The Bible. Why hadn't she started her morning with God? Spending time with God always gave her peace. She wasn't too familiar with all the books in the Bible yet, so she searched on Pinterest for Bible verses about peace. She turned to Philippians 4:6-9. "Don't worry about anything; instead, pray about everything. Tell God what you need, and thank him for all he has done. Then you will experience God's peace, which exceeds anything we can understand."

Aubrey remembered Pastor Davis talking about this verse before. Prayer and gratitude were the keys to receiving God's peace in any trial or situation.

She shook her head. How had she forgotten to turn to God, the one who was in control?

She bowed her head and closed her eyes.

God, I trust you. I've already asked for your forgiveness, and you've showed me there are consequences from drinking. There are consequences

*when I don't obey your Word, and I know I have to accept the conse-
quences, even if it means getting fired.*

*Thank you for changing my desire to drink. Thank you for blessing
me here in San Diego even when I don't deserve it. Thank you for blessing me with so much in this job, even when I've been ungrateful. Thank
you, God, that no matter what happens, you are in control and you have
a plan for me. Amen.*

It was finally Friday morning. Instead of waking up with knots
in her stomach, Aubrey woke up with a confidence that could only
come from God. She had already decided on her outfit the night
before—dark jeans, booties, and a blazer. A look that said she was a
functioning adult who had her life together, instead of a drunk girl
who was a hot mess.

As she drove to work, she listened to a sermon from her old
church in Chicago, Soul City Church, about obeying God. It had
resonated with her before, and she needed a reminder of God's
faithfulness before her fate would be decided.

"So, we all know the story of Jesus' birth and how an angel told
Mary, a virgin, that she would give birth to the Messiah. You hear
this story every Christmas, but today I want to focus on Mary's
response." She loved how Pastor Jeanne preached. So confident yet
so gentle and full of love at the same time.

"After the angel explained that the Holy Spirit would come
upon her, Mary's response was 'may it be Lord, I am your faithful
servant.' Mary didn't question whether God had chosen the wrong
girl. She didn't object and tell God he was ruining her wedding
plans with Joseph. Mary simply responded with obedience to God.

"'May it be Lord, may it be.' When was the last time you said that to God? We should have the same response to God when he calls us to do something. He knows the plans he has for us, and we are called to obey him, no matter how crazy it sounds. We can trust God and the timing of his plans for us, and that if it's his will, he will provide a way."

Aubrey put her car in park and closed her eyes.

God, may it be. I surrender this job and my life to you, God. May your will be done, God. If it's time to leave my company, I trust you, God. I trust the plans and future you have for me. You know I want to stay and that I don't want to leave the company yet. But God, if this is your way to get me to leave Assets & Beyond Consulting, may your will be done. You are in control, God. May it be.

Aubrey repeated "May it be, Lord; may it be" as she walked into the office building. As she rode in the elevator. And as she knocked on the door of the conference room.

"Hi, Aubrey. I'm Rebecca. Thank you for coming in today. Have a seat." She shook Aubrey's hand a little too forcefully as she attempted a smile.

Aubrey didn't know what to say. She didn't want to seem like she wasn't taking this seriously by making small talk, so she sat down across from Rebecca at the long conference table as she gave a polite smile in return.

"Stacey is in New York today, so we are just going to call her on her office phone." Rebecca avoided making eye contact with Aubrey as she dialed on the office phone in front of her.

"Sounds great." Aubrey attempted to smile as she noticed the pieces of paper lying face down next to the phone.

This was it. Her last potential hour at Assets & Beyond Consulting. Her last hour before everyone found out. If they wanted to think she was a drunk who got out of hand, so be it. She knew who she really was, now that God had showed her who he was. She was a church girl now, not the bar girl she used to be. If they didn't understand that, then there was nothing she could do.

Thankfully, nobody else she worked with would see her in the conference room this early. She would see what Stacey had to say, and then she would be on her way before anyone could see her.

It's in your hands now, God. It's in your hands. You are with me. You are with me. May it be Lord, may it be.

She prayed silently in her head and focused on taking deep breaths as the phone rang on speaker. Don't cry. Don't cry. Don't cry.

"Hello. This is Stacey."

"Stacey, yes, this is Rebecca, from the San Diego office. I have Aubrey sitting with me." She folded her hands and then unfolded them as she stared at the phone. "Shall we begin?"

"Yes, thanks, Rebecca. Why don't you kick things off?"

"So, Aubrey," Rebecca said, "we are here today to discuss the incident at the happy hour at training. Due to the incident, we've asked Stacey to speak to you personally, and I am here to help explain and answer any questions you have from an HR perspective."

Aubrey nodded. Time for the interrogation to begin.

"Thanks, Rebecca." Stacey chimed in. "Aubrey, we are aware that this is your second violation against the firm's code of conduct two years in a row at training, and due to the nature of the incidents and since we've known each other a while, I wanted to discuss this matter with you myself. Your behavior showed that you were crying and upset with Devon at the happy hour and that you were intoxicated. We've discussed this incident with Devon and others who were at the happy hour, and we have issued you a written write-up and statement to follow.

"Since both of your incidents at training involved alcohol, in order to remain employed with the firm, you must contact the firm's employee assistance program for an initial alcohol counseling screening session. Aubrey, can you please read the write-up and let us know if you have any questions?"

Rebecca passed Aubrey one of the papers that had been sitting in front of her.

Was she supposed to read this out loud? It was too silent; she couldn't focus on the letter as Rebecca stared at her.

"Please read through this and let us know if you have any questions," Rebecca continued. "As Stacey explained, you must schedule an initial alcohol counseling session within seven days of this meeting to remain employed by the firm."

Alcohol counseling session? Aubrey couldn't help the tears from escaping as she skimmed the letter.

Violation of the firm's code of conduct. Intoxicated at a happy hour while getting noticeably upset with Devon. Someone had reported the incident to HR. She had called Devon a horrible leader and a cheap ass. Still on probation from an incident at training a year prior. Alcohol involved at both events. A phone number to contact within seven days to set up an alcohol counseling session. Failure to comply with the letter would result in termination from the firm.

Aubrey straightened her blazer as she continued staring at the letter. She couldn't believe she had said those things to her boss. Even though she didn't remember saying them, and she would never say those things to him sober, she couldn't take it back. Just like she couldn't undo all the tequila shots she had taken. And now her work thought she had a drinking problem. But at least it appeared that she still had a job. And that they weren't taking away her bonus again.

How was she supposed to respond to this? Was it even worth mentioning that she was not that person anymore? That she had given her life to God and he was already showing her not to drink as much? She was not the person this letter described. She didn't want them to think she was a terrible person or had a drinking problem. But she had to face the consequences.

"I understand the letter and the consequences," Aubrey said, sounding more professional than she felt. "I accept full responsibility for my actions and want to apologize for my behavior. I was unprofessional and was out of line and I take full responsibility."

"Great," Stacey said. "So, Rebecca will follow up with you, making sure you've complied with the steps in the letter, and we will put this in your file."

Rebecca gave Aubrey a weak smile as Aubrey signed the letter.

"Here is your copy," Rebecca said, handing her one. "Let me know when you've scheduled your counseling session."

"Will do. Thanks."

Aubrey walked past her cubicle to the elevator. There was no way she could work in the office today. It wasn't even nine yet; she could still leave without any of her coworkers showing up.

She needed time to process everything. She still had a job. She wasn't getting fired. And she had seven days to schedule an alcohol counseling session, whatever that was.

The elevator pinged. She prayed as she made her way down to the parking garage.

Thank you, God, for letting me still have this job. Thank you for showing me grace and not letting me get fired. God, thank you for softening their hearts to extend grace to me, even when I didn't deserve it. Thank you, Lord.

Chapter 37

⚓

Aubrey checked her phone. She still had a few minutes before her alcohol counseling session. She had scheduled the session right after she got home from her meeting with HR. Time to get it over with and move on with her life.

She paced back and forth in her living room. What kinds of questions would they ask her? Should she be honest about all the drinking problems she had had in the past?

Her drinking had been out of control in the past, but she was different now. She didn't drink like that anymore. She stayed in most weekends, and she had only slipped up and gotten drunk twice this year so far. Once at the happy hour at training and then again on her birthday. And she didn't even miss drinking.

She wanted to be honest, but she didn't want to make this a bigger deal than it already was.

Her phone rang. Time to face her fears.

"Hi. This is Aubrey."

"Hi, Aubrey. My name is Diane. I'm the counselor who has been assigned to your case. Let me explain how this process will work before we begin the questioning."

Aubrey gulped. "Okay, sounds good."

"According to the report from your employer, you are required to have this initial alcohol counseling session in order to remain employed by the firm. They mentioned that you've had a few incidents at work events involving alcohol and your employer recommended the session to see if additional help is needed. Is that correct?"

Aubrey nodded. "Yes, that's right."

"Great. I'm going to ask you several questions related to drug and alcohol use to determine the next steps and treatment, if applicable. Do you have any questions before I begin?"

Treatment? What kind of treatment did they think she needed? She wasn't an alcoholic!

"Um, no. No questions. I'm ready to begin."

"Great. Let's get started. For all questions, unless otherwise indicated, please respond based on your current alcohol and drug use. First question I have for you Aubrey, how often do you drink alcohol?"

"Um, only a few times a month."

"And where do you typically drink? Do you drink at your home or with friends?"

"I only drink socially with other friends. Usually when we all go out for a special occasion or dinner."

"How many drinks do you typically drink on the occasions that you do drink? For clarification, a drink is defined as twelve ounces of beer, one-and-a-half ounces of hard liquor, or five ounces of wine."

Aubrey had a flashback of tailgating in college. She and her sorority sisters would easily consume six to ten drinks before and during a football game. And every night they went out. Who was able to keep count after three or four?

"Um, I would estimate that I drink two or three drinks when I do drink." She decided not to mention the number of drinks she had drank on her birthday. That was an exception, not the norm anymore.

"And what kind of alcohol do you typically drink?"

Aubrey used to drink everything. Beer, wine, mixed drinks, shots, and hard liquor. She grimaced just thinking about it.

"I typically only drink wine or mixed drinks now."

"What kinds of mixed drinks do you drink?"

Was this lady serious? What did it matter what kinds of mixed drinks she drank?

"I try to stick to clear liquors. Like a vodka soda or Moscow mule." That was true. Vodka drinks made her less nauseous now, and it was better for her beach diet.

"Thanks for clarifying. Just so you are aware, some mixed drinks count as multiple drinks because they contain several shots of hard liquor. You need to be careful when drinking any mixed drink to ensure you aren't underestimating the amount of alcohol being consumed."

Great, now she was lecturing her. When was this going to be over? She wanted to tell her it was really none of her business, but she knew she needed to cooperate.

"Okay, great."

"Now I'm going to ask you some questions based on your past alcohol and drug consumption. Aubrey, have you ever blacked out from drinking?"

"Yes."

"Have you ever hurt yourself from drinking?"

"No." Aubrey's face went flush. She didn't want to lie, but she didn't want her company to think she had a drinking problem.

Diane continued with the questions. Had she ever drank on the job? Had she ever showed up to work drunk or hungover? Did her parents drink? Had she ever used drugs? What was her current drug use? Had she ever experienced depression or anxiety from drinking?

Aubrey answered as honestly as she could. She didn't do drugs, and she didn't suffer from any mental health disorders. She had showed up to work hungover before, but that was back in Chicago.

"Great. So that concludes the questioning. Now, we discuss next steps and any necessary treatment."

Diane hesitated as Aubrey heard paper shuffling in the background.

Please, God, let this be over. Please let this whole thing be over.

"So based on your responses, the amount of alcohol you consume is slightly higher than average alcohol consumption and considering your alcohol behavior at work, I recommend either taking a ten-hour online course about alcohol and drug use or setting up an in-person appointment with a counselor to determine if any additional help is needed."

Two to three drinks at one time were slightly higher than average? What database was Diane basing this on? Clearly, Aubrey wasn't the only one who lied about the number of drinks she consumed at once.

"Um, I'll sign up for the online course. Thanks for explaining the options."

Aubrey wanted to get this done with as soon as possible. Even if she did need more help controlling her alcohol, she didn't know how it would impact her job. She didn't want anyone telling her job that she needed help. Besides, she had God. He would help her overcome this.

"So, you'll have thirty days to complete the online course. I'll email you the instructions for how to access it. Once you've completed the course, email me a copy of your exam results, indicating you've passed, and I'll send the final report back to your employer, informing them you've complied with the requirements."

After they hung up, Aubrey breathed a sigh of relief. This was almost over. Ten more hours of facing the consequences and it would all be behind her. At the end of the day, she still had her job and could live on the beach.

Aubrey treated herself to a vanilla latte from the coffee shop next door and settled in on her couch. Time to click through this online course as fast as she could and move on.

The introduction informed her that the course was educational on the impact drugs and alcohol have on a person's life, as well as awareness of alcohol and drug abuse in America. There would be a final exam at the end, and she needed to score 70 percent or higher to pass the course.

The course first covered types of drugs and their effects upon a person's body. Different categories of drugs. Effects on the brain. Percentage of people addicted in America.

Click. Click. Click.

More drugs. Effects to impairment and other bodily functions. Effects to fetuses.

Click. Click. Click.

Wow, there were so many types of drugs Aubrey had never heard of before. This was messed up. Why would people put these sub-

stances into their bodies with all these effects? She was grateful she
had never really gotten into drugs and didn't have to worry about it.

So many people smoked weed like it wasn't a big deal, but
nobody talked about the side effects, like losing brain cells and body
impairment when you're high. It sounded downright dangerous.

She shook her head. She was never smoking weed again, no
matter how harmless it seemed or how many of her friends were
doing it.

The next section focused on alcohol and the side effects of drinking on the brain. Aubrey clicked on a video.

"Alcohol abuse continues to be a serious issue and cause of
death. Each year, 95,000 people die from alcohol-related causes,
making alcohol the third leading preventable cause of death in the
United States.

"And alcohol use for students has had significant impacts on the
younger population. Thirty-three percent of college students, ages
18-22, reported binge drinking in the past month, and 696,000
students, ages 18-24, are assaulted by another student who has
been drinking every year. Binge drinking is defined as a pattern of
drinking that brings blood alcohol content levels to .08 percent.
This typically occurs after four drinks for women and five drinks for
men, if consumed in about two hours."

Dang. Drinking that many drinks at once pretty much
summed up everyone she had met in college. And most of the
people she worked with. And all her friends in Chicago. Did they
all misuse alcohol?

"Alcohol abuse is pretty widespread," the video continued. "It's
important to understand people have different types of drinking

problems. We will now discuss each one and how to recognize whether a person has a specific drinking problem."

Click.

"First, we will discuss alcoholics. Alcoholics have an addiction problem to alcohol. It is hard for alcoholics to have just one drink or even one sip of alcohol before they lose control. It is common for alcoholics to drink every day and not be able to avoid drinking alcohol if it's within reach. The problem with alcoholics is the first sip. An alcoholic will want more and more. Isolating alone at home to drink or drinking throughout the day is not uncommon for an alcoholic."

That made sense. Some of her friends' parents seemed like they fell into this category. Thankfully, she was not an alcoholic. She hardly drank alone in her apartment, and she had never gotten into the habit of wanting or needing a glass of wine at the end of the day.

Some of Aubrey's friends liked to drink every day after work, but she just didn't understand the need to have a glass or two of wine a day. In the past, she drank to get drunk; she hadn't seen the point of drinking only a few glasses if she wasn't going to get buzzed or drunk.

Click. Another video.

"The next type of drinking problem we will discuss is binge drinking. People who consume at least four drinks in one period of time are considered to be binge drinkers. There are different causes of binge drinking, including social drinking."

Didn't most people drink at least four drinks at a time? Were all her friends and the people she used to see out at the bars on weekends binge drinkers?

"Now, a lot of Americans drink socially; it has become a part of culture to consume a few alcoholic beverages when you go out to dinner or out with friends. The key to identifying someone as a social binge drinker is whether they know how to control or stop drinking. Some drinkers know how to control themselves when they drink and they know how to stop. Social binge drinkers have a problem because they don't know how to stop. Frequent blackouts or getting physically hurt are common symptoms of binge drinkers."

Aubrey closed her eyes. Her chest ached. Her palms were sweating. Tears started to fall down her face.

She had never thought her drinking was a big deal since everyone around her drank as much as she did. They all went out on the weekends, taking shots and having fun. Waking up hungover. Repeating it again the next night. But her friends had never made mistakes like she had made. They never blacked out as hard or as often as she had.

Aubrey had gotten more out of control as she got older. The mistakes and consequences had gotten greater. While others around her were still functioning adults as they drank, she had almost lost everything—her job, her reputation, her life.

It had all started in high school. All of her friends had started drinking, so she started drinking and going to parties too. But she had gotten caught by the cops twice and been given a "minor in possession."

By Aubrey's senior year in college, it wasn't uncommon for her to go out to the bars three or four nights a week. With God's grace, she had somehow managed to graduate with her bachelor's with a 4.0.

Nothing really bad ever had happened her five years in college until her last day. On the morning of her master's graduation, she woke up in the hospital bed with an IV in her arm. She had no idea how she had gotten there, and she was alone. The nurses had told her she had ridden in an ambulance, but she didn't remember. They told her that her blood alcohol content was a .389, a level where death was possible.

Aubrey knew that was her first real wakeup call. God had been trying to get her attention and warn her all the way back in college.

"You have a drinking problem," her parents had warned her. "You need to stop drinking so much."

But she had shrugged it off. It was only one time at the hospital. She would cut back on her drinking and she would be fine.

While living in Chicago, Aubrey had done what all her friends and the other young professionals did. They worked hard and partied harder. The college and sorority life resumed in the real world, except they were older and had more money to spend on booze at the bar.

Instead of buying handles of cheap vodka like in college, they bought fifths of Patrón at swanky places in River North after work or indulged in bottle service on the weekends. They drank to relieve stress and to escape work and get laid.

But the nights started to get more out of control. The night Aubrey peed on her friend's floor after her boyfriend broke up with her. The night she fell off the bed of a guy she had just met, getting a bloody nose and breaking his lamp. The night strangers drove her to the emergency room after she hit her head on the concrete while making out with a coworker.

Not to mention the incidents that had happened at her work trainings.

These types of nights didn't happen to everyone. Drinking like this was not normal.

The description of a social binge drinker in the video described her. They were talking about her. She had been a social binge drinker her entire adult life. She'd had a drinking problem for so long and hadn't even known. She couldn't deny it anymore. She had had a problem for years and now, at twenty-nine, it was staring her in the face.

The tears fell harder as she remembered what all those drunken nights had cost her.

The opportunity to walk across the stage at her graduation for her master's degree. The thousands of dollars lost from the bonus that was taken away. Her reputation after she had hooked up with her coworker. The five staples in her head. All the hospital bills her insurance didn't cover. Her reputation at work as someone who got kicked out of hot tubs and mouthed off to her boss. All the brain cells that were destroyed by the alcohol. All those mornings wasted that she had spent hungover in bed.

Why hadn't anyone told her? Why hadn't anyone warned her about her behavior?

She set her laptop on her couch and collapsed on the floor.

God had been trying to get her attention all along. He had opened her eyes, and now she was finally seeing the truth. She had a drinking problem, and she couldn't keep living like that.

She had been hospitalized and almost gotten fired twice, yet God had saved her. All those drunken nights, all those drunken hookups and mistakes, and God had still decided to save her.

He had already started to change her desire for alcohol, but did that mean she still had a problem? Would she have this problem forever?

Aubrey had heard people talk about alcoholics before, saying once you were an alcoholic, you were always an alcoholic. But the Bible talked about freedom and the power of Jesus to set anyone free from their sin. Just like with sexual sin, could she be set free from drinking too?

Aubrey got chills all over her body as she bowed her head.

God, thank you for saving me and waking me up. Thank you for forgiving me for all my drunken mistakes and changing my desire to drink. Thank you for giving me the strength to stay away from drinking and to resist temptation. I don't want to live that life anymore, God. Thank you, God, for saving my life those nights when I could have died or gotten hurt.

Thank you for showing me that my purpose and identity is not found in drinking. It is found in you, Lord. Thank you for waking me up to the life I was living and the life I get to live with you.

I will not let drinking ruin my life, God. I choose you and the life you have for me. Change me, God. Set me free from this drinking problem. I never want to drink like that ever again.

God was giving her a second chance. Well, maybe a fifth or sixth chance. And she wasn't going to waste it.

Despite all her mistakes, God had always been there with her, protecting her and extending his favor and grace. Allowing her to get a 4.0 as an undergraduate. Allowing her to get a $10,000 scholarship she hadn't even applied for when her dad got laid off during the recession. Allowing her to earn six figures her second year after college. Allowing her to travel the world and move to California to live at the beach.

God had showered her with grace, even when she was still stuck in a lifestyle of sin. He had showed her grace when she had needed it most, even when she hadn't deserved it.

God had given her a new life, a fresh start because of Jesus, and she wasn't going to waste it by drinking or sleeping around. The fact that she still had a job was a miracle. God could have taken her job and beach life away, but he hadn't. But it was no mistake; God still wanted her at Assets & Beyond Consulting for a reason, so she would honor God and use her job for good as she figured out what God wanted her to do next.

Chapter 38

⚓

Over the next month, Aubrey fell into a routine of reading the Bible and praying every morning, working at the office to be with the team, and working out and spending more time with God in the evenings. She devoured all the Christian books and podcasts she could find. She learned more about purity, how to find her purpose and calling, how to love others, and how to have an intimate relationship with God.

Instead of feeling lonely on weekend evenings, she felt empowered staying in. Sometimes she would go for a run, running past all the bars by the beach that she had previously gone to. And she didn't miss being there or drinking alcohol. She finally felt like she had the strength to say no to the party world and yes to the plans God had for her. She would rather be alone with God on her couch than at a bar, drinking in hopes of meeting friends.

But as she ran by some of the bars, she couldn't help but think of Jake. Some nights she feared she would run past him on the boardwalk, walking with another girl, but God reminded her not to think about all the what-ifs. She didn't understand why her heart still longed for Jake after all he had done. She didn't understand how she could feel so angry and miss him at the same time. While she was glad he hadn't reached out to her, it still hurt knowing he didn't want her or that he hadn't fought to have her in his life.

After completing one of her longer Friday night runs, Aubrey had gotten up at 7 a.m. that Saturday and already felt like a new person. She no longer slept until noon and wasted the day being hungover. Now, she read the Bible and journaled at her favorite park along the ocean. The whole day and a new life were ahead of her without drinking.

She prayed out loud as she stared at the palm trees around her.

God, please bring me true friends who are also Christians. I need new friends here, Lord. Friends who care about other things besides drinking and having sex. God, help me make new friends. Help me meet other loving people who also love you.

She closed her eyes as she waited, picturing Jesus sitting with her on the bench. What would Jesus say to her right now?

Search again.

Her eyes shot open. Why hadn't she tried out more churches? She had already been going to the Freedom Church for months now and still hadn't met anyone to hang out with. There had to be other churches she could try. And they all had social media accounts by now. Where did all the people her age go to church?

She opened Instagram and searched for Christian women in San Diego. The first account that popped up was about a women's ministry called Cherish at Awaken Church.

She had never been part of a women's ministry, but this didn't look so bad. There were images of women dressed up at a photo booth, performing in a talent contest, and singing at church.

Wasn't this the same church she had found on Google when she first moved to San Diego? If God was guiding her to go to a new church, what did she have to lose?

As Aubrey arrived at Awaken Church, she told herself, *Don't be nervous. God is with me. This is church, the place where the most welcoming, loving people hang out. I don't need to worry about feeling weird showing up alone. God is with me. Just smile and act natural.*

Then she said a quick prayer, *Please, God, let people be nice. Let me meet new people, Lord.*

Aubrey still had a few minutes before the service started. She had always shown up late before, slipping in and sitting in the back of church while worship had already started. A whole half hour of not knowing what to do with her hands had always felt like too much before. But she needed to give this new church a shot. She couldn't keep hiding in the back.

She took a few deep breaths as she walked up to the church's front doors. She wore a shirtdress and low-heeled wedges to boost her confidence without looking like she was dressing up too much.

A group of smiling people, all wearing bright orange shirts with "Hi" written across the front smiled at her.

"Welcome to church!" they waved in unison.

Aubrey smiled and waved back. As long as they didn't single her out as the new person, this would be fine.

She glanced around the lobby. Parents were leading their kids to kids' church. People were waiting in line to order coffee at the café. Volunteers were passing out free donuts as people made their way into the auditorium.

At least it wasn't as big as the other church. She made her way into the auditorium and forced herself to sit somewhere in the middle.

"Excuse me; is this seat taken?" Aubrey smiled at an older woman who was sitting alone.

"No, it's yours, my dear!" The woman patted the empty seat next to her.

The worship music started, so Aubrey didn't have to make awkward small talk. Similar to the other church, it didn't take long for people to raise their hands as they sang along with the worship team.

There was a full band, complete with guitarists, a drummer, and even a violin. More people started to lift their hands. People at the front of the stage even started dancing.

Aubrey swayed back and forth as she got into the music. Were these singers professional worship artists? She had never heard people sing like this in church.

A woman who sounded like she could win *American Idol* started speaking as the first song ended.

"Good morning, Church! God is with us this morning. Hallelujah!"

Everyone in the church clapped and hollered.

"Let's give God praise this morning as we stand and worship in his presence. When we worship, we praise the Lord and thank him for all that he has done. And worship is one of our most powerful weapons as we sing his praise. God moves at the sound of our praise; he sends down his presence when we worship him. So have your way in us this morning, Lord, have your way in us!"

She lifted her hands to the ceiling as more shouts and cheers filled the auditorium.

The band started playing one of Aubrey's favorite songs, "Reckless Love." She closed her eyes and got lost in the melody. As they sang the lyrics, Aubrey felt a wave of heat wash over her.

She felt like she had when she surrendered her entire life to God in her living room. Without thinking, Aubrey lifted her hands in worship. She stuck them straight up in the air as she sang along with the chorus. Tears were falling down her face as she smiled up at God.

Thank you, God, for never giving up on me. Thank you for loving me even when I wasn't pursuing you, even in all my mistakes. I love you, Lord.

Aubrey forgot she was in an auditorium full of other people. It was just her and God. Worshiping the one who had saved her. Thanking him for waking her up to who he was and who she was as a daughter of God.

The song ended, and then everyone was asked to greet the people sitting around them.

What had just happened? Aubrey felt like a surge of energy had gone through her during worship. Like her whole body was tingling.

The older woman next to her shook her hand.

"I'm Pam. Nice to meet you. What great worship today!"

"Hi, I'm Aubrey. Yes, worship was so good! They could be on *American Idol.*"

They both laughed.

"Have you been coming to the church for a while?" Aubrey asked.

"Oh, yes, for many years. My kids live here, so I moved here to be closer to my grandbabies, and I fell in love with this church. What about you?"

"It's my first time actually."

Pam gasped. "Oh, I am so excited for you! I'm so glad you came today, my dear. This church will change your life. And you came at the perfect time. They have a Cherish Night this Wednesday where all the ladies get together for a ladies' night at church. Cherish is our women's ministry. You need to be here!"

Pam seemed genuinely interested in getting to know her, not like the people Aubrey had met at Freedom Church who had made no effort to make real conversation.

"Thanks for letting me know. That sounds fun."

"The righteousness of God is on you, my dear; keep seeking his righteousness. Don't lose faith."

Huh? What was she talking about? This lady didn't know her.

Before Aubrey could ask Pam what righteousness meant, a couple took the stage and welcomed everyone to church.

"Good morning, Church! We are so glad you decided to join us today. We have so many exciting events coming up. Where are all my ladies at?" The woman searched the crowd as some women cheered.

"It's a very special month for you, ladies. Not only is Cherish Night happening this week, but we also have our Cherish Conference coming up in a few months! Don't forget to register by next week to receive the discounted price."

The man next to the woman speaking chimed in. "Yes, ladies, you do not want to miss the conference. After three days at Cherish, my wife comes back a whole new woman. Men, buy your ladies a ticket to Cherish!"

A three-day conference? To talk about Jesus? She could talk about Jesus at church, but talking about him for three days in a row seemed a bit much.

"Now, it's time to welcome our new guests!" The woman smiled. "If you are here at Awaken Church for the very first time, raise your hand; one of our volunteers will give you a welcome card to fill out, and after the service, they will give you a special gift."

A few people raised their hands as the smiley people in orange shirts ran around and gave them a card.

Aubrey figured she would grab a card and her gift after the service. No way was she raising her hand again in front of everyone.

"She's new; right here!" Pam waved her hand in the air and pointed at Aubrey as a young man ran over to give her a card.

Aubrey blushed. *Thanks a lot, Pam.*

"Now, get ready for a powerful message today. If you could all stand, it's time to welcome our lead pastor, Pastor Leanne, to the stage!" The couple walked off the stage as the church stood and erupted with applause.

Pastor Leanne took the stage. Aubrey immediately liked her— her Australian accent made everything she said more interesting, and she looked warm and welcoming in her hunter green jumpsuit.

"Now, some of you already know this story," Pastor Leanne said, "but I'm going to tell it again because it's a good one. My dashing husband and I were doing well at our church in Australia as young adult pastors when we felt God calling us to move and start a church in San Diego. Now, we had never been to San Diego before and didn't know a single soul. And we had finally felt settled in with our family at our church and home in Australia. So we were like, God, are you sure? And God was like, 'Yeah, I'm sure; get moving.'

"So we decided to trust God and obey his call for us. We said goodbye to our life and community back in Australia, and packed up our belongings with our young children to start a church in San

Diego. We started hosting church in someone's family room, and now, fifteen years later, we have six churches in America and growing. Churches where people have given their life to Jesus. Where people have experienced an encounter with God and been filled with the Holy Spirit. Churches where people have been miraculously healed and set free.

"All because we trusted God and obeyed his call for our lives. Obedience is the key to unlocking the supernatural power and presence of God in your life. When you choose to surrender or let go of things in your life out of obedience to God, you allow him to open up new doors and opportunities."

Pastor Leanne picked up the Bible that had been sitting on the podium.

"When you choose to obey God's Word and his commands, you allow him to do the supernatural in your life through your obedience."

A few people stood up and cheered her on.

"We are called to trust and obey God, no matter how crazy it seems. The world around us may not understand, but we have to trust that God has a plan and purpose for us. Let's pray."

Everyone bowed their heads as Pastor Leanne led them in prayer. Aubrey decided she would obey God, no matter what she had to give up. Drinking and having sex just to have friends or a boyfriend wasn't worth it. She had been disobeying God's will for her life for so long, and he had showed her the consequences of choosing to do things her way.

Aubrey smiled as she closed her eyes.

I put my trust in you, Lord. I will obey your will for my life and the call you have for me, Lord.

Her eyes were still closed but she saw Jesus speaking to her, as if he were standing on the altar.

I'm so proud of you, my daughter. I'm about to take you to places you've never been before. You can leave the past behind and trust me, my beloved. Trust that I will open up doors that you can't even imagine. This church is one of those doors. This is where you belong. I will show you the friends I have for you. I will show you the way.

Aubrey felt a burst of warmth all over her body. She knew God had been speaking to her when she felt this way—a strong sense of peace and reassurance.

She was exactly where she needed to be.

Chapter 39

⚓

"Welcome to Cherish Night, ladies!" The church erupted in cheers as Pastor Leanne took the stage. She immediately got everyone's attention with her smile and her T-shirt that said "Fun & Holy."

Aubrey had never seen so many women her age at church before. She felt like she was at a secret club for Christians, a club she hadn't known existed for so long. A club where they worshiped Jesus instead of taking shots and dancing with guys. This was where she belonged. Not at the bar.

"We are in for a special treat this evening. Our guest speaker tonight is a pastor and author of seven best-selling books, and she flew all the way from Nashville to spend time with us tonight. Ladies, I am so excited to welcome to the stage my dear friend and sister in Christ, Pastor Jackie!" Pastor Leanne clapped as a petite brunette woman took the stage.

"I am so thrilled to be here tonight with all of you. Awaken has such a special place in my heart, and God spoke to me very clearly this morning about what to share with you," Pastor Jackie said.

"Now, you ladies are Awaken Cherish ladies. You already know Jesus died for your life so you can be set free from sin to live the life God intended for you. A life of abundance, to prosper and thrive in what you were put on this Earth to do. But tonight, I'm here to talk about one of the Enemy's tactics that may be holding you back. The Enemy is smart; he's sneaky and cunning, and he tries to hold us back without us even realizing it. While Jesus came to give you life, the Devil tries to take it away. His sole purpose is to steal, kill, and destroy the life and plans God has for you. But today, we are going to expose his lies! We are going to learn how to be set free and how to fight back!"

Several women stood and cheered.

"That's right!"

"Let's go, Jackie; let's go!"

"There's been a stronghold over many of you, some of you for several years. Some of you have been feeling trapped, like you can't move on from the past. The Enemy loves to keep us in bondage to this stronghold because he knows how destructive it is."

She paused. The entire audience was silent.

"Ladies, it's time to fight back. It's time to be set free from the spirit of offense and unforgiveness."

A few gasps went around the room.

"Jesus already forgave you for all the sins you've already committed and all the sins that you will still commit in your lifetime. The Bible commands us in Ephesians 4:32 to forgive others since Jesus has forgiven us. Ladies, it's time to forgive. It's time to forgive those who have hurt you. It's time to forgive those who have wrongfully accused you. It's time to forgive family members for rejecting you. It's even time to forgive those who have sexually abused you. And ladies, it's time for you to forgive yourselves.

"Ladies, if we don't surrender our unforgiveness or offense to Jesus, it will fester in our Spirit. What seems like a small offense will grow over time. It will take root and cause bitterness and resentment in our hearts. Anger. Some of you have had unforgiveness growing for a while in you; it's time to uproot it and leave it at the foot of the cross!"

The place was electric. Half the ladies were standing, cheering her on.

Aubrey's heart was racing. She had asked for God's forgiveness for all her drinking mistakes, but she still didn't know how to forgive herself. She couldn't shake the shame from what she had done. She was still worried about what others would think of her at work if they knew what she had done. Every day she went to work, she worried what others would think of her. She worried that all the other partners might know about what had happened. She worried that she would never get promoted since Devon approved all the candidates up for promotion.

What was with all these tears? She needed to get ahold of herself.

Pastor Leanne took the stage again. "Wow, what a word! Thank you, Jackie, for speaking God's truth so boldly with us tonight. What a much-needed message in this season. I know it spoke to me. If God spoke to you tonight, I encourage you to come up to the front for prayer. As women of God, we are called to pray for each other with power and authority. It's time to surrender any unforgiveness to Jesus. It's time to lay it as his feet and ask for his help so you can move on from whatever has hurt you in the past."

A group of ladies positioned themselves at the front of the altar as the worship team started playing a song about new wine. The rows started to clear out as the women made their way up to the ladies in the front for prayer.

Why were they singing about new wine? What was happening? Aubrey had never seen people pray for each other like this. Her mom didn't even pray for her like this. They usually always prayed alone, quietly.

Women were laying hands on each other, shouting while the women receiving prayer raised their hands in the air. Some girls were already crying. Some were shouting cries of joy.

Aubrey had never known that church could be like this. A place where you could have a relationship with God while being a part of a community of people who genuinely cared.

A woman with curly hair and red lipstick who looked to be Aubrey's age came and sat in the empty seat next to her.

"Hi. I'm Layla! What's your name?" she asked with a huge smile.

"Um, hi. I'm Aubrey. Nice to meet you. Sorry, I don't even know why I'm crying right now." She wiped the tears from her cheeks.

Layla laughed. "Don't worry, babe; happens to me all the time. God always gets me like that, especially at nights like these. So glad you could make it! How long have you been at Awaken?"

Who was this girl? And why was she being so nice to her when she was sitting there crying?

"It's my first week actually. My first time was on Sunday, and I heard about this, so I figured I would check it out. I've never seen anything like this before; I've never seen people pray like this before, and it's a bit overwhelming."

Layla laughed again. "Girl, I hear ya. I didn't know churches could be like this either until I moved here a few years ago. I came here by myself, and I couldn't believe that this whole other life with God existed. Now, this is my family here." She gazed around the church.

"I just moved here by myself too," Aubrey replied. "I've been looking for a church that feels like home for a few months, and I have a good feeling about this place."

"Well, welcome to San Diego! I believe God has great things in store for you here. Are you interested in trying a connect group? I lead a women's group on Saturday mornings. We meet at someone's house for brunch and to talk about what God is doing in our lives. You should totally join us!"

"I would love that," Aubrey said. "Thank you. I've been wanting to meet new friends who also love God for months now, and I feel like God brought me here for a reason."

"Oh, of course he did. God is always bringing the right people into your life. Won't he do it."

They exchanged numbers—another sign that this church was where Aubrey belonged.

"So, are you going to go up for prayer? I know it may seem like a lot right now, but it will be very powerful. Trust me. Come on." Layla reached for her hand.

Aubrey hesitated. Her heart raced again, but she didn't move. Other than receiving prayer on Easter, she had never prayed with a stranger like this before. What if they judged her for her past? What if they couldn't help her?

God is with me.

She grabbed Layla's hand and let her lead her to the front. Layla nudged her to pray with a tiny, older woman.

"Hello, dear. I'm Jen. How can I pray for you? What's your name?" Jen put her hand on Aubrey's shoulder.

Aubrey immediately started crying again.

Jen rubbed her back. "Now, now, it's going to be all right. That's what we are here for. What's on your mind, love?"

"I've never done this before," Aubrey said. "Sorry I'm crying. I'm fine really. Just been going through a lot and trying to leave my old life behind. I really screwed up drinking. I almost got fired because of it, and I need to forgive myself. I was also in an unhealthy relationship where I couldn't stop having sex even though I knew it was bad, and I just want to move on and for God to heal my broken heart. I'm still new to San Diego, and I don't really have true friends here, and it's been hard moving on from the past."

Once she had started talking, Aubrey couldn't stop. This woman knew all her secrets and her past, yet she kept smiling at her.

"It's okay, love," Jen said. "You are in the right place and I'm proud of you for coming here today and for seeking God through this. He is going to work all things for good for your future; you just wait. I'm going to pray for you, and I just want you to open up your hands to heaven and receive. Can you do that?"

Aubrey nodded.

"Awesome. And I want you to get some new friends. Don't hang out with those people who still drink and have sex all the time. You don't need those people in your life anymore. You're in the right place here. Look all around you—these are people who will become your friends. True sisters in Christ who will love and support you. Are you in a connect group?"

"Not yet, but I'm going to one on Saturday." Aubrey looked over at Layla, who was already receiving prayer from the woman next to her.

"Good, that's great. All right, enough talking. Let's pray."

Aubrey closed her eyes and lifted her hands into the air.

"Father God," Jen prayed, "we come to you today in the name of Jesus. We thank you that your daughter Aubrey has been forgiven and wiped clean of her past. Father, we bind and break any strong-holds in Jesus' name, and we command the Devil to get out of her life. We command any spirit of offense to flee, and we thank you for healing her heart from any unforgiveness, Lord. She is a new creation in Christ and the Devil has no authority over her life. No weapon formed against her shall prosper. In Jesus' name.

"And God," Jen continued, "we thank you for bringing the right people into Aubrey's life, and that she will reap a harvest of new friends to support her in her walk with Christ. For he knows the plans he has for you, plans for hope and a future. A future that involves true, loving friends, and a future without sexual sin or alcohol. Aubrey, you have been set free as a daughter of Christ. Amen!" she shouted.

Aubrey felt like her knees were about to give out. Her body felt tingly all over. She gave Jen a hug before walking away.

It felt like fire had gone through Aubrey's body, from her head and out through her toes. She stumbled into the lobby area, wiping the remaining tears from her eyes. Was she seeing things now? Had this woman's prayer teleported her to some church in the future?

A DJ was spinning music in the corner. The lobby was filled with women dancing to the song "Wobble" and dressing up in the photo booth. A few ladies were passing around pink lemonade and chocolate strawberries. Pastor Leanne was in the middle of the dance floor, dancing along with the girls.

It was like being part of Aubrey's college sorority, but without all the alcohol and provocative outfits. And these women were actually nice. And they knew how to pray.

Aubrey felt joy bursting through her. She laughed as she looked up. "Oh, God, you're full of surprises. I have so much to learn, and I have a feeling it's only the beginning."

Layla grabbed Aubrey's arm and led her to the dance floor.

Chapter 40

⚓

Aubrey couldn't believe she was heading to a church group on a Saturday morning. No more sleeping until noon and wasting the day being hungover. She got up early now to read the Bible and meet new friends.

God, thank you for bringing the right people into my life. Thank you for bringing me true friends, Lord. Please let them be nice, and please let them like me, Lord. I just have to be myself. You are with me, God.

Aubrey prayed as she walked up to the front door of Layla's house. She had made her chocolate-chip, banana muffins, but she had no idea what was appropriate for this type of gathering.

Would they sit around reading the Bible? Would the other ladies be warm and welcoming like Layla? Were they struggling with drinking and purity like she was? Would they drink mimosas? She didn't know if Christians at her new church drank at all, but she wasn't going to be the first one to mention it. And she wasn't going to drink even if they did have mimosas. She still hadn't had the desire to drink since taking that alcohol course.

"Good morning, beautiful!" Layla smiled as she opened the door. "So glad you could join us!"

A handful of other ladies were already there, gathered around the kitchen table, chatting and sipping coffee. Everyone gave Aubrey a hug after Layla introduced her. A few ladies seemed like they were in their forties, but most looked like they were in their late twenties and early thirties.

"Welcome to connect group, ladies!" Layla said, taking command of the room as everyone found a seat. "We are women of intention, intentional about growing in community as we become the women God created us to be. We are here to support and encourage each other as sisters in Christ; remember, we love and don't judge. This is a safe place where we can be vulnerable and share what we are going through while we pray and support our sisters. Suzanne, would you please open us up in prayer?"

Layla gestured for the woman next to her to pray.

"Father God, we thank you for bringing us all here together today in your presence. God, we ask that you open our hearts to receive you today. We thank you that you are with us here, and we thank you for moving through us with the Holy Spirit. And we thank you for all the new ladies who came here today, God. We thank you for all the divine friendships that are being formed in this group. In Jesus' name. Amen."

Suzanne looked over at Aubrey and smiled. Her prayer had instantly put Aubrey more at ease.

One by one, everyone introduced themselves and shared a story about how God had been moving in their lives that week. One girl talked about how God had set her free from anxiety. For years, she had struggled with controlling her thoughts and being able to sleep at night, but she told the group that she had felt this weight come off of her when she went up for prayer at Cherish Night and had been able to sleep through the entire night since then. They all clapped as a few girls shouted praise to God with their hands in the air.

Another woman shared that her husband had finally gone to church with her. She admitted that she hadn't been walking with the Lord when they got married, but that she had been praying for her husband to turn to God for years, ever since she had been saved. More claps and cheers around the room.

Dang, Aubrey thought. *This is already intense.* She knew others must have their own junk to deal with, but she wasn't expecting people to share like this. What should she say when it was her turn? She wasn't ready to share what she had been through. She didn't even know these women. Why would they care about what she was going through?

A girl named Lexi went next. She was in the Navy and seemed like she had known God for a while.

"I just got back from my recent deployment. I was on the ship in Asia for nine months, and basically, God healed me from my past, and I'm pretty sure I met my future husband."

The girls squealed. "Tell us more!" "Details, please!"

Lexi laughed. "Well, right before the trip, I had ended an on-again, off-again relationship. I was so sick of sleeping with guys who didn't want to commit, and I was sick of meeting all the guys at work who wanted to sleep with everyone. I knew I was supposed to wait until marriage, but I always struggled with boundaries, especially when I felt lonely. Having sex was always my escape—my chance to feel loved and accepted. But on the ship, I started spending more time in the Bible and really studying purity and God's design for sex. And God healed me. I experienced his love in a way I hadn't felt before, and I recommitted my life and purity to him. I prayed and broke off all previous soul ties I had with the men I had slept with.

"A few men tried to hit on me, but I wasn't having it. But then I met this guy John my last month on the ship. He just seemed different. He asked me out on an actual date, and he didn't try to sleep with me. We've been on several dates since then, and he supports my decision to wait until marriage to have sex; he didn't think it was weird at all. And then I had this dream where God basically told me that he's my husband."

Layla stood up with her hands raised. "Won't he do it! Yes, he will!"

A few other girls got up and hugged Lexi as the others clapped.

"Aubrey, are you okay?" Suzanne passed her a tissue.

Aubrey hadn't realized she had been crying. She thought she was the only one struggling with sex, but here was Lexi, talking about it so openly. And she knew how Lexi felt, wanting to feel loved and accepted. But no guy had ever truly loved her. They had only used her.

"Sorry. I don't know why I'm crying. I can't stop crying with all this new God stuff." Aubrey dabbed at her eyes.

"Girl, it never stops. Join the club. What's on your mind, girl?" Layla said.

What did she have to lose? She didn't even know these women. It wasn't like she had to see them again.

"It's just that Lexi's story spoke right to me. I've been struggling with sex for so long, especially recently with this one guy who really hurt me. I'm still trying to move on and not think about it, but I keep thinking about what he did and how badly things ended."

"Is he still in the picture? Are you guys still talking?"

"No. God made it clear I had to cut him out of my life. But it still hurts. I still feel so attached to him, and I can't stop thinking about him. I even read Proverbs, and where it talks about the ways of the wicked, I think of him, but I still can't help feeling the way I do."

Aubrey was ugly crying by now.

Suzanne patted her leg. "Thank you for sharing with us—you're very brave. I knew exactly how you felt when I couldn't move on from some guys I had dated before I met my husband. Aubrey, do you know what a soul tie is?" Suzanne asked.

Aubrey shook her head. Lexi had mentioned soul ties, but she had no idea what it meant.

"When we have sex, a bond is created with the other person that is intended to bond us for life. This bond is called a soul tie. God created sex for husbands and wives to bond in a special, intimate way—God created sex to bond a husband and wife together in marriage. When people have sex, certain hormones are released. For women, oxytocin is released, making a woman naturally want to bond to the man she was intimate with. For men, vasopressin is released, which makes the man naturally want to protect and provide for the woman.

"But when people have sex outside of marriage, these hormones are out of balance. A bond is created between two people that was not intended to be created, so it's like there is this pull or connection that sticks the two people together. So, this creates an unhealthy and ungodly soul tie, which should be a bond between two people God intended to bond for life. Sex isn't just physical; it creates an intimate bond between two people that is not intended to be broken. When people have casual sex and then sleep with other people, it creates bonds that were not intended to be formed, leaving people hurt, confused, and alone."

What? So this was why she and her friends continued getting hurt after sleeping with someone?

"Is this," Aubrey asked, "why friends who try to be only friends with benefits in the movies always end up falling for each other? Because sex was never meant to be just casual sex? It was meant to bond them for life?"

"Exactly. Friends with benefits don't exist. That wasn't God's intent."

Dang. No wonder she couldn't move on from Jake. She wasn't crazy for still missing him after what he had done. It was all because of their soul tie. Why hadn't anyone told her this in her sex education class growing up?

"Well, how do I get rid of this thing?" Aubrey asked. "Is it possible to get rid of it?"

"Of course it's possible. All things are possible with God. Let's break that soul tie, girl!" Layla fist-pumped the air.

The girl next to Aubrey handed her another tissue. "Here; you'll need this."

"Aubrey," Suzanne said, "you mentioned that you still get upset when you think of him. I understand that he hurt you, but have you decided to forgive him for what he did?"

Forgive him? Why would she forgive Jake after all he had done? After all the pain he had caused? Then she heard a voice inside her.

Forgive others as I have forgiven you. I've already forgiven you for all your mistakes; you can forgive Jake too.

The tears wouldn't stop. It was a lot, discovering she had a soul tie she didn't know existed, and now she was to supposed to forgive Jake?

"I haven't forgiven him yet. It hurts too much." She blew her nose.

"Well, that's what we are here for," Suzanne said. "We are your sisters in Christ and we are here to pray and stand in authority with you to help set you free. So God can heal your heart." Suzanne lifted Aubrey to her feet.

They all formed a circle around Aubrey and laid hands on her. Aubrey lifted her hands to heaven and closed her eyes.

"Father God," Layla prayed, "we thank you for bringing our sister Aubrey here today. You promise to work all things for good for those who love you, and we thank you that you are working this for good. We thank you for healing her broken heart and for forgiving her sexual past. We come against any shame or guilt from the Enemy, and we rebuke it in the name of Jesus. We stand in agreement, and we break the soul tie with Jake in Jesus' name, and we ask that Aubrey will walk in freedom from this relationship. She has been set free and she has been purified with the love and blood of Jesus. In Jesus' name. Amen."

Aubrey felt that warm and tingly feeling again, like their prayers had gone right inside to her heart.

"Now," Suzanne said, "I want you to pray to God. If you want to forgive Jake for what he's done, pray to God that you forgive him and ask for him to help you forgive. Surrender it to Jesus."

Aubrey had never prayed out loud in front of anyone before, but she knew she couldn't say no. She needed to deal with this. It was time to move on. Aubrey closed her eyes again as she raised her palms to the ceiling.

"God, I forgive Jake for what he has done. I forgive him for hurting me and for sleeping with other women." She hesitated as she caught her breath between sobs. She felt the arms around her, helping her to continue standing.

"I forgive the other woman as well. Thank you God for giving me the strength to forgive him. Thank you for freeing me from any unforgiveness, and thank you for healing my broken heart. In Jesus' name. Amen."

Aubrey felt like a weight had been lifted off her chest. She felt lighter, and she felt peace that hadn't been there before. The ladies clapped and gave her a hug.

They continued sharing about God and praying for each other for the next hour. Finally, it was time to leave.

As Aubrey grabbed her bag to go, Lexi came up to her and gave her another hug.

"You're very brave, my friend. It took courage to come here today and to share what you've been going through. Let's go grab a smoothie this week and talk more about sex."

"I would love that. Thank you."

Aubrey continued to cry, but they were happy tears. Tears of joy and awe. She had found somewhere she belonged, with people who actually cared about her and who cared about other things besides drinking on the weekends. And she finally felt peace when she thought of Jake. She finally felt like her heart was being put back together again.

Epilogue

⚓

A few months later…

"Bring on the new wine, God—bring it on." Aubrey swayed to the music as the worship team finished singing.

She had listened to the new wine song on repeat all week when she prayed in the morning. She was the offering, a vessel for God to use for his glory, to make this world a better place. And she would figure out how God wanted to use her.

"Ladies, I can't believe we are finally here! Welcome to Cherish Conference!" Pastor Leanne took the stage as everyone stood and cheered.

Aubrey still couldn't believe that pastors like Leanne existed, pastors who helped her understand the Bible while having fun at the same time. They had already had worship and a few messages from a few guest speakers, and between the messages, they had a dance contest on stage.

Pastor Leanne surveyed the crowd.

"It is so good seeing all of your beautiful faces. I had no idea what God had in mind when he told me to start a women's prayer group, yet here we are today."

More cheers. "We love you, Pastor Leanne!"

"I'm so excited to share the Word that God downloaded for you, ladies. Just like I was trying to figure out what God wanted me to do early on in my ministry, he wants to help you figure out your purpose and calling as a daughter of God. He has a unique plan and calling on each of your lives, and today, we are going to unpack how to discover that."

Layla grabbed Aubrey's arm. "He will speak to you. Get ready, girl."

Last week, Layla and Aubrey had been talking about finding their purpose with God. Aubrey had told her she was frustrated that she still didn't know what she was supposed to do.

"Each one of you standing here today is a masterpiece, created by God to do good works. Each one of you was created with a unique set of gifts, talents, and passions to use for God's glory. Even before you were born, God knew the plan for your life, and he has equipped you with everything you need to fulfill those plans. But some of you are not sure what those plans are yet. You know you are special as a daughter of God; you know you were created on purpose for a purpose, yet you still aren't clear what God wants you to do with your life."

Aubrey nodded as she listened to every word.

"And that is okay," Pastor Leanne continued. "God knows exactly where you are at, and he wants you to know you have purpose right where you are. As you wait for God to reveal your calling, he will show you how he wants you to serve him. You can serve him in school as you get your degree. You can serve him in your current job, even if you don't like what you are doing. You can serve him when you volunteer at church. You can serve him as a stay-at-home mom as you raise young babies and teach them the way they should go. As you step out in faith, God will reveal the gifts and calling he's given you. And each one of us must keep doing what he's already told us."

Pastor Leanne read the Bible verse that appeared on the screen behind her.

"'You must love the Lord your God with all your heart, all your soul, and all your mind.' This is the first and greatest commandment. A second is equally important: 'Love your neighbor as yourself.'

"While we wait for God to reveal what he wants us to do, he tells us in Matthew 22:37-39 to focus on loving him and loving others. Growing in God's love and sharing that love with others should never be second to the calling he has for you. God's love is the foundation to everything else you will do, and if you don't understand how to live and abide in God's love, you will not be ready for the calling he has for you."

Aubrey felt like her spirit jumped inside of her. This was what she needed to focus on. It was so simple. Love. Loving God and loving others.

"I want us to worship to 'New Wine' again," Pastor Leanne said, "and I want each one of you to pray and ask God how you can focus on his love and sharing that love right where you are."

The worship team took the stage as everyone stood up.

New wine. New power. A new life with God, trusting him with everything.

Lord, thank you for loving me even when I didn't deserve it. Thank you for saving me and rescuing me from my old life. Show me how to grow in your love so I can share that love with others. Show me my purpose here, God, and what you created me to do.

Aubrey swayed to the music with her eyes closed. Arms raised out to the sky, her starfish worship position. And she heard a whisper from within.

I am showing you what love is, my daughter. A love you've never seen before, a love you didn't know existed. I am healing your heart from the past and making it whole. Whole in my love.

I love you so much, my daughter. It broke my heart to see yours broken, but I am already working it for good. You will know what true love is. Love from me as your father, and one day love from a husband. I have been protecting you, keeping you safe, your whole life. I have been protecting you from the world. All those men couldn't love you because they didn't love me. They would not accept my love, so they were unable to love in return.

There is nothing wrong with you, my beloved. You are wonderfully and remarkably made. Love will become one of your greatest gifts. The love so many people desperately need. The transforming love of Jesus Christ.

Aubrey sat in her chair, crying long after the worship team had gone off stage and the room started to clear out. She had written everything God had spoken in her journal. She wanted to look back and remember this moment. The most beautiful words God had ever spoken to her. The day she understood her purpose. And the day she understood why none of those guys had ever loved her.

She heard the music playing in the lobby. She was ready to join the dance party, but she needed to make a phone call first. She found a quiet place outside by the parking lot.

Who was that cute Asian guy serving in the parking lot? She hadn't seen that smile at church before. She shook her head. She wasn't going to worry about that kind of love yet. God's love came first.

"Hey, girl! How are you?"

"Tina! You'll never guess what just happened!"

Tina laughed. "I can only imagine after the last few months you've had. Did you burn all those trashy romance novels you told me you were never reading again?"

"No, but thanks for reminding me that I still need to throw them in the dumpster. Tina, this is serious. God really spoke to me at my church conference. I finally feel like I know what I'm supposed to do with my life."

"What is it?"

"Well, I had been lost for so long, and I didn't even know it. I was caught up in the party scene—drinking, sex, and not knowing my purpose at work for so long until God woke me up. And now, I know that this whole other world exists, a world with God. I know he has plans for us, that we are loved, that we have purpose. But I didn't know this for so long, you know? Like how did I waste twenty-nine years without realizing this? So, I feel like I'm supposed to help others know that this life with God exists. That they don't have to drink and have sex with men who don't love them. That they can live a life on purpose with God and live the life they were created to live."

"Wow," Tina said. "That's so beautiful, Aubrey. I know how you feel, like, why did we live that way and not turn to God sooner? I used to think I wasted a lot of years partying, but now I know God works all things for good. Everything you went through is part of your testimony, and you will get to help others through this. You are living proof of what the power and love of Jesus can do!"

"What's a testimony?" Aubrey asked. She hadn't quite learned all of the Christian language yet.

"A testimony is the story of how you were saved, how you surrendered your life to Jesus," Tina explained. "Where you talk about your life before God, what made you seek him, how he saved you, and how he has changed you."

"Yes! I will share my story so others can see for themselves. The girl who used to love tequila shots and sleeping around, forever changed by the love of Jesus Christ."

"Exactly!" Tina laughed.

"But how do you share a testimony?"

"God will show you."

"Yes, yes, he will."

Note to Reader

⚓

One Transforming Love is based on a true story, my own story of how Jesus saved and transformed my life. My hope for you reading this book is that you have your own transforming relationship with Jesus and that you discover the life and plans God intended for you.

It doesn't matter how far you are right now from God or what you've done in the past, Jesus is for all of us. He died for each one of us so we could be reconciled to God and for our sins to be forgiven. He died so we could become new creations; so we could live the lives we were created to live and so we could spend eternal life with him.

As you know, deciding to surrender my life to Jesus was no simple decision. And choosing to surrender my old life to God was not easy. But God showed me it was the only way.

If you want to surrender your life to Jesus, you can find resources on how to surrender your life and follow Jesus at www.funandholy.com/followJesus. If you are ready to invite Jesus into your life, you can pray the prayer on the following page. If you've made the decision to follow Jesus from reading this book, email me at erinelisekiu@funandholy.com so I can celebrate this monumental decision that you've made!

I talked a lot about my struggle with surrendering my sex life to God because it was the hardest thing for me to give up to follow Jesus and I see so many other women struggling with sexual sin. My hope is that you know you are not alone if you are struggling to obey God in this area and that it is possible to walk in purity. If my journey pursuing purity and overcoming my sexual past spoke to you and you have the desire to learn more about purity and how you can surrender this area to God, you can find resources on how to pursue purity at www.funandholy.com/pursuingpurity.

If you've already surrendered your life to Jesus, I am thankful I get to call you my sister in Christ. My hope is that my testimony inspires you to boldly and fearlessly share the love and truth of Jesus with others around you. Perhaps God is calling you to share your own testimony. Perhaps God is calling you to step out in faith for such a time as this. Whatever God has put on your heart, let's encourage each other as sisters in Christ. Let's stay in touch at www.funandholy.com as we continue to seek the plans God has for us. If you want to share what God has done in your life or if you have questions about how to take your faith to the next level, you can email me at erinelisekiu@funandholy.com.

Thank you for reading this book and for sharing the transforming love of Jesus with others around you.

With Love,
Erin Elise Kiu

Prayer to Follow Jesus

⚓

If you are ready to surrender your life to Jesus, pray the prayer below as you ask Jesus to come into your life.

Prayer

God, I thank you for sending your son Jesus to die for my sins.

I confess that I am a sinner and I need a Savior. I believe that Jesus died on the cross for my sins and that I am forgiven.

Today, I surrender my life to Jesus Christ. I accept Jesus as my Lord and Savior and I choose to follow him with my whole heart. Jesus, I invite you to come into my life.

I thank you that I am filled with the Holy Spirit, and that the same power that raised Jesus from the dead lives in me.

As a child of God, I declare that I am saved and that heaven is my home. In Jesus' name. Amen.

Acknowledgments

⚓

I cannot describe in words how much time, effort, and prayer went into this book. But to give you a glimpse of how this book came into the world, I'd like to thank a few special people.

To the team who helped this book come to life, I couldn't have done it without you. It takes a small village to publish a book and I am forever grateful for all the wisdom and advice you shared along the way. Thank you to my book coach, Christine Gail; I know it was a divine encounter meeting you that one night at Church when God had been leading me to write a book. Thank you to my editor, Tyler Tichelaar, for helping finesse the words of my story so others can laugh and cry as they read my testimony. Thank you to the cover design and interior layout team at Fusion Creative Works; thank you for helping my book look beachy and beautiful.

To my husband, Jeff Kiu, thank you for praying for me and believing in me every step of the book-writing journey. Thank you for being my prayer warrior, for praying for me before you even met me, and for believing that all things are possible with God. Thank you for speaking God's Word and promises over my life on those days when I wanted to stop writing and nap on the couch. And thank you for joining me and cuddling me on those days when I did need to nap on the couch.

To my family, Kathy, Dirk, Tom, Ashley, Mason, Olivia, and Dawson, thank you for always loving and supporting me even when I moved all the way across the country. Mom, thank you for always praying for me, and never giving up that I would come to know Jesus. Thank you for always loving me and supporting me when I needed it most, even during the time when you put bubble wrap by the front door to catch me from sneaking out. Dad, thank you for always being my biggest fan and for teaching me to swing hard at whatever dreams God has put on my heart. Tom, Ashley, Mason, Olivia, and Dawson, thank you for putting up with the old me for so many years before I had the benefit of knowing God. Thank you for always being there out of love my whole life, no matter what mess I had gotten myself into. And thank you for bringing the three most adorable babies into this world.

To my Awaken Church family in San Diego, thank you for empowering me to step into my purpose and calling as a daughter of Christ and for giving me the faith and courage I needed to step out and write this book.

To my lead pastors, Jurgen and Leanne Matthesius, thank you for following the call of God on your lives to start a church in San Diego. Thank you for always standing up for God's truth and for awakening my identity in Christ as a warrior for God's Kingdom. Thank you for establishing the Emerge and Cherish ministries where my husband and I were able to become the husband and wife we are today. And thank you for showing us what God can do when we believe in the impossible to happen in our lives.

To my campus pastors, Jon and Becky Heinrichs, thank you for leading a church that became my family. Thank you for not being afraid to talk about the messy parts of life and for leading by example. Thank you for teaching me about the power of the Holy Spirit and for showing me that I am a fully loaded weapon for God's glory. Thank you for teaching me that I can be both a prayer warrior and boss in the marketplace as I set out to accomplish what God is calling me to do.

To all the original Women of Intention, thank you for welcoming me into your lives and hearts with open arms. Thank you for loving me and not judging me and for inviting me into the family. And thank you for not being afraid to talk about sex.

To all the other Women of Intention and my sisters of Christ at Awaken and across the country, thank you for all your prayers as this book came to life. Thank you for all your words of encouragement when I needed it most to keep writing the story that needed to be written.

To all my coworkers at my former accounting firm, you know who you are. Thank you for always encouraging me and believing in me as I set out to find my purpose and passion in life. Thank you for loving me and for wanting me to be a part of the team, even when you knew I didn't like accounting. Thank you for all those phone calls and texts when I thought I was about to lose my job, and thank you for not letting me quit before I was ready. I miss you all so much and I'll never forget all our laughs and memories together in the accounting world. And to all my bosses along the way, thank you for your grace and patience and for allowing me to still have a job.

To Jarrett and Jeanne Stevens at Soul City Church in Chicago, thank you for initiating my transforming relationship with Jesus.

Thank you for teaching me about the love and grace of God at such an early stage in my journey. And thank you for encouraging me to say yes to God by running the Chicago marathon; that was the first time God showed me that all things are possible with him, even running 26.2 miles.

To all my sisters in Christ who partnered with God to make my salvation and transformation possible, thank you for obeying the call of God on your life and for the ministries you've launched.

To Priscilla Shirer, thank you for writing the *Discerning the Voice of God* Bible study. Thank you for obeying what God put on your heart through this study and thank you for teaching me who God really is. Thank you for all the other books, Bible studies, and conferences you've ministered through as you helped me grow in my faith.

To Kristen Clark and Bethany Beal, the founders of GirlDefined Ministries, thank you for teaching me what God's Word says about sex, purity, and womanhood. Thank you for not being afraid to talk about the hard topics that nobody wants to talk about. Thank you for addressing all the questions I had about Christian dating and for showing me that it is possible to do things God's way, including waiting to have sex until marriage.

To my favorite Christian fiction authors, Karen Kingsbury and Francine Rivers, thank you for inspiring me and showing me that it is possible to write novels that show the love of God, and thank you for sharing the stories God has put on your heart with the world.

About the Author

⚓

Erin Elise Kiu is passionate about helping women have a transforming relationship with Jesus. After experiencing her own transformation with God, Erin's mission is to help other women live the fun and holy lives they were created to live.

Erin empowers women to have their own transformation with God through her writing. She is an author and blogger at Fun & Holy, a blog and community for women to grow together as they become the women God created them to be.

At Fun & Holy, Erin talks about dating, purity, and living set apart in this world as a woman of faith. No question or topic is off limits at Fun & Holy—if you're looking for honest, biblical answers, this blog and community is for you.

Erin also has a heart for single ladies to help them attract their future husbands while learning how to date and build Christ-centered relationships. God wrote her love story and showed her how to pursue a godly marriage, and Erin hopes to help other women do the same.

When she's not writing, you can find Erin on the beach or biking along the coast with her husband in San Diego.

To connect with Erin, email her at erinelisekiu@funandholy.com.

For updates on upcoming books and to check out the Fun & Holy blog and community, visit www.funandholy.com.